RECITATIVE

Prose by James Merrill

EDITED AND WITH
AN INTRODUCTION BY

J. D. McClatchy

ix

NORTH POINT PRESS
San Francisco
1986

Cover illustration: Debora Greger
Cover design: David Bullen

North Point Press
850 Talbot Avenue
Berkeley, California
94706

Contents

Introduction

Critics have read James Merrill's dramatic monologue "Mirror," his knowing inquiry into the order of appearances, as a contrast between the poem and the novel, verse and prose. The mirror in its gilded frame—the reflective voice of poetry—speaks to the facing window's tall transparence:

> If ever I feel curious
> As to what others endure,
> Across the parlor *you* provide examples,
> Wide open, sunny, of everything I am
> Not. You embrace a whole world without once caring
> To set it in order. That takes thought.

The poem sets up a kind of rivalry. But in Merrill's own career there has been an enriching contract between the expansive reach of prose and the speculative intensity of his poetry.

Some readers may forget the regularity with which Merrill, quintessentially a lyrical and autobiographical poet, and sometimes a hermetic one, has from the beginning turned his hand to prose. *Jim's Book*, a gathering of juvenilia privately published in 1942 (Merrill was sixteen), is about evenly divided between poems and stories, and testifies to the divided attention, or ambition, of its precocious author. In 1950, having finished work on *First Poems*, he started and then abandoned a novel. A quarter-century later, he lost his drafts and notes for another novel. That loss is recounted in "The Will" and in "The Book of Ephraim," where its summarized plot is included as an alternate version of events in the poem—a literally embedded novel-in-verse. In between these two abandoned projects, Merrill completed and published two other novels: his dark comedy of manners *The Seraglio* (1957) and the experimental *The (Diblos) Notebook* (1965). The narrative amplitude, the energies of portrait and scene, the disposition of circumstance and motive, of irony and disclosure in *The Seraglio* found their way next into the poems of *The Country of a Thou-*

sand *Years of Peace* (1959) and *Water Street* (1962), the volumes that secured his mature style. *The (Diblos) Notebook* takes the form of a novel-in-progress, what happens in a fictional life slowly forged into a more life-like story. The tale is the telling, and it takes advantage of a layering at once ingenious and revealing: over the dreamlike wisdom of myth (in versions by Racine and Proust, as well as by Freud) is laid a patina of the anti-novel's textuality, "indecisions, pentimenti, glimpses of bare canvas, rips & ripples & cracks which, by stressing the fabric of illusion, required a greater attention to what was being represented." It is no wonder the Greek word for "novel"—Merrill's novel is set in Greece—is *mythistorema*. The refracted narrative first tried in *The (Diblos) Notebook* came to characterize the structure of the long poems in *Nights and Days* (1966) and later the self-revising complexities of his masterwork *The Changing Light at Sandover*.

In his introduction to *The Poet's Story*, Howard Moss proposes the reason a poet is drawn to writing fiction: so that he may be *less* himself. The centripetal force of a poem, narrowly centered on the lyrical ego, pulls him inward, whereas in the novel the self is dispersed into characters, freed and various. But it can as well be said that, when he is writing fiction, or really any prose, the poet may be *more* himself. Freed of the constraints of lyricism, the channels of convention and metaphor, from the demands of a "poetic voice," which invariably raises the pitch and status of utterance, he may be allowed opinions and hesitations, allowed more time and leeway with the whole of his personality. This miscellany of prose pieces, selected from the work of four decades, is intended to give the reader of James Merrill's poetry, even the reader who knows the poet's novels and plays, a still more comprehensive view of his work—and of his personality, or that side of it evident in the range of his enthusiasms, aversions, and affiliations. It is meant to be a background to further study, but also to highlight a critical intelligence of unusual subtlety, buoyant wit, and rare eloquence.

At one point in *The (Diblos) Notebook* its narrator, the novice novelist, takes stock: "I should have made some sort of scheme to refer to. This is my 1st *long* piece of work, & the problems it raises are new & different from those of short stories (the single mood or action). Yet I keep imagining, wrongly perhaps, that, once I arrive at the right 'tone,' the rest will follow." In a sense, it is *tone*, as both subject matter and manner, that is central to most of what follows. Merrill has portrayed himself in his poems as someone shy of ideas. This collection belies that; or belies the pose. It would be more accurate to say he is suspicious of ideas, of their tendency to blur distinctions, to inhibit clarity or nuance. So it is to tone he attends—inflection, style, the *feel* of thought. "No thoughts, then, but in things?" he asks in his essay on Francis Ponge. "True enough, so long as the notorious phrase argues not for the suppression of thought but for its oneness with whatever in the world—pine woods, spider, cigarette—gave rise to it." Merrill's ideas are always grounded in metaphor, poetry's primary language to render the world and to recover, control, and heighten feeling.

> Ah, but styles. They are the new friend's face
> To whom we sacrifice the tried and true,
> And are betrayed—or not—by. For affection's
> Poorest object, set in perfect light
> By happenstance, grows irreplaceable,
> And whether in time a room, or a romance,
> Fails us or redeems us will have followed
> As an extension of our "feel" for call them
> Immaterials, the real right angle,
> The golden section—grave proportions here,
> Here at the heart of structure, and alone
> Surviving now to tell me where I am.

It is the traditional task of any poet's prose to create that taste by which his own work may be appreciated and judged. And Merrill turns in these essays to those writers who have influenced his work (like Dante or Wallace Stevens) and his sensibility (like Cavafy and Elizabeth Bishop). A poet's— or this poet's—critical writing is neither accidental nor programmatic. It comes into being when an invitation from someone else crosses an impulse of his own. There are essays that one wishes were here, but aren't. His splendid meditation on Corot makes one long for more general pieces on painting and music. I would like to read Merrill on, say, Byron's letters and journals, or on Henry James, or Mallarmé, or Frost. But homage takes other forms. Some poets Merrill might have written about—Valéry or Montale—he has translated. Others—Auden and Yeats—he has literally incorporated into his own poems. And throughout the essays and interviews in this book one will find succinct tributes and incidental remarks— here on Marianne Moore, there on T. S. Eliot—that say a good deal more than many prolix studies do. Merrill is drawn most, as we would expect him to be, to congenial temperaments, locales he is at home in. His interest, for example, in Greek society and in the French language, is both explored and celebrated in his essays on Cavafy and Ponge—writers whose own gifts overlap his but don't entirely coincide. "New landscapes express the new ideas I have in their presence," he once wrote. Other poets are as much new landscapes for Merrill as New Mexico or New York City. It is worth noting, too, that what engages him is more often than not the outsider—writers to one side, modest or strange in their demands on us. His prevailing aversion is to the "giants who seem in their life's work to transcend human dimensions," or to what he elsewhere calls "featureless" poetry. What he usually has in mind is the heritage of High Modernism. It is the "human dimension" that attracts Merrill to poets like Cavafy, whom he praises for "limiting his subject to human deeds and desires," or Elizabeth Bishop, whose life and art were each a refreshment and perspective on the other. The claims on Merrill's attention derive, in the pieces that follow, from study, from emulation, from friendship. The figures brought together here—Cavafy but also an Alexandrian dilettante, Dante *and* a Stonington neighbor—will recall for many readers the supporting cast of the *Sandover* trilogy.

A poet's prose is not necessarily "poetic," but more often than the novelist's prose, it plays on what Mallarmé called a "concealed keyboard." Certainly Merrill's does. Metaphor and anecdote combine; indirection, irony, and image, not argument, make the connections. It is commentary raised to the level of implication. Auden once said that any poem has both "an immediate meaning and a possible meaning." So too do Merrill's essays. They present their subjects, explain and expand on them. But the suggestions he makes in passing, and the themes he dwells on, have everything to do with his own work as well. His description of Dante's *Commedia*, for instance, is clearly made in light of the sources and structure of his own *Sandover* trilogy:

> In an age that discouraged the heretic, his vision reached him through the highest, most unexceptionable channels. Its cast included saints, philosophers, emperors, angels, monsters, Adam and Ulysses, Satan and God. To these he added a poet he revered, a woman he adored, plus a host of friends and enemies whose names we should otherwise never have heard; and garbed them in patterns of breathtakingly symmetrical lights-and-darks woven from a belief everybody shared.

This is an obvious warrant. But when, later in the same essay, he singles out Dante's "eclectic middle style" that mediates between divine revelation and mundane particularity, the mystic and the scientist, he is also describing, albeit implicitly, the style of his own poem. In this and the other essays here, Merrill is continually and subtly characterizing himself. If he is, as he says, "a man choosing the words he lives by," so too does he choose writers whose work manifests those qualities that have given life to his own work—intelligence, equilibrium, a dramatic instinct, an enharmonic wit, the "desire, compassion, and regret" he relishes in Cavafy, the sharp-eyed descriptions that metaphor inspires, and those conventions of poetic form that clarify the conventions of the emotional life.

Not all of James Merrill's critical prose is collected here. Early student work, interesting for its preoccupations, has been left out. The curious reader may want to track down "The Transformation of Rilke," written as a class assignment in 1945 and published the next year in *The Yale Poetry Review*. Or Merrill's 107-page senior thesis at Amherst, "*A la recherche du temps perdu*: Impressionism in Literature," an astute study of Proust's style, which uses the analogy of impressionist painting to explore the two elements of metaphor, subject and image, as they relate to the economy of sensation and memory that constitutes Proustian reality. In the course of his argument, he alludes to Dante and Hart Crane, Wordsworth and T. S. Eliot to help make his points. Also omitted from this collection are small items—statements, appreciative paragraphs, and the like. His continuing series of introductions for the Yale Younger Poet volumes he has chosen (since 1983) are not included, but are easily available. And there have been published several more interviews than those (lightly edited to avoid repetitions) reprinted here. Why interviews at all, it might be asked, in a book of prose? Because in all but two instances (the Ashley Brown interview and the symposium "On Literary Tradition"), Merrill *wrote* his answers. The illusion of spontaneous conversation is after all attainable at the writing-desk. The model might be, or might as well have been, Nabokov, who scorned the verbatim transcript and said that "even the dream I describe to my wife across the breakfast table is only a first draft." Each paragraph of "talk" in these interviews represents, then, a considered opinion. And it is characteristic—of this entire collection, in fact—that Merrill wants prompting: a question, an invitation, an assignment. It is as much the desire for an audience as for a dialogue with another voice. Haven't his poems been similarly prompted? It comes back to tone. To respond is, for Merrill, a way to test, to temper his ideas; to make certain they suit an occasion and are telling the truth. The transmuted talk of the interviews makes them essays-in-entries.

Merrill's ideas have developed, but not fundamentally changed over the forty years of writing which this book collects. They have grown more tolerant perhaps, more canny; his tastes have broadened, and his ambition taken on larger proportions. Certainly he would not have considered an essay on Dante ten years earlier, before having written a demanding epic of his own. But the consistency of his allegiances is remarkable. This collection offers a privileged look into the poet's imagination, into his working methods and interpretations, into short stories that foreshadow larger narratives, into the autobiographical and literary backgrounds of his career. Any writer, Merrill tells David Kalstone in their interview, leads a double life: "Not so much in the obvious division between experience and its imitation on the page as in the two sides . . . of the creative temperament. That which conceives and that which executes." There are analogous divisions and doublings everywhere in Merrill's work, but these essays and interviews and stories make still more explicit that side of Merrill—of his life, and of his creative temperament—that "conceived" his art. And if poems and the private life serve finally to illuminate each other, then both take their light from reading. The pages that follow are a lifetime's encounters with writers who have stood by James Merrill as he wrote the poems that have come to find a place beside theirs.

Foreword

There are after all things to be said for prose. I still read it, often with more profit than I do poetry. I go on using it for letters, conversation, the recording of dreams, and so forth. It is not *that* much harder to write than verse, or (as a seventeen thousand-line poem goes to show) that much less concise. Yet I persist in seeing it as a mildly nightmarish medium, to which *there is no end*: conterminous with one's very life, and only at rare and irregular intervals affording that least pause in flight whereby a given line of poetry creates the desire for another, and renews through all-but-subliminal closure the musical attack. With prose, as I saw it, the aria never came. All was recitative which, however threatened by resolution, continued self-importantly to advance the plot, explaining, describing, discriminating, while at least this listener, in the grip of his untenable prejudice, held out for song, for opera, for *opera*—works no longer made up of set pieces but *durchkomponiert* according to the best post-Wagnerian models. In retrospect, however, it must be granted that certain evenings were much enlivened by those skittish interludes, and I shall be glad to have these of mine assembled, whenever *Una voce poco fa* finds itself with nothing to say, or *Il mio tesoro* falls outside the tenor's range.

James Merrill
Stonington
July 1985

xiii

Acknowledgments

Grateful acknowledgement is extended to the publications in which these pieces originally appeared, in somewhat different form: "Acoustical Chambers," under the title "Condemned to Write About Real Things," appeared in the February 21, 1982, *New York Times Book Review*, copyright © 1982 by The New York Times Company. Reprinted by permission. "On Literary Tradition," excerpts from the "Literary Tradition" symposium at George Mason University, appeared in *Shenandoah*, vol. 33, no. 3 (1982), copyright © 1982 by Washington and Lee University, reprinted from *Shenandoah: The Washington and Lee University Review* with the permission of the Editor. "On the Country of a Thousand Years of Peace" appeared in the book *Poet's Choice*, edited by Paul Engle and Joseph Langland, copyright © 1962 by Paul Engle and Joseph Langland. Reprinted by permission of Doubleday & Company, Inc. "On 'Snapshot of Adam' " from the symposium "Ecstatic Occasions, Expedient Forms" appeared in *Epoch*, vol. 33, no. 1 (Fall–Winter 1983), and is reprinted by permission. "On Yánnina," under the title "The Poet: Private," appeared in *The Saturday Review*, vol. 55, no. 49 (Dec. 1972), copyright © 1972 by *Saturday Review* magazine. Reprinted by permission. "An Interview with James Merrill" by Donald Sheehan appeared in *Contemporary Literature*, vol. 9, no. 1 (Winter 1968). Reprinted by permission of the University of Wisconsin Press and by permission of the author. "An Interview with James Merrill" by Ashley Brown appeared in *Shenandoah*, vol. 19, no. 4 (Summer 1968), copyright © 1968 by Washington and Lee University, reprinted from *Shenandoah: The Washington and Lee University Review* with permission of the Editor and the author. "James Merrill's Myth: An Interview" by Helen Vendler appeared in *The New York Review of Books*, vol. 26, no. 7 (May 3, 1979), copyright © 1979 by N.Y. REV., Inc. Reprinted by permission of the publisher and the author. The "Interview with Fred Bornhauser" is reprinted from *Contemporary Authors New Revision Series*, vol. 10 (Detroit, 1983) edited by Ann Evory and Linda Metzger (Copyright © 1962, 1963, 1964, 1965, 1966, 1967, 1968, 1969, 1970, 1971, 1973, 1974, 1975, 1976, 1977, 1978, 1979, 1980, 1983 by Gale Research Company; reprinted by permission of the publisher), Gale Research, 1983, pp. 326–329. The "Interview with J. D. McClatchy" originally appeared in *The Paris Review*, no. 84 (Summer 1982) and was reprinted in *Writers at Work: The Paris Review Interviews*, edited by George Plimpton. Copyright © 1984 by The Paris Review, Inc. Reprinted by permission of Viking Penguin, Inc. "Divine Poem" appeared in *The New Republic*, vol. 183, no. 22 (Nov. 29, 1980). Reprinted by permission. "Unreal Citizen," under the title "Marvelous Poet," appeared in *The New York Review of Books*, vol. 22, no. 12 (July 17, 1975), copyright © 1975 by N.Y. REV., Inc. Reprinted by permission. "Object Lessons" appeared in *The New York Review of Books*, vol. 19, no. 9 (Nov. 30, 1972), copyright © 1972 by N.Y. REV., Inc., Reprinted by permission. "Elizabeth Bishop (1911–1979)" appeared in *The New York Review of Books*, vol. 26, no. 19 (Dec. 6, 1979), copyright © 1979 by N.Y. REV., Inc. Reprinted by permission. "The Transparent Eye," under the title "The Clear Eye of Elizabeth Bishop," appeared in *The Washington Post Book World*, vol. 13, no. 8 (Feb. 20, 1983). Reprinted by permission. "Robert Bagg: A Postscript" appeared in the July, 1961, *Poetry*. Re-

RECITATIVE

Reprinted by permission. "The Beaten Path" appeared in *Semi-Colon*, vol. 2, nos. 5 and 6. Reprinted by permission. "Notes on Corot" was originally published in The Art Institute of Chicago, *Corot 1796–1875* (exh. cat.), Chicago: 1960. Reprinted by permission. The "Foreword" to *Le Sorelle Brontë* by Bernard de Zogheb, published by Tibor de Nagy Editions, 1963, is reprinted by permission of Tibor de Nagy Editions. "Driver" first appeared in *Partisan Review*, vol. 29, no. 4 (Fall, 1962). Reprinted by permission. "Peru: The Landscape Game" appeared in *Prose*, no. 2 (Spring 1971). Reprinted by permission of Prose Publishers Incorporated.

Excerpts from the letters of Elizabeth Bishop are printed with permission of Alice Methfessel, Literary Executor of the Bishop estate. The poem "Exchanging Hats" and other lines by Elizabeth Bishop are from *The Complete Poems, 1927–1979* by Elizabeth Bishop, copyright © 1983 by Alice Helen Methfessel. Reprinted by permission of Farrar, Straus and Giroux, Inc.

I.
WRITING

Acoustical Chambers

Interior spaces, the shape and correlation of rooms in a house, have always appealed to me. Trying for a blank mind, I catch myself instead revisiting a childhood bedroom on Long Island. Recently, on giving up the house in Greece where I'd lived for much of the previous fifteen years, it wasn't so much the fine view it commanded or the human comedies it had witnessed that I felt deprived of; rather, I missed the hairpin turn of the staircase underfoot, the height of our kitchen ceiling, the low door ducked through in order to enter a rooftop laundry room that had become my study. This fondness for given arrangements might explain how instinctively I took to quatrains, to octaves and sestets, when I began to write poems. "Stanza" is after all the Italian word for "room."

Foreign languages entered my life early in the person of my governess. Although we called her Mademoiselle she was not a spinster but a widow. Neither was she French, or even, as she led us to believe, Belgian, but part English and part, to her undying shame, Prussian. She had lived in Brussels at least, and her sister, who now taught music in Pennsylvania, had been decorated for playing duets with the old Queen Mother of Belgium. Mademoiselle's maiden name was Fanning. This meant some distant kinship with the explorer who discovered—I can see her finger poised above the open atlas—*those* tiny Pacific islands, and whose house a block away from mine in Stonington, Connecticut, I would be able to point out to her when she spent a day with me thirty years later.

I worshiped this kind, sad woman: her sensible clothes, her carrot hair and watery eyes, the sunburnt triangle at her throat, the lavender wen on her wrist. She taught me to say the Ave Maria and to sing Carmen's habanera. I got by heart the brother heroically dead, the sister in Johnstown,

Published under the title "Condemned to Write about Real Things" in *The New York Times Book Review* (February 21, 1982), as part of its "The Making of a Writer" series, a feature in which writers were invited "to comment on various aspects of their craft: their imaginative and autobiographical sources, their practices of composition, the origin of their sense of vocation."

3

the other sister in Copenhagen. I resolved as soon as I grew up to marry her daughter, Stella, at that age plain and rather disagreeable, who was boarded out to a refined Catholic family in East Hampton—the light of love suffused even *them*. I heard all there was to hear about Mademoiselle's previous charges and prayed every night to grieve her less than spoilt Constance M. or devilish Peter T. had done. While she talked a needle flashed—costumes for my marionettes. Stories that ten years later would have convulsed me, I drank in solemnly. For instance: Having to relieve herself at a border checkpoint during the war, Mademoiselle had overlaid the *"infecte"* toilet seat with some family letters she happened to be carrying in her purse. In the course of the "formalities" her innocent buttocks were bared by a uniformed matron and found to be stenciled with suspicious mirror writing, which triggered a long and humiliating interrogation. *"Figure-toi!"* she exclaimed, gravely fixing me through her gold-rimmed spectacles. I could indeed imagine. I too was being imprinted, there and then.

By the time I was eight I had learned from her enough French and German to understand that English was merely one of many ways to express things. A single everyday object could be called *assiette* or *Teller* as well as *plate*—or were plates themselves subtly different in France and Germany? Mademoiselle's French and Latin prayers seemed to invoke absolutes beyond the ken of our Sunday school pageants. At the same time, I was discovering how the everyday sounds of English could mislead you by having more than one meaning. One afternoon at home I opened a random book and read: "Where is your husband, Alice?" "In the library, sampling the port." If samples were little squares of wallpaper or chintz, and ports were where ships dropped anchor, this hardly clarified the behavior of Alice's husband. Long after Mademoiselle's exegesis, the phrase haunted me. Words weren't what they seemed. The mother tongue could inspire both fascination and distrust.

But back to those octaves and sestets. Words might frustrate me, forms never did; neither did meter. Children in my day were exposed to a good deal of competent verse. Each first grader at St. Bernard's memorized his hundred lines of Walter Scott and received an apple for so doing. Before graduation he would speak deathless poetry in the annual Shakespeare play. The masters somehow let meaning take care of itself, a chip borne along by the rhetorical surge. Accordingly, frustration was reserved for the content, or lack of it, in what I'd begun to write at boarding school. Gerrish

4

Thurber, the mild and merciful librarian who "advised" the young editors of the *Lawrenceville Lit*, read through my first submission and nodded, saying only, "We can always use a well-made sonnet." It took me a while to fathom what he hadn't said.

My classmate Frederick Buechner wrote his poem first. In a flash I thought: I can do that too! And away we went. Luckily perhaps, since it allowed us to polish without much thought for what (if anything) we were communicating, our callowness led us to second-rate, *fin de siècle* stuff— Wilde, Heredia, Alice Meynell. These writers didn't figure in the Lawrenceville curriculum, although they met its chief requirement by having died. The living poets (unlike Milton or Keats, on whom white-haired Mr. Raymond had given us the last sonorous word) were still scandalously eluding definition in the pages of anthologies never seen in the classroom. Would our style ever mature? Or rather, dripping and sugary, would it ever unripen? Long after Freddy had gone on to Blake and Whitman, I dawdled behind with Elinor Wylie and the gaudier bits in Baudelaire.

On the threshold of our senior year the *Lit*'s graduating editor summoned his two least trustworthy successors. Sucking at a pipe, this man of eighteen urged us to recant. "Write about *real things* for God's sake: blondes and pistons!"—fetishes no less conventional than the moonlit foliage, masquerades, mad crones, and pet monkeys that clotted our own poems and stories. We left his room with scornful smiles.

The airs I was giving myself ran in the family. My father had offered his Aunt Grace the sum, unheard-of in those Depression years, of five dollars a page for memoirs of her Mississippi girlhood. She couldn't do it; the truth froze her pen. Not that she stopped writing. One summer a flier came in the mail from a vanity press in New York, announcing Aunt Grace's novel, *Femme Fatale*. "Set against the turbulent background of the French court, this tale of searing passion. . . ." My mother and I, alone that year and needing diversion, at once ordered our copy—several copies: Christmas was coming. Before it did, German troops overran a real France Aunt Grace wouldn't have crossed the street to see, and *Femme Fatale* was never published or our money refunded.

Like Aunt Grace, and like many adolescents, I needed to feel that I was fulfilling myself in the face of heartless indifference. In fact my mother was both proud and critical of my early writing. She had taken a summer course in the short story at Columbia, worked on the Jacksonville newspaper and edited until her marriage a weekly gazette of her own. Some

5

satirical doggerel she dashed off about the preparations for my sister's wedding dazzled me, at nine, with its zany, end-stopped rhyming. My father, who could compose long lucid letters in his beautifully rounded hand and read with X-ray eyes the to me impenetrable editorials in the *Herald Tribune*, looked to literature for a good cry. His favorite author was J. M. Barrie—indeed, Alice and her port-sampling husband may be found in Barrie's play '*Dear Brutus*.' My father had a way of his own with rhyme. Here is how he acknowledged one of my letters when I first went abroad:

> Though we're apart,
> You're in my heart—
> I too love Chartres.

He was also a powerful and unpredictable man, never more so, in my young eyes, than when, pretending to want for his scrapbook the poems and stories I'd written up to then, he had a small edition of them handsomely produced during my senior year at Lawrenceville. *Jim's Book*, as he titled it, thrilled me for days, then mortified me for a quarter-century. I wouldn't put it past my father to have foreseen the furthest consequences of his brilliant, unsettling gesture, which, like the pat on a sleepwalker's back, looked like approbation but was aimed at waking me up.

It partly succeeded. I opened my eyes enough at least to see how much remained to be learned about writing. Presently I was at Amherst, reading Proust, Dante, and *Faust* in their various originals, Jane Austen and Pope with Reuben Brower, Shakespeare and Darwin with Theodore Baird. Here also Kimon Friar put before me the living poets and gave the nine-day wonders that shot up like beanstalks from this richest of mulches their first and only detailed criticism. Many hands made light work. Four years after graduation my *First Poems* had appeared. I was living alone and unhappy in Rome and going to a psychiatrist for writer's block.

The doctor wanted to hear about my life. It had been flowing along unnoticed in my absorption with the images that came and went on its surface. Now its very droplets were being studied on a slide. "Real things"—was I condemned to write about them, after all?

Of course I had been doing nothing else. Symbolist pastiche or makeshift jotting, our words reveal more than we think. The diary kept during my first year away at school reports a Christmas-break visit to Silver Springs, Florida. I'd like to go back there one day and ride again in the glass-bottomed boat, peering down at the cold pastoral of swaying grasses and glinting schools. There would be much to say about "unconscious depths," about my zodiacal creature the Fish, above all about the heavy pane of glass that, like a kind of intelligence, protected me and my mother from that sunken world while revealing its secrets in magical detail. But in 1940 the artless diarist records only this: "Silver Springs—heavenly colors and swell fish."

Two banalities, each by itself bad enough, and hopelessly so in conjunction. Yet in their simple awfulness they broach the issue most crucial to this boy not quite fourteen. Two years earlier my parents have been divorced and Mademoiselle amicably sent packing: I am thought to need "a man's influence." We hear how children suffer under these circumstances. I am no exception; my grades plummet, I grow fat gorging on sweets. "Heavenly colors and swell fish." What is that phrase but an attempt to bring my parents together, to remarry on the page their characteristic inflections— the ladylike gush and the regular-guy terseness? In reality my parents have tones more personal and complex than these, but the time is still far off when I can dream of echoing them. To do so, I see in retrospect, will involve a search for magical places real or invented, like Silver Springs or Sandover, acoustical chambers so designed as to endow the weariest platitude with resonance and depth. By then, too, surrogate parents will enter the scene, figures more articulate than Mademoiselle but not unlike her, either, in the safe ease and mystery of their influence: Proust and Elizabeth Bishop; Maria and Auden in the Sandover books. The unities of home and world, and world and page, will be observed through the very act of transition from one to the other.

On Literary Tradition

In response to a question from William Matthews about literary appren-
ticeship:

I want to start with a phrase you used. You were saying about the young
poet that the best he or she could do was to write what was truly felt and
could be clearly said. I think probably my ambition, when I was an adoles-
cent, was to do almost the opposite. Because I didn't know what I felt, it
seemed to me that what was obscurely said had a kind of resonance that
charmed me and led me at least down that dangerous path toward the impenetrable quatrains of Mallarmé, trying deliberately to create a surface
of such impenetrability and, at the same time, such beauty that it wouldn't
yield up a meaning easily, if at all. Maybe eventually one gets tired of that
kind of thing, though in my weak moments I still find myself drawn to it.
My point is that one needn't have any idea what one feels when one starts
to write a poem. The poem is, in a way, an act of self-purification. The
clarity you may arrive at is unforeseeable. . . .

The feeling, too, can surface at the end. The feeling you begin with is
very often just the feeling of wanting to write a poem. With any luck you
can put it together with a so-called real emotion, love or anger.

About tradition—Bill was talking about the reaction of one generation
to another against the tone, everything, to use a clumsy word, *human*, that
has been brought by the poet to his work. I think this changes, and one
reacts against tone much more automatically and rapidly than one reacts
against form. Descartes may have wanted to turn his knowledge inside out
but he still was using the form of the French sentence and the language.
The forms in writing are what tide one over these periods of reaction. . . .

Excerpts from the transcript of a symposium held at George Mason University, April 4–5,
1982. The topic was "Literary Tradition," and the participants were Nadine Gordimer,
David Kalstone, William Matthews, Myra Sklarew, Susan Sontag, D. M. Thomas—and
James Merrill. The transcript was published in *Shenandoah*, vol. 33, no. 3 (1982).

They *do* change, but they change as slowly as the forms in Darwin, whereas the pendulum of individual tone from one generation to the next keeps moving briskly.

To a question about passion in poetry:

Life will teach you passion. I agree with Lytton Strachey when he was asked what the most important thing was in the world and he said passion. Unfortunately, when we've been in workshops, or looked at beginner poems, we've seen poems full of passion which neither we nor their authors would want to read a few months later. And yet the great poems, in our language or in any language, are the passionate poems. As a young person, I didn't know what I felt. I was a very backward child and I practiced simply the skills; whatever came to hand filled in the frame. As I grew older, I had stronger, more trustable emotions, things that came to me with life, from life, not from reading or from the classroom, and those feelings went into my frame. I don't deny that we all felt intensely at the age of fifteen or twenty, but it's a feeling that doesn't always bear inspection a few years later because we grow so rapidly at that time in our lives. It's really the artistry that sustains the passionate poem that we would read from one century to the next. What I might have wanted to learn in a workshop was precisely as much as I could about artistry, trusting life to take care of the rest.

To a question about some earlier remarks Merrill made about Elizabeth Bishop:

I was talking about Elizabeth Bishop and wondering what sets her apart from the male giants—Eliot, Pound, Wallace Stevens who seem in their life's work to transcend human dimensions; somehow wondering whether the light that philosophy casts made a greater shadow on the wall behind them. I've noticed in my own work, to my horror, writing this trilogy, that suddenly everything was getting much bigger than I thought a life should be. I kept clinging to the idea of Elizabeth with her sanity and levelheadedness and quirkiness of mind.

To a question about modernism:

The modernist work is like one of these plate-glass banks where you can look in and see the vaults, see all of the workings and all the precautions they've taken against being robbed. The only thing you don't see is what happens to the individual safe deposit box. Sometimes I wish we still had those heavy marble facades that kept everything a mystery.

RECITATIVE

To a question about discipline:

My discipline is that of a terrible untidiness. I never know what piece of paper I've written yesterday's note down on or what little notebook I should be looking into for this or that. Back to workshops—Auden used to say that he didn't believe in them, except that one might learn at an age young enough for it to take how to keep a tidy desk, and from then on everything would follow.

To a question about strategies of allusion:

I think perhaps there's the same amount of embarrassment attached to alluding overtly to other writers as there would be in alluding to your own work. It's a bit snotty to nudge the reader too obviously with reference to Virgil or Eliot. In our day resonance has become, thanks to Freud and Jung, more the property of the unconscious than a conscious manipulation of the body of literature. So that whenever I've alluded to either another part of my own work or to a poem from the past, I've been happiest about it when I realized *after* I'd done my work that the allusion was there. Whether I wanted to bring it to light or not, to make it explicit or not, was entirely up to me. I think of a poem I wrote twenty years ago, a description of a willowware teacup. Luckily I didn't connect my poem, until I had finished it, with a famous poem about a vessel with figures on the outside and images that were both idyllic and violent.

On "The Country of a Thousand Years of Peace"

THE COUNTRY OF A THOUSAND YEARS OF PEACE

Here they all come to die,
Fluent therein as in a fourth tongue.
But for a young man not yet of their race
It was madness you should lie

Blind in one eye, and fed
By the blood of a scrubbed face;
It was madness to look down
On the toy city where

The glittering neutrality
Of clock and chocolate and lake and cloud
Made every morning somewhat
Less than you could bear;

And makes me cry aloud
At the old masters of disease
Who dangling high about you on a hair
The sword that, never falling, kills

Would coax you still back from that starry land
Under the world, which no one sees
Without a death, its finish and sharp weight
Flashing in his own hand.

Published in *Poet's Choice*, edited by Paul Engle and Joseph Langland (New York: Dial, 1962).

RECITATIVE

In 1950, at the beginning of nearly three years abroad, I went to Lausanne
for an hour with my friend the Dutch poet Hans Lodeizen. He had been
reading George Sand's autobiography; there was Roussel on the phonograph and a Picasso etching of acrobats on the floor. The June sunset filled
up his hospital room. He spoke with carefree relish of the injection they
would give him presently. Before I left we agreed to meet in Italy sometime
that fall. He had leukemia and died two weeks later, at twenty-six. It was
my first deeply felt death. I connected it with the spell of aimless living in
Europe to which I was then committed and to which all those picturesque
and novel sights corresponded painfully enough. As the inevitable verses
took shape, strictness of form seemed at last beside the point; my material
nevertheless allowed for a good deal of paring and polishing. Eight years
later, a word from Barbara Deming led me to rephrase the last four lines;
another, from Benjamin DeMott, to make use of the second person. The
poem still surprises me, as much by its clarification of what I was feeling,
as by its foreknowledge of where I needed to go next, in my work.

On "Snapshot of Adam"

SNAPSHOT OF ADAM

By flash in sunshine "to reduce contrast"
He grins back from the green deck chair,
Stripped, easy at last, bush tangle rhyming
With beard and windblown hair;
Coke sweating, forearm tanned to oak,
Scar's lightning hid by flat milk-blaze of belly
—But all grown, in the sliding glass
Beyond him, unsubstantial. Here I dwell,

Finger on shutter, amid my clay
Or marble ghosts; treetops in silhouette;
And day, his day, its vivid shining stuff
Negated to matte slate
A riddle's chalked on: Name the threat
Posed never long or nakedly enough.

Imprinted over centuries upon the sestet of a sonnet is a change of mood
or direction. The example at hand modulates from solid to flat; Adam to
his maker; the opener (if only of a Coke) to the camera's shutter, etc.
Rather than plan ahead as the eighth line approaches, I'm apt to recall a
moment at the Kabuki in Tokyo decades ago. A long ramp (the *hamamichi*
or "flower way") cuts through the public to join the stage at right angles.
This transitional point challenges the actor who crosses it. That day we
had seen Benten the Thief at work plundering a house from top to bottom.
Frightened, furtive, eyes darting, sleeves full of loot, he ran from the
scene, set foot upon the ramp, paused, straightened, tidied his clothing,
stuck out his chest. An imaginary thoroughfare took shape around utter
probity, now striding out of sight to loud cheers.

A contribution to a poets' symposium "Ecstatic Occasions, Expedient Forms," edited by
David Lehman. Published in *Epoch*, vol. 33, no. 1 (Fall-Winter 1983).

On "Yánnina":
An Interview
with David Kalstone

YÁNNINA

For Stephen Yenser

There lay the peninsula stretching far into the dark gray water,
with its mosque, its cypress tufts and fortress walls; there was
the city stretching far and wide along the water's edge; there
was the fatal island, the closing scene of the history of the once
all-powerful Ali.   EDWARD LEAR

Somnambulists along the promenade
Have set up booths, their dreams:
Carpets, jewelry, kitchenware, halvah, shoes.
From a loudspeaker passionate lament
Mingles with the penny Jungle's roars and screams.
Tonight in the magician's tent
Next door a woman will be sawed in two,
But right now she's asleep, as who is not, as who . . .

An old Turk at the water's edge has laid
His weapons and himself down, sleeps
Undisturbed since when? 1913?
Nothing will surprise him should he wake,
Only how tall, how green the grass has grown
There by the dusty carpet of the lake

Published under the title "The Poet: Private" in *Saturday Review*, vol. 55, no. 49 (December 1972).

Sun beats, then sleepwalks down a vine-festooned arcade,
Giving himself away in golden heaps.

And in the dark gray water sleeps
One who said no to Ali. Kiosks all over town
Sell that postcard, "Kyra Frossíni's Drown,"
Showing her, eyeballs white as mothballs, trussed
Beneath the bulging moon of Ali's lust.
A devil (turban and moustache and sword)
Chucks the pious matron overboard—
Wait—Heaven help us—SPLASH!

The torch smokes on the prow. Too late.
(A picture deeply felt, if in technique slapdash.)
Wherefore the Lion of Epirus, feared
By Greek and Turk alike, tore his black beard
When to barred casements rose the song
Broken from bubbles rising all night long:
"A ton of sugar pour, oh pour into the lake
To sweeten it for poor, for poor Frossíni's sake,"*

Awake? Her story's aftertaste
Varies according to the listener.
Friend, it's bitter coffee you prefer?
Brandy for me, and with a fine
White sandy bottom. Not among those braced
By action taken without comment, neat,
Here's how! Grounds of our footnote infiltrate the treat,
Mud-vile to your lips, crystal-sweet to mine.

Twilight at last. Enter the populace.
One little public garden must retrace
Long after school its childish X,
Two paths that cross and cross. The hollyhock, the rose,
Zinnia and marigold hear themselves named

---

*"Time was kind to the reputation of this woman who had been unfaithful to her husband, vain, and grasping. She came to be regarded as a Christian martyr and even as an early heroine in the struggle for Greek independence. She has been celebrated in legend, in poetry, in popular songs and historical fiction, and surrounded with the glamour which so often attaches to women whose love affairs have been of an intense nature and have involved men of political or historical importance." William Plomer, *The Diamond of Jannina*.

RECITATIVE

And blush for form's sake, unashamed
Chorus out of *Ignoramus Rex*:
"What shall the heart learn, that already knows

Its place by water, and its time by sun?"
Mother wit fills the stately whispering sails
Of girls someone will board and marry. Who?
Look at those radiant young males.
Their morning-glory nature neon blue
Wilts here on the provincial vine. Where did it lead,
The race, the radiance? To oblivion
Dissembled by a sac of sparse black seed.

Now under trees men with rush baskets sell
Crayfish tiny and scarlet as the sins
In any fin de siècle villanelle.
Tables fill up. A shadow play begins.
Painted, translucent cut-outs fill the screen.
It glows. His children by a jumping bean
Karaghiozi clobbers, baits the Turk,
Then all of them sing, dance, tell stories, go berserk.

Tomorrow we shall cross the lake to see
The cottage tumbling down, where soldiers killed
Ali. Two rugless rooms. Cushions. Vitrines
In which, to this day, silks and bracelets swim.
Above, a painting hangs. It's him,
Ali. The end is near, he's sleeping between scenes
In a dark lady's lap. Vassilikí.
The mood is calm, the brushwork skilled

By contrast with Frossíni's mass-produced
Unsophisticated piece of goods.
The candle trembles in the watching god's
Hand—almost a love-death, höchste Lust!
Her drained, compliant features haunt
The waters there was never cause to drown her in.
Your grimiest ragamuffin comes to want
Two loves, two versions of the Feminine:

16

One virginal and tense, brief as a bubble,
One flesh and bone—gone up no less in smoke
Where giant spits revolving try their rusty treble,
Sheep's eyes pop, and death-wish ravens croak.
Remember, the Romantic's in full feather.
Byron has visited. He likes
The luxe, and overlooks the heads on pikes:
Finds Ali "very kind . . . indeed, a father . . ."*

Funny, that is how I think of Ali.
On the one hand, the power and the gory
Details, pigeon-blood rages and retali-
ations, gouts of fate that crust his story;
And on the other, charm, the whimsically
Meek brow, its motives all ab ulteriori,
The flower-blue gaze twining to choke proportion,
Having made one more pretty face's fortune.

A dove with Parkinson's disease
Selects *our* fortunes: TRAVEL AND GROW WISE
And A LOYAL FRIEND IS MORE THAN GOLD.
But, at the island monastery, eyes
Gouged long since to the gesso sockets will outstare
This or that old timer on his knees
Asking the candlelight for skill to hold
The figures flush against the screen's mild glare.

Ali, my father   both are dead.
In so many words, so many rhymes,
The brave old world sleeps. Are we what it dreams
And is a rude awakening overdue?
Not in Yánnina. To bed, to bed.
The Lion sets. The lights wink out along the lake.
Weeks later, in this study gone opaque,
They are relit. See through me. See me through.

---

*Letter to his mother, November 12, 1809. Plomer observes: ". . . even allowing for Oriental effusiveness, it seems doubtful whether [Ali's] interest in Byron was exactly as paternal as he pretended, for a father does not give his son sweets twenty times a day and beg him to visit him at night. It is worth remarking that Ali was a judge of character and a connoisseur of beauty, whether male or female, and that the like of Byron, and Byron at twenty-one, is not often seen."

For partings hurt although we dip the pain
Into a glowing well—the pen, I mean.
Living alone won't make some inmost face to shine
Maned with light, ember and anodyne,
Deep in a desktop burnished to its grain.
That the last hour be learned again
By riper selves, couldn't you doff this green
Incorruptible, the might-have-been,

And arm in arm with me dare the magician's tent?
It's hung with asterisks. A glittering death
Is hefted, swung. The victim smiles consent.
To a sharp intake of breath she comes apart
(Done by mirrors? Just one woman? Two?
A fight starts—in the provinces, one feels,
There's never that much else to do)
Then to a general exhalation heals

Like anybody's life, bubble and smoke
In afterthought, whose elements converge,
Glory of windless mornings that the barge
(Two barges, one reflected, a quicksilver joke)
Kept scissoring and mending as it steered
The old man outward and away,
Amber mouthpiece of a narghilé
Buried in his by then snow-white beard.

KALSTONE: Can you say something about the circumstances surrounding "Yánnina"?

MERRILL: It's a town I'd wanted to visit for years and had begun to fear I never would, like Proust and Parma. So that I must have worked myself into a fairly receptive state by the time I got there. No research, mind you—a phrase or two out of Lear, a dim echo of Byron, the foreknowledge of a lake. It never hurts, does it, to have a body of water up one's sleeve, something that flows or reflects? Ali Pasha was just a name. Later on, halfway through the poem when I needed a biography of him, I was delighted to find the wonderful William Plomer had written it. In any case the day came—less than a day: I didn't spend twenty-four hours on the spot. But the piano had been prepared, and only the notation remained. That whole element—do we dare call it reality?—had to be unforeseeable, accidental, something to fill in then and there. I'd counted on that.

KALSTONE: Did you have a theme already in mind? Is that what you're saying?

MERRILL: No, not really. . . . Wait—yes, I did! How odd not to have made the connection. Earlier that year I'd been concerned for a friend, a woman whose son had disappeared. He'd been teaching somewhere—a man in his thirties—and one day absolutely vanished without a trace. Weeks passed, months passed, his friends imagined the worst, his mother was beside herself. I was already in Greece when two letters came from her. In the first she had just heard from a friend of Bruce's that he was well and living under an assumed name—she didn't yet know where. Her second letter, not long afterwards, said that she'd heard from Bruce (or Tom, as he now wanted to be called); he'd given her his address, told her he'd found work there. What he'd wanted was no less than a brand-new life, and it looked, at that point, as if he'd found it. Now it may sound—it may be—childish, but haven't we all dreamed of doing exactly that? To disappear and reemerge as a new person without any ties, the slate wiped clean. Sometimes one even puts the dream into action, in a less dramatic way than Bruce's, or do I mean Tom's? In my own case I began going to Greece—over ten years ago—very much in the spirit of one who embarks upon a double life. The life I lived there seemed I can't tell you how different from life in America. I felt for the first time that I was doing exactly as I pleased. How we delude ourselves! As if there were ever more than one life. Tom is as close to Bruce's mother as Bruce had ever been. He's in touch with many of his former friends—all this after scarcely a year of his new identity. I myself, after ten years of moving back and forth, can hardly distinguish, now, between Athens and Stonington, Connecticut. Anyhow, you might say that these "scissorings and mendings" are the theme of "Yánnina."

KALSTONE: Does this notion of playing different roles connect with the shadow play in the poem? I'm not altogether sure what a shadow play is.

MERRILL: They're dying out, like everything. The one I describe was set up out of doors—a proscenium framing a long, white screen lit from behind. The puppets are two-dimensional figures of colored parchment, or maybe plastic nowadays, somewhat articulated but mainly relying on the verve and bounce of the manipulators who hold them flat against the screen with rods. Rather the effect of a primitive animated cartoon. Lots of contemporary allusion, popular songs, political jokes, but the main action generally refers back to the Turkish occupation. There's always a pompous, dim-witted Pasha whom Karaghiozi makes a fool of. Karaghiozi's the hero—a wily little Greek, terribly demotic and down to earth. The play Byron saw in Yánnina reminded him of morris dancing, it was so indecent. I'm afraid things have changed since his day.

KALSTONE: About these changing roles. You appear to identify with the manipulator in one stanza—"to hold the figures flush," etc.—and in the next with the translucent puppet itself—"See through me . . . ."

MERRILL: Yes. It was greedy of me to want that double life. A writer already has two lives, don't you think? Not so much in the obvious division between experience and its imitation on the page as in the two sides of—well, I'll have to trust you, when this gets transcribed, to put in some less inflated term—the two sides of the creative temperament. That which conceives and that which executes. There are moments when the light *does* seem to shine through us. The rest of the time we spend trying to keep our images steady.

KALSTONE: The poem is full of paired figures, isn't it? Frossíni and Vassilikí, the speaker and his companion. And it's not just your poet who has a double life; many of the characters do as well. Frossíni in the text comes off as a chaste martyr, but as "unfaithful, vain, and grasping" in the footnote. Vassilikí gives her body to Ali but "goes up in smoke"; we never know what she was thinking. Ali himself is both gentle and cruel.

MERRILL: Isn't it odd? I mean, how one tries—not just in writing—to escape from these opposites, from there being two sides to every question!

KALSTONE: But you also show things being made whole. The magician—

MERRILL: The magician, yes, performs the essential act. He heals what he has divided. A double-edged action, like his sword. It's what one comes to feel that life keeps doing.

KALSTONE: You said once that your poems are not "historical." Yet I'd say that this poem is almost *about* history, that it's a kind of stand against people locked into the present. Not history as public record, mind you, but—

MERRILL: A kind of time-zoo?

KALSTONE: The vividness of your Ali—

MERRILL: Historical figures are always so well lighted. Even if one never gets to the truth about them, their contradictions, even their crimes, are so expressive. They're like figures in a novel read by millions of people at once. What's terrifying is that they're human as well, and therefore no more reliable than you or I. They have their blind, "genetic" side, just like my boys and girls in Yánnina.

KALSTONE: That's the point, isn't it? Not just that historical figures enter the poem, but that they're *creatures* of history ("oblivion/dissembled by a sac of sparse black seed"). There's no clear present in your poem; the past shadows it. It's as if you always need the past as a sounding board.

MERRILL: I liked that sense of sleeping presences. Ali, Frossíni, Vassilikí, the old Turk at the beginning—they're merely asleep. The woman to be sawed in half. Even "you and I" toward the end seem half-absorbed into the dreaming landscape.

Maybe there's something worth saying about tenses here, how one handles them. Last winter I visited a workshop in which only one out of fifteen poets had noticed that he needn't invariably use the first-person present active indicative. Poem after poem began: "I empty my glass . . . I go out . . . I stop by woods. . . ." For me a "hot" tense like that can't be handled for very long without cool pasts and futures to temper it. Or some complexity of syntax, or a modulation into the conditional—*something*. An imperative, even an auxiliary verb, can do wonders. Otherwise, you get this addictive, self-centered immediacy, harder to break oneself of than cigarettes. That kind of talk (which, by the way, is purely literary; it's never heard in life unless from foreigners or four-year-olds) calls to mind a speaker suspicious of words, in great boots, chain-smoking, Getting It Down on Paper. He'll never notice "Whose woods these are I think I know" gliding backwards through the room, or "Longtemps je me suis couché de bonne heure" plumping a cushion invitingly at her side.

KALSTONE: You're talking about—against?—so-called confessional poems. Yet the present is still *the* lyric tense, isn't it? Isn't the point that it aims at an ecstatic, timeless state? "Earth has not anything to show more fair. . . ."

MERRILL: Ah, but that's in the third person; that's another matter. No, you're right, and I don't want to paint myself into a corner. Yet I can't help. . . . Think how often poems in the first-person present begin with a veil drawn, a sublimation of the active voice or the indicative mood, as if some ritual effacement of the ego were needed before one could go on. "I wonder, by my troth, what thou and I . . ."; "Let us go then you and I. . . ." The poet isn't always the hero of a movie who *does* this, *does* that. He is a man choosing the words he lives by.

KALSTONE: Your own way of veiling the first person here has to do with the way you present the landscape, doesn't it?

MERRILL: You hardly ever need to *state* your feelings. The point is to feel and keep the eyes open. Then what you feel is expressed, is mimed back at you by the scene. A room, a landscape. I'd go a step further. We don't *know* what we feel until we see it distanced by this kind of translation.

KALSTONE: So, people and places fade into one another. Like the sun in "Yánnina" sleepwalking down the vine and the provincial boys who wilt on it? In Yánnina—*your* Yánnina—we're doomed to repeat certain experiences. Human contradictions appear to root themselves in nature.

MERRILL: No wonder Nature revenges herself. Those lines in Jarrell—remember?

> A quarter of an hour and we tire
> Of any landscape, said Goethe; eighty years
> And he had not tired of Goethe. The landscape had,
> And disposed of Goethe in the usual way.

KALSTONE: Is that why you don't write protest poems?

MERRILL: I don't know. Auden says they do no good, except to get you an audience among people who feel the same way.

KALSTONE: Wouldn't you like a larger audience?

MERRILL: When I search my heart, no, not really. So why invite it, even supposing that I could? Think what one has to *do* to get a mass audience. I'd rather have one perfect reader. Why dynamite the pond in order to catch that single silver carp? Better to find a bait that only the carp will take. One still has plenty of choices. The carp at Fontainebleau were thought to swallow small children, whole.

As to protest poems . . . they aren't poems first of all, so much as bits of honorable oratory. A protest *poem* would be one written against a poem of a different kind, one that reflected a different tradition. Wordsworth against Pope, Byron against Wordsworth.

KALSTONE: Would you like to say what kind of poem "Yánnina" is written against?

MERRILL: You must be joking. Well . . .

KALSTONE: There's a phrase in your second novel. You say about Racine—"the overlay of prismatic verse deflects a brutal, horrible action." Not that the underlying action of "Yánnina" is brutal or horrible.

MERRILL: No, but you mean it's implicit rather than presented as narrative? Yes. I'd wanted to let the scene, the succession of scenes, convey not meaning so much as a sense of it, a sense that something both is, and isn't, being said. I hoped that a reader's own experience would remind him that some things can go without saying. I was trying for an intimacy of tone, not of content. People are always asking, Was it real? Did it happen? (Thank *you* for not asking that, by the way.) As if a yes-or-no answer would settle the question. Was is really Yánnina I went to? Was my companion real or imaginary? I can only say yes *and* no to questions like that.

KALSTONE: You used the image of a veil earlier, talking about reticence. Does your veiling of tense and voice have to do with your feelings about "real" experience in a poem?

MERRILL: I suppose it would have to. We've all written poems that imitate a plausible sequence of events. "I go out" for a walk and find these beautiful daffodils or this dead songbird and have the following feelings. But, for better or worse, that walk is in fact taken—or Yánnina is visited—by a writer in hopes of finding something to write about. Then you have not simply imitated or recollected experience, but experience in the light of a projected emotion, like a beam into which what you encounter will seem to have strayed. The poem and its occasion will have created one another.

An Interview
with Donald Sheehan

SHEEHAN: I'd like to start by asking you about your poetry course at the University of Wisconsin this semester. What did you teach in it?

MERRILL: It was described as a poetry workshop, though there was little actual writing done. The eight weeks were mostly spent reading things I liked, then toward the end we took up some student work. We spent half of the time at least on Elizabeth Bishop's last book, *Questions of Travel*. And then we read some of Berryman's *Dream Songs* and some Lowell, and we had a glorious day on *The Rubáiyát*.

SHEEHAN: What do you think *The Rubáiyát* offers in teaching?

MERRILL: An anonymous poem, really, where the language, the content, is drawn from a whole universe much older, say, than Greek mythology, a kind of Old Testament, as old as language itself. The wine, the bread, the wilderness, the rose—all that of course translates beautifully into just what a Victorian audience wanted to hear: those Christian words, I mean. The vocabulary of the poem works both ways, for piety and paganism alike, which perhaps explains why Fitzgerald's translation sank so quickly into everybody's consciousness. People know lines from it who have never heard of Fitzgerald or Omar—or of poetry, for that matter.

SHEEHAN: This seems to be something of a comment about the so-called confessional poetry of late. Do you have any feelings about it?

MERRILL: It seems to me that confessional poetry, to all but the very naive reader or writer, is a literary convention like any other, the problem being to make it *sound* as if it were true. One can, of course, tell the truth, but I shouldn't think that would be necessary to give the illusion of a True Confession.

Conducted on May 23, 1967, in Madison, Wisconsin, where Merrill was poet-in-residence for the spring term at the University of Wisconsin. Published in *Contemporary Literature*, vol. 9, no. 1 (Winter 1968).

SHEEHAN: So the division between confessional and objective poetry is, you would say, artificial in the sense that both modes are conventions.

MERRILL: Precisely. Now and then it's been *true* what I wrote. Often, though, it's been quite made up or taken from somebody else's life and put in as if it were mine.

SHEEHAN: Critics today are asserting that in poetry the period of experimentation is over and a period of consolidation has set in, the Second World War being the Great Divide. Does this have any meaning to you? Is this true?

MERRILL: I've always been suspicious of the word experimentation. It partakes too much of staircase wit. People who talk about experimentation sound as if they thought poets set out deliberately to experiment, when in fact they haven't: they've simply recognized afterwards the newness of what they've done. William Carlos Williams talks about breaking the back of the pentameter as if this had been the first step in a program. It's something I should think he'd have been more likely to recognize well after doing it—if he ever did do it. The pentameter has been a good friend to me; you'd think I'd have noticed a little thing like a broken back. As for consolidation, I'm not so sure. Anybody starting to write today has at least ten kinds of poem, each different from the other, on which to pattern his own.

SHEEHAN: What kinds would you say?

MERRILL: There would be the confessional, if you will; or the personal nature lyric along the lines of Roethke; or the Chinese-sage manner, full of insects and ponies and small boats and liquor and place-names; or the kind of stammered-out neo-epigram of people like Creeley—to name only a few. And there are all sorts of schemes on the page to reproduce—the broken line, Williams' downward staircase, three paces to a step; the tight stanza; the heavy garlands of Perse; the "expressionist" calligrams of Pound or Olson. . . .

SHEEHAN: Perhaps this is a false abstraction to keep pursuing, but the sort of poetry that, say, Eliot and Pound wrote, doesn't seem to be getting written today. At the same time, though, I can't imagine, without some of Pound at least, any poets writing as they do today. Do you think there exists an "influence" (if I can use that tricky word) of Eliot and Pound on poets today?

MERRILL: Yes, if only as something to react against. Eliot and Pound, though, seem to be so terribly different in the long run. With Pound, in the *Cantos* at least, we find precious little unity except the contents of a single, very brilliant, and erratic mind. Whereas Eliot gives what may be only an illusion—I haven't read him for twenty years—of being infinitely in control of his material: so much so, that you have the sense of the whole civilization under glass. As, indeed, Eliot's poems are under glass for me. The temptation to reread them, though it's growing, is still fairly slight.

SHEEHAN: How about Wallace Stevens?

MERRILL: Stevens seems much more of a poet, that is to say, a nonhistorian. There's a nice distinction in a poem of A. D. Hope's, where he says that he wanted to be a poet, the "eater of time," rather than that "anus of mind, the historian." I'm an enemy of history, by the way—absurd thing to say, I'll be condemned to repeat it if I'm not careful. Repeat history, that is. Well, my position's open to analysis; I even have a poem about Father Time. However. Back to Stevens, I think he continues to persuade us of having had a private life, despite—or thanks to—all the bizarreness of his vocabulary and idiom.

SHEEHAN: I here think of the term used constantly, "voice." As a critical term, do you think it has meaning?

MERRILL: I think it does. "Voice" is the democratic word for "tone." "Tone" always sounds snobbish, but without a sense of it how one flounders!

SHEEHAN: Is voice a function of metrics, would you say?

MERRILL: I notice voice a good deal more in metrical poetry. The line lends itself to shifts of emphasis. If Frost had written free verse, I don't think we'd have heard as much of the voice in it.

SHEEHAN: I'd like to ask you about your own development. I notice in your four published volumes that you seem to have gone from a rather strict, symmetrical poem to a much looser, freer poem. Do you agree with this, and if you do, I wonder what led you in this direction?

MERRILL: I always relapse into the strict poem. I'd like to think I would continue to write a strict poem when I felt like it. But what you say is true. I remember—this might modify what I said about experiment—I remember, after *First Poems* was published, having in mind the kind of poem I wanted to write. I could picture it to myself only by seeing an unbroken page of blank verse, the density of the print trailing down the page; and long before any of these poems began to turn up in the little *Short Stories*, there was this picture I had of a certain look to the poem. And with these poems came various new conversational elements—the first earmark, perhaps, of blank verse.

SHEEHAN: This is related, I think, to another point. You're probably one of the few poets who has written completely successful novels, ones that can't be termed "poetic" in the usual sense of that word. What about the prose element in poetry, in your verse particularly?

MERRILL: I've enjoyed reading novels more often—or more profoundly—than I've enjoyed reading poems. There seems to be no poet except perhaps Dante whose work has the extraordinary richness of Tolstoy or Proust; and there are very few poets whose work gives as much fun as James. Oh, there's always a give and take. For instance, though a lot of the sound of James is prose, can't one tell that he'd read Browning? You hear a voice talking in prose, often a very delightful voice which can say all kinds of odd things. For me, to get something of that into poetry was a pleasure and even perhaps an object.

SHEEHAN: That would seem to contradict what some reviewers have said about your poems, that they have become more personal, perhaps even autobiographical. If the point is, as you were saying, to get a voice in poetry, what would you say to the critics and reviewers who claim this voice to be autobiographical?

MERRILL: To *sound* personal is the point—which is something I don't believe, by the way, that Pound and Eliot do very often; rather, they have impersonal, oracular voices. But so does an Elizabethan lyric sound impersonal. I'm not making judgments.

SHEEHAN: What about Auden's remark that if the poet raises his voice, he becomes phony or dishonest. Is that what you're saying?

MERRILL: If it's raised in all earnestness, dishonesty usually follows.

SHEEHAN: You know many European languages and speak a number of them, including modern Greek. Are you drawn to any of the modern foreign literatures? If so, which ones do you like especially?

MERRILL: I began caring more about French poetry than I did about English, no doubt because there was no question of completely understanding it. But, again, my feeling for it ends with Apollinaire and Valéry. I find very few living French poets intelligible—my French has withered on the vine.

SHEEHAN: I noticed you recently translated Eugenio Montale.

MERRILL: My Italian is even worse than my French, but I liked his poems very much and felt close to the feeling behind them.

SHEEHAN: What is the feeling behind Montale's poems that struck you especially?

RECITATIVE

MERRILL: The emotional refinement, gloomy and strongly curbed. It's surprisingly permeable by quite ordinary objects—ladles, hens, pianos, half-read letters. To me he's *the* twentieth-century nature poet. Any word can lead you from the kitchen garden into really inhuman depths—if there are any of those left nowadays. The two natures were always one, but it takes an extraordinary poet to make us feel that, feel it in our spines.

SHEEHAN: You mentioned Elizabeth Bishop before. A number of other poets today have singled her out. Would you say, in terms of form, that she has provided valuable examples for poets, especially in your own poetry?

MERRILL: The unpretentiousness of her form is very appealing. But I don't know if it's simply a matter of form. Rather, I like the way her whole oeuvre is on the scale of a human life; there is no oracular amplification, she doesn't go about on stilts to make her vision wider. She doesn't need that. She's wise and humane enough as it is. And this is rather what I feel about Stevens. For all the philosophy that intrudes in and between the lines, Stevens' poetry is a body of work that is man-sized. Whereas I wouldn't say that of Pound; he tries, I think, to write like a god. Stevens and Miss Bishop merely write like angels.

SHEEHAN: Do you think it might have something to do with wit and humor? Reviewers have used the term "witty" to describe your poetry; and Stevens' is surely filled with various sorts of jokes. Reed Whittemore once claimed that, in recent poetry, there was an unbridgeable split between light and serious verse. Do you agree?

MERRILL: Hardly unbridgeable. Aren't we used by now to the light poem that has dark touches and the serious poem shot through with lighter ones? The Canadian George Johnston comes to mind as an example of the first. His material is all quite shallow and amusing indeed, but leaves a sense of something unspoken, something positively sinister. . . .

SHEEHAN: Can the joke control that sort of oracular voice of Eliot and Pound, tone it down, make it more human?

MERRILL: That is my fond illusion.

SHEEHAN: Whittemore was referring in part, I think, to the *New Yorker* sort of exclusively light verse as created by Ogden Nash. John Updike's poems come to mind.

MERRILL: Updike's are light indeed. Ogden Nash may be taken more seriously by another generation. The prosody—if you can call it that—is really such a delight. To me, it's a very American form—that interminable line with the funny rhyme.

SHEEHAN: In two recent poems of yours, "The Thousand and Second Night" and "From the Cupola," you've written what's called a long poem. Do you feel any distinctions between the long and short poem in terms of style, structure, and form?

MERRILL: The length of those poems is partly accidental. I never dreamed, when "The Thousand and Second Night" began to take shape, that it would be as long as it is. I couldn't foresee the structure of the poem. I was working on what seemed rather unrelated poems, then suddenly an afternoon of patchwork saw them all stitched together. What emerged as the final section had been written quite early in the process.

SHEEHAN: This account almost seems to have a musical metaphor under it. Would you say there's any relation between music and your poetry?

MERRILL: There's to me a tremendous relation. Certainly I cared about music long before I cared about literature. When I was eleven years old, I began being taken to the opera in New York; and the sense of a feeling that could be expressed without any particular attention to words must have excited me very much. I daren't go into the effect Mrs. Wix would have pounced upon, of the opera on my moral sense. All those passions—illnesses, ecstasies, deceptions—induced for the pure sake of having something to sing beautifully about. Whenever I reach an impasse, working on a poem, I try to imagine an analogy with musical form; it usually helps. For instance, in "The Thousand and Second Night" the last thing I had to write was the passage at the end of section three beginning "Love. Warmth." I had no idea how to write it; I thought I would do it in free verse and made all kinds of beginnings, before the six-line stanza finally evolved. But the moment for which I'm most grateful is in the third of those five stanzas, when it came to me to make the meter trochaic rather than iambic—a stroke I associated quite arbitrarily with that moment at the end of the Rondo of the "Waldstein" Sonata, where the tempo is suddenly doubled or halved (I'm not sure which), and it goes twice as fast. "An Urban Convalescence" is in the form of an Introduction and Allegro. In between comes a trill (on the word "cold"), an organ point (following "self-knowledge"), then the rhymes, the quatrains begin, in 4/4 time, as it were. Need I say how subjective this all is?

SHEEHAN: I'm reminded of a brief essay of Valéry's, "On Speaking Verse," in which he instructs the actor to approach the line from the state of music, understanding musical form first, then letting the words and the meaning come through. Does music take us back again to voice?

MERRILL: It does, if we're poets. The next step, for me, was listening to French art songs: especially Maggie Teyte's records of Debussy, Fauré, and Duparc, where, once more, though most of the words were intelligible, they made no great demands on the intelligence. It was only the extreme beauty of the musical line that was spellbinding. At first I hadn't known any German songs, but when I began to hear Schubert and Schumann, the text would often as not have some independent merit. Unlike Albert Samain and Leconte de Lisle, Heine was intense and psychological. By then, a way of uttering a line to have it make real sense, real human sense, had come into my musical education.

These were all things I could have learned from my teachers. I remember a course at Amherst that Reuben Brower gave. I now see it was chiefly a course in tone, in putting meaning and the sound of meaning back into words. He made very clear connections, so that by the time we read some Frost poems, we could see certain relationships to E. M. Forster and Jane Austen, whom we'd read earlier.

SHEEHAN: If, as you say, rhythm often has its own sense and meaning and energy, could it sometimes so shape the line or stanza (or even whole poem) that it dictates what words will work? Has this ever been your experience?

MERRILL: Oh, absolutely. Words just aren't that meaningful in themselves. *De la musique avant toute chose*. The best writers can usually be recognized by their rhythms. An act of Chekhov has a movement unlike anything in the world.

SHEEHAN: I think here of Frost's idea of "sentence sounds." Is this more or less relevant to what you're saying?

MERRILL: I think so. The point about music and song is that theirs is the sound of sheer feeling—as opposed to that of sense, of verbal sense. To combine the two is always worth dreaming about.

SHEEHAN: I'd like to ask you about "From the Cupola." The poem uses Greek myth, but (perhaps to distinguish it from an Eliot poem) one couldn't say it was at all "propped up" by the Eros-Psyche story. What shifts and transformations were involved in making the myth relevant to the poem?

MERRILL: Again, this is all afterthought. In the poem there are, let's see, three stories going. There's the story of Eros and Psyche, which is, if not known, at least knowable to any reader. Then there is the contemporary situation of a New England village Psyche and her two nasty sisters and of somebody writing love letters to her. And finally there is what I begin by describing as an unknowable situation, something I'm going to keep quiet about. But, in a way, the New England village situation is transparent enough to let us see the story of Eros and Psyche on one side of the glass and, perhaps, to guess at, to triangulate the third story, the untold one.

SHEEHAN: Then it's the contemporary situation that unified the mythic and the unknowable situations?

MERRILL: If anything does. I suppose the two twentieth-century writers who have used myth most brilliantly are Joyce and Cocteau. Joyce teaches us to immerse the mythical elements in a well-known setting; Cocteau teaches us to immerse them in a contemporary spoken idiom. Although I can't pretend I planned on doing this, what pleases me in the poem are precisely those two effects: a great deal of setting and a great deal of contemporary idiom.

SHEEHAN: *The (Diblos) Notebook* also uses myth. Is the same thing involved?

MERRILL: Not really, because there's no myth underneath; that is, there's no structural use of myth in *The (Diblos) Notebook*. Rather, it is used as ornament; the central character's attitude toward myth is the issue, not myth itself.

SHEEHAN: Does this apply to "From the Cupola"? The poem is perhaps the most difficult of yours to understand in that its experience (which may well be the speaker's attitude toward it) seems to be so elusive.

MERRILL: It is elusive. As I said, the poem begins with the statement that it's not going to be a confessional poem. To be honest, I don't understand the poem very well myself—at least not the first third. I've been helped, though, by the times I've read it aloud. I trust the way it *sounds* at any rate; though I find that I have to read sections of it very rapidly indeed, like that long speech of Alice's: there's next to no meaning in the speech, except for a few nuggets for a clever reader to unearth. She does ramble and that may be part of her terror. In this sense, her speech is a device out of theatre: a ranting scene that goes on for its own sake, in which every word doesn't count.

SHEEHAN: I seem to hear vague echoes somewhere of Plato: the poet composing without understanding his poem, in a kind of inspired frenzy.

MERRILL: In a way, yes. I'm not sure about frenzy, though: "From the Cupola" was not composed in a frenzy. Yet certainly there wouldn't be as much pleasure in writing poems if one understood exactly what one had in one's heart and head. The process of writing discovers this—if we're lucky.

SHEEHAN: Would you say that "From the Cupola" represents anything new in your career? Is a new idea involved in this poem, a new technique?

MERRILL: The newness would have to do with the narrative elements, I suspect. Without these to carry it forward, "From the Cupola" mightn't seem drastically different from those two sets of "variations" in *First Poems*.

SHEEHAN: The speakers in a number of your recent poems seem to be concerned with the difficulties or joys of being a poet. Is this a new subject for you?

MERRILL: It's one I've tried to resist. In principle, I'm quite against the persona of the poem talking about the splendors and miseries of writing; it seems to me far too many poets today make the act of writing one of their primary subjects. Obviously I'm following the crowd myself, but I've hoped as much as possible to sugar the pill by being a bit rueful and amusing about having to do so.

SHEEHAN: The fourth section of "The Thousand and Second Night"— the academic parody—is surely quite amusing about it.

MERRILL: A friend of mine urged me to take that section out, saying it was hard enough to create an illusion, and that to shatter one would be disastrously perverse. I left it in, though, because, well, I wanted something to delay the final section. Also, the parody of the classroom was a structural equivalent, it occurred to me later, of the use of quotation, interspersed throughout the poem—the little snippets from Eliot, Yeats, Hofmannsthal, and so forth. It did in terms of structure what those did ornamentally. Once I thought of that, I had a sounder reason to leave it in.

SHEEHAN: You've used the words "ornament" and "decoration" a number of times. Would they possibly relate to what a number of readers have felt in your work: that the novels, plays, and poems project *in toto* a particular sort of social milieu? I'd define the term along the lines, say, of taste, intelligence, and manners rather than class or family. Am I right in saying that there is a more or less unified social world in your work?

MERRILL: We all have our limits. I draw the line at politics or hippies. I'd rather present the world through, say, a character's intelligence or lack of it than through any sort of sociological prism. It's perhaps why I side with Stevens over Eliot. I don't care much about generalizing; it's unavoidable, to begin with. The point about manners is that—as we all know, whether we're writers or not—they keep the ball rolling. One could paraphrase Marianne Moore: using them with a perfect contempt for them, one discovers in them after all a place for the genuine. In writing a novel or poem of manners you provide a framework all the nicer for being more fallible, more hospitable to irony, self-expression, self-contradiction, than many a philosophical or sociological system. Manners for me are the touch of nature, an artifice in the very bloodstream. Someone who does not take them seriously is making a serious mistake. They are as vital as all appearances, and if they deceive us they do so by mutual consent. It's hard to imagine a work of literature that doesn't depend on manners, at least negatively. One of the points of a poem like Ginsberg's *Howl* is that it uses an impatience with manners very brilliantly; but if there had been no touchstone to strike that flint upon, where would Ginsberg be?

And manners—whether good or bad—are entirely allied with tone or voice in poetry. If the manners are inferior, the poem will seem unreal or allegorical as in some of Stephen Crane's little poems. Take the one in which the man is eating his heart and the stranger comes up and asks if it's good. Those are bad manners for a stranger. Consequently the poem ends shortly after it begins because they have nothing more to say to each other. On the other hand, a poem like George Herbert's "Love" goes on for three stanzas; in a situation fully as "unreal" as Crane's, two characters are being ravishingly polite to one another. Manners aren't merely descriptions of social behavior. The real triumph of manners in Proust is the extreme courtesy toward the reader, the voice explaining at once formally and intimately. Though it can be heard, of course, as megalomania, there is something wonderful in the reasonableness, the long-windedness of that voice, in its desire to be understood, in its treatment of *every* phenomenon (whether the way someone pronounces a word, or the article of clothing worn, or the color of a flower) as having ultimate importance. Proust says to us in effect, "I will not patronize you by treating these delicate matters with less than total, patient, sparkling seriousness."

SHEEHAN: Reviewers have sometimes used the word "elegant" to describe your poetry. How would you react to this term?

MERRILL: With a shrug.

SHEEHAN: I'd like to ask you about *The Seraglio*. I'm tempted at times to read Francis Tanning as something of a paradigm. That is, I see a young man who struggles to see the world singly, but somehow seems doomed to see it doubly; mirror and dreams figure prominently. Is this young man a sort of Ur-character? And are his struggles some sort of Ur-plot in your work?

MERRILL: He seems to me, with a few superficial differences, the kind of young man one finds in nearly any first novel. As far as an Ur-character goes: well, four or five years after I'd written the novel, I came upon some books from my childhood. I reread one of them, having no particular memory of ever reading it before, yet I must have, since I found—to my horror and amusement—that, by and large, its plot was that of *The Seraglio*. Both novels involved the effort to reintroduce an exiled mother into an atmosphere of ease and comfort; both scenes were dominated by an irascible grandfather-figure. Of course, the children's book was *Little Lord Fauntleroy*.

SHEEHAN: Again, one hesitates to use the word influence. To return to *The (Diblos) Notebook*, the novel has raised what is perhaps a side issue: how it actually was composed. Did it really grow out of a notebook?

MERRILL: Yes. I had the story in mind several years before I found myself writing the book. During that time I had no idea how to write it, although I made a few conventional beginnings. Then, one summer, when I'd been traveling in Greece, unable to do any real work, I kept a journal. But whenever I tried to inject any of those impressions into my conventional narrative, they went dead on me. The notebook itself, though, still seemed comparatively full of life. It took a while to realize that this was a possible technique, and use it. It's a technique I might have discovered much earlier from, say, that edition of Keats' letters where the deletions are legible; and, of course, from letters one receives oneself: the eye instantly flies to the crossed-out word. It seems to promise so much more than the words left exposed.

SHEEHAN: You've written for the theatre as well, one of your plays—*The Immortal Husband*—receiving highest critical praise. Have you an opinion on the "verse drama" so many modern poets have attempted—Eliot, Yeats, Pound, even Wallace Stevens, as well as Ted Hughes and Robert Lowell more recently? What aesthetic problems does a poet face in writing plays?

MERRILL: I loved the first act of *The Cocktail Party*—that unmistakable sound of Eliot, his line, hired out in the service of small talk. You couldn't imagine a suaver bartender. The poet writing plays faces the same problem that the playwright does. Borges has a piece on Aeschylus as the man who introduced a second actor onto the stage, thus allowing for an infinite dialogue. The problem from then on has been to decide on the dimensions of that dialogue for one's particular purpose. We spoke of structural rhythm a while back. One responds to that in plays more immediately than in poems. It's virtually one's entire first impression of any play by Beckett.

SHEEHAN: Have you found any older—that is, pre-twentieth-century—poetry relevant to your work?

MERRILL: Actually, I'd read little twentieth-century poetry until I'd been writing for several years. My first efforts, sonnets of course, were written at fourteen when I knew only bits and pieces of Shakespeare, Mrs. Browning, some Pre-Raphaelite verse. My first twentieth-century passion, two years later, was Elinor Wylie. I was a retarded child. No reflection on her—I still think she's marvelous, far and away the most magical rhyming we've ever had. There's a glaze of perfection to contend with, but I ate it up; it never put me off—not at least until I went on to Yeats. Older poets, though. Pope, Keats, "Lycidas." I was out of college by the time I read Herbert. Much later, though I'd never looked at more than a page of *Don Juan* and knew about Byron only through Auden's "Letter" to him, I *knew* that he had been an influence on "The Thousand and Second Night." When I checked, I found very much the tone I'd been trying for: that air of irrelevance, of running on at the risk of never becoming terribly significant. I see no point, often, in the kind of poem that makes every single touch, every syllable, count. It can be a joy to write, but not always to read. You can't forego the whole level of entertainment in art. Think of Stevens' phrase: "The essential gaudiness of poetry." The inessential suddenly felt as essence.

SHEEHAN: This attitude is directly counter, isn't it, to the one underlying so much earlier twentieth-century poetry: the desire for concentration and concision in poems.

MERRILL: Yes, it may well involve a fatigue with all that. How can you appreciate the delights of concision unless you abuse them?

SHEEHAN: One of the perennial questions asked any artist is whether he has any particular method of composition. Would you care to reply?

MERRILL: Usually I begin a poem with an image or phrase; if you follow trustfully, it's surprising how far an image can lead. Once in a great while I've seen the shape of the whole poem (never a very long one, though) and tried simply to follow the stages of plot, or argument. The danger in this method is that one knows so well where the poem is going that one hasn't much impetus to write it. In either case, even before the poem is fully

35

drafted, my endless revisions begin—the one dependable pleasure in the whole process. Some poets actually say they don't revise, don't believe in revising. They say their originality suffers. I don't see that at all. The words that come first are anybody's, a froth of phrases, like the first words from a medium's mouth. You have to make them your own. Even if the impersonal is what you're after, you first have to make them your own, and only then begin to efface yourself.

SHEEHAN: Novelists sometimes speak of characters "taking over" and the work "writing itself." Has this been your experience, either as a novelist or a poet?

MERRILL: As a novelist, no, I'm not good enough. That kind of submission must be one of the darkest secrets of technique. With poems I don't know who or what takes over, unless it's I who do, and that's not what you mean. Sooner or later one touches upon matters that are all the realer for not being easily talked about.

An Interview
with John Boatwright
and Enrique Ucelay DaCal

BOATWRIGHT/DACAL: At what age did you first begin to write poetry and why? Do you consider it a justified reason for having started, in terms of yourself today?

MERRILL: I began at fourteen or so. My best friend at school was writing poems, and I must have thought: Why not me? Years of pleasing himself have properly wrinkled the brash little Narcissus who made that choice. And yet I stand by it, for better or worse. To write is "me," and not to write is "not-me." One does what one can.

BOATWRIGHT/DACAL: Much of the work done by students today in poetry could be called neosurrealist, in that automatic psychological imagery, even Oriental-mystical imagery is used. How do you feel about these trends?

MERRILL: All imagery allows for a psychological reading. You can analyze Wordsworth until he sounds like Freud's first patient, if you like. As for automatism, I'd hope there was enough in all of us without our needing to cultivate it.

These things come and go. The Orient has kept breaking upon the scene in *nouvelles vagues* for centuries. Beautiful styles may result, which are about as Oriental as a Chinese Chippendale chair. Since they are not truly part of us, these ideas seem more attractive company than those of our guilt-blackened West. Remember how Ogden Nash put it?—

The interviewers were students at Hotchkiss and Bard. The interview was conducted in 1968 and published that year in *Stage IV*, a small interscholastic literary magazine.

RECITATIVE

There would be less danger
From the wiles of the stranger
If one's own kin and kith
Were more fun to be with.

BOATWRIGHT/DACAL: The war in Vietnam particularly, but the Negro revolution as well, have sparked a lot of markedly social poetry among both student and professional poets. What is your opinion on the relation of poetry to social or political realities? What is the power or use of social poetry?

MERRILL: Oh dear. These immensely real concerns do not produce *poetry*. But of course one responds. A word-cluster like *napalm-baby-burn* stimulates the juices as infallibly as the high C of a Donizetti mad scene. Both audiences have been prepared for what they get and are strongly moved. The trouble with overtly political or social writing is that when the tide of feeling goes out, the language begins to stink. In poetry I look for English in its billiard-table sense—words that have been set spinning against their own gravity. Once in competition with today's headlines or editorial page you just can't sustain that crucial, liberating lightness without sounding like a sick comedian. The wisest resources appear to be those of song (Lorca, Brecht, rock groups) or those of extreme obliquity—which last, however, can all too easily bewilder the reader who expects a message rather than a poem.

BOATWRIGHT/DACAL: There seems to be, among those of our generation, a distaste for anything that might seem a strictly aesthetic approach to poetry, not only in its writing, but also in its reading. Poetry, it is argued, should be a majority art form, and the fact that it is not is seen as a function of the emptiness of our culture. How do you feel about this?

MERRILL: Popular art, in a society without ritual, can only be that which entertains, is consumed, and is replaced at once by the next thing. Its admirers include, to a man, us aesthetes. That the admiration isn't mutual needn't bother anyone. Some will always have a more complex emotional or intellectual life than others, which a more complex art will be called upon to nourish. What's fascinating today is the communization of the aesthete—his drugs, his adornments, his arrogance, his whole allure taken over from Baudelaire or Robert de Montesquiou as a group project, like a private house turned into a school. Perhaps after all the majority *can* be tenderized by sprinklings of these neural equivalents of the papaya enzyme.

BOATWRIGHT/DACAL: In the same vein, how personal do you feel poetry should be, not only thematically, but imagistically? As a corollary, how do you feel about the tendency, since Joyce, toward strongly hermetical poetry?

MERRILL: Total, clear-eyed immersion in one's own little world produces (especially if one is Joyce, or Montaigne, or Tolstoy) an excellent likeness of the universe. Under Joyce's difficult surface there's an old, old story, a family scene with himself at the head of the table. My own ideal of the hermetic artist is Mallarmé. Under his difficult surface there's the midnight sky, a skull of stars. John Ashbery is closest in our language to that tradition, nowadays. His work is precious in most senses of the word.

The means—imagery, tone, and so forth—can be as personal as you like, so long as the end is not to express personality.

BOATWRIGHT/DACAL: Do you feel that there is any real possibility in our technological society for traditional poetry, or that some form of new poetry must be evolved?

MERRILL: New forms evolved in nontechnological societies, just as they seem to be doing in ours. With fewer and fewer people, even bright ones, who know what traditions are, my old-fashioned kind of poem may soon be mistaken for something much newer than it is, and read with appropriate cries of delight.

BOATWRIGHT/DACAL: How do you feel about the potentialities of mixed media poetry? Can poetry be a physical experience?

MERRILL: It was for Housman. He felt it in the pit of his stomach without any mixing of media. I feel about the mixers like a student when the Dow Chemical man turns up on campus. I don't want any part of it. I want full control over my own product.

An Interview
with Ashley Brown

BROWN: I'd like to ask you about your literary education. Did your family and teachers encourage you to write, or did you take it up on the sly?

MERRILL: My family weren't exactly averse to it, but I suspect if they had encouraged me more than they did, I would have stopped then and there. When I went away to school in Lawrenceville, I wrote my poems out of envy of my friend Freddy Buechner, who was already writing lovely poems. This soon became a habit, and before long I worked up to a poem a day. My very first efforts were sonnets, which I wrote as much with French models as with English—the melodic, empty-headed *fin de siècle* sort of thing.

BROWN: How was Amherst as a training ground? Richard Wilbur and two or three other literary students were there in your time, weren't they?

MERRILL: Wilbur had already graduated when I entered. I started in the summer of 1943, when there were only ninety students. You remember how the colleges were during the war. Kimon Friar was teaching languages at that time—he was not on the regular faculty—and he encouraged the campus poets. Nobody on the faculty was particularly helpful. George Whicher was always pleased to see a poem. There were classes in writing, but the best training one got was in reading, and this was important to me. Nobody ever taught the works of a living poet—except Frost, of course. Reuben Brower once mentioned the name of Marianne Moore.

BROWN: Things have certainly changed, haven't they? Nowadays many students seem to read nothing but the moderns. Even Frost seems like a

Published in *Shenandoah*, vol. 19, no. 4 (Summer 1968). This interview was oddly conducted. At regular intervals during their conversation, Brown would leave the room and write down what he remembered of Merrill's answers.

40

nineteenth-century poet to a lot of them. Was he teaching there when you were a student?

MERRILL: He was always in and out, but I never saw much of him. I met him through G. R. Elliott. I was a student in Elliott's Spenser class, and he once had me to tea to meet Frost. Frost always liked students—not faculty. He usually had fifteen students at his feet every evening. It was rather sad, in a way, for both sides, because he eventually would have to begin repeating himself, and the students weren't as interchangeable as he may have thought.

BROWN: You've actually taught writing courses yourself two or three times, haven't you?

MERRILL: Only once in a great while. I spent a year at Amherst, and there was a year at Bard, which was interesting, and recently I had a short period at Madison—the University of Wisconsin.

BROWN: Do you have any opinions on this general subject of young poets in the universities? A lot of people, including some of their teachers, think they ought to get out in the world more and cut loose from fellowships and graduate schools and even writing courses.

MERRILL: One of the best poets at Madison actually did that. I felt sorry for a lot of those students. The more advanced ones were graduate students, and they were too busy keeping up with their teaching to do much writing. They are under terrible pressures to get degrees.

BROWN: Do you think the universities foster an excessively cautious sort of poetry?

MERRILL: That hasn't been my impression. But I guess I'm an arch-conservative. More arch than conservative, I'm sometimes made to feel. At any rate, I've come to the conclusion that most people aren't helped by writing courses.

BROWN: By the time you started publishing, back in the 1940s, some young poets were almost painfully aware of the achievement of their predecessors—Eliot and Stevens and Auden and the rest—two generations of modernists. Did you feel their presence was something to resist?

MERRILL: No, I don't think I ever felt that. They seemed very much their own men. They represented the immediate past. I felt no sense of competition, if you could call it that. If I had any sense of competition, it was with people at most five years older than I was. My reaction to Stevens, for instance, was merely that it was wonderful to mention strange colors along with big abstract words. I was, to begin with, more influenced by Elinor Wylie, whom I worshiped when I was fifteen or sixteen.

BROWN: Stevens and Auden had a large influence twenty years ago, didn't they? I guess I'm right in saying that you were touched by both of them. I was recently rereading your "Medusa," which is a wonderfully supple poem and fairly characteristic of your work then. It has something of Stevens' rhetorical splendor, but toned down a little, as it were, by Auden's understatement.

MERRILL: I certainly liked them both and still do! The first Stevens I read was *Notes Toward a Supreme Fiction*. I teethed on that. I read Auden by stages. I remember reading *The Sea and the Mirror* when I was in the army (just the place for that) and being dazzled by the range of forms, which meant most to me at that time. Certainly I was inspired to try some of these things myself. *The Age of Anxiety* was so murky by contrast.

To come back to "Medusa": I wrote it over not long ago, I can't think why. It's a poem without content, really. I wrote so easily in those days. The stanza is one of Elinor Wylie's. But you are right in mentioning Stevens. You remember the passage about the stone mask in the *Notes*. I must have had that in mind, the image, I mean, as distinct from Stevens' glorious sound effects. I thought of poems as visual artifacts back then.

BROWN: Elizabeth Bishop doesn't much care for reading poetry aloud. Do you?

MERRILL: She doesn't need to! In the old days it never occurred to me to read aloud—the vogue for public recitation started later. I didn't even read aloud to myself. What was I thinking of? If you value tone, how else can you get the effects of irony and understatement? Still, I always felt I was turning out a poem for the eye rather than the ear.

BROWN: Did you ever hear Stevens read? On the recording it's not quite satisfactory.

MERRILL: In Florida once he visited Marjorie Kinnan Rawlings, who was a friend of my mother. He started reading at someone's request, but it was unendurable, and after twenty minutes Marjorie Rawlings snatched the book from his hand. She was going to show him how! No, I never heard him read.

BROWN: You really were formal in those early days, weren't you? In *First Poems* you managed terza rima, triplets, and some rather intricate stanzas (for example in "The Peacock"). I suppose much of the pleasure of writing came by way of the forms themselves.

MERRILL: Yes, I liked that "Peacock" stanza—I used it four times. I'm no less formal now, but I no longer dote on elaborate stanzas.

BROWN: Did you find yourself much involved in your early poems? The one I find most affecting (just my own reaction) is the "Elegy" which begins, "Sickness, at least, becomes us. . . ." Significantly perhaps, it's the most irregular poem you had written. But even here you generalize the experience, don't you? "We" rather than "I" is the characteristic pronoun. Indeed "I" scarcely appears in the early poems.

MERRILL: Oh, you know, the "Elegy" is really part of something longer—the "Variations and Elegy." The way it's set up in the book it looks separate. I'll admit that part of the "Elegy" was trumped up. It was a task I set not to use rhyme. But that sort of thing didn't pay off for a number of years, perhaps not till my *Short Stories*. I felt humanly more involved in "The Willow" and "The House," the last poems in my early book. "Real" experience had grazed them, somehow. They are very formal poems in triplets, too.

Your remark about "we" opens up quite a subject. A generation ago "we" was *the* pronoun. It probably started with Auden—let's say it conveyed the sense of a political elite. But there was another and to me more important source—Rilke in the *Duino Elegies*. The "we" there is an elite of sufferers. I didn't know German very well then, but Rilke was five times more poetic to me than Yeats. Yeats seemed by comparison somewhat external to one's situation. Auden, you know, must have learned a lot from Rilke, even the excessive personification. So maybe the two "we's" are one.

BROWN: I've always felt one had to know German rather well to read Rilke—he eludes translation much of the time. But maybe I'm being too strict about this.

MERRILL: I don't know German any better now. In fact the point may be *not* to know German well enough where Rilke is concerned! So as still to feel, I mean, the overture of abstraction in all those capitalized nouns. In mentioning Yeats, by the way, I must say that I read and admired him a lot in my youth. I read "Sailing to Byzantium" when I was in the army. It got through to me because of the circumstances. I couldn't wait to get "out of nature" myself. But what I got from Rilke was more than literary; that emphasis on the *acceptance* of pain and loneliness. Rilke helps you with suffering, especially in your adolescence. . . .

BROWN: I wonder if you agree with Ransom about the virtue of having little dramatic situations in short poems?

MERRILL: Not altogether. I always find when I don't like a poem I'm writing, I don't look any more into the human components. I look more to the *setting*—a room, the objects in it. I think that objects are very subtle reflectors. When you are in an emotional state, whatever your eye lights on takes on something of the quality of a state of mind.

BROWN: But to what extent do you think a poem depends on objects? Can't you have the reverse—say Sonnet 129 of Shakespeare, which is almost a poetry of statement? And a lot of Stevens is statement.

MERRILL: Perhaps. But in my case the objects are important, more so than ever.

BROWN: Quite a few of your poems—even recent ones—are built up out of human situations which are themselves almost metaphors—"The Lovers" for instance in your second book. Do you defend this kind of indirection? You seem to be pointing toward something else beyond the ostensible subject of the poem.

MERRILL: "The Lovers" is one of a great number of my poems where the human situation *is* a metaphor or perhaps even a vision. I must have some kind of awful religious streak just under the surface. "The Doodler," for instance, turns out to be God looking at his creatures. I've had to conclude that these buried meanings help. Without something like them, one ends up writing light verse about love affairs. "In the Hall of Mirrors" is a fairly obvious case. It was written during the 1950s when the "myth" poems were popular. It's about the expulsion from Eden. I won't say the buried meaning came first; probably it didn't. I'm never altogether pleased to see this happen, but it does again and again.

BROWN: During the 1950s you moved into playwriting and prose fiction—and very gracefully, in my opinion. Your *Short Stories* poems like "A Narrow Escape" are the obvious result. Did you find the blank verse of these poems an advantage?

MERRILL: I wanted to write blank verse—even before I wrote the poems. Why? Because I wanted to get some of the pleasures of prose into poetry. The influence of playwriting came a bit later.

BROWN: I've had the impression for some time that older writers of prose—for instance Katherine Anne Porter—often took their tonal effects from the poets, say Eliot and Pound and Yeats. But now American poets are tapping the resources of prose more than ever. Do you agree?

MERRILL: Absolutely. Prose feeds into poetry much more than the reverse. I was thinking this way in the 1950s, and I was already trying for something new in "About the Phoenix," even though this poem is slightly modeled on Elizabeth Bishop's "Over 2,000 Illustrations and a Complete Concordance."

BROWN: What *about* your playwriting? *The Immortal Husband* had a successful production off-Broadway, didn't it? I didn't see it, but I thought your manipulation of Tithonus' sad story through several period settings was a delight to read. You seem to work best in drama and fiction when you reverse the naturalistic illusions. *The Seraglio* is the exception—that's rather Jamesian.

MERRILL: It was *fairly* successful. I wrote the play for Anne Meacham, a marvelous actress. Well, about naturalistic illusions: In *The Immortal Husband* the doubling of characters gives a unity that Aristotle knew about but never bothered to mention: the unity of the performer. His reality is often far more immediate than that of his material. Just as in my second novel, *The (Diblos) Notebook*, the writing of the novel is the immediate reality. In that sense I'm not reversing the illusion at all.

BROWN: Do you plan another novel?

MERRILL: No, I can't invent, and I think a novelist must have that talent. Right now I'm working on a ballad about Stonington. It contains four local characters, the people in fact that *Water Street* is dedicated to. It's a substitute for a novel.

BROWN: Something like Elizabeth Bishop's "Burglar of Babylon"?

MERRILL: In a way, yes. Since I've been living in Greece I've found myself thinking a lot about human behavior. It's because of the language barrier—when you can't ascertain the full range of people's motives and feelings, they are simplified in a sense. This particular experience of being with people may have led to a ballad—in traditional ballads the characters *are* properly simplified. I think I like either those people who completely understand whatever I say—at all levels—or those who understand hardly any of it, for whom I am simplified into a dream-figure, as they no doubt are for me. Understanding has more than one face.

BROWN: I guess one of the turning points in your poetry came with "An Urban Convalescence" in *Water Street*. It's perhaps the most innovative and the most personal poem you had yet written.

MERRILL: Yes, it was a turning point. I remember writing half of it and thinking it was going to be impossible to finish. Then I had the idea of letting it go back to a more formal pattern at the end. I was helped by a musical analogy—a procedure I've used several times since. In this case it was a Toccata (or introduction) and Allegro, and so I let my quatrains wind up a poem which threatened to fall away. Although I am very personal in this poem (more so than in the "Elegy" in the first book), I feel I'm inventing things here and there.

BROWN: Have you been attracted to the dramatic monologue as a way of getting a lot of experience into poetry? "Roger Clay's Proposal" and "1939" are two of these among your more recent poems. Or does this seem like the easy way out?

MERRILL: I like Browning's monologues; they seem more natural than Lowell's. Those little *données* about the Canadian nun and the old man falling asleep over the *Aeneid* would never occur to me as a way of getting a poem started. I approach the dramatic monologue with diffidence; I feel happier not restricting myself to the single speaker. The overt monologue serves well enough only when I know exactly where I'm going. For instance, "1939" is an actual transcription of an anecdote told by a woman here in Stonington. I wanted to get away from pentameter, too. Do you know that wonderful poem by Elizabeth Bishop called "The Riverman"? It's in *Questions of Travel*. Wonderful, fluid, pulsing lines—you hardly feel the meter at all.

BROWN: In your last book, *Nights and Days*, you've certainly come a long way from *First Poems*, but your formal experiments are pretty clearly developed out of "An Urban Convalescence," aren't they?

MERRILL: Yes, I think so. I can tell you precisely the point when I felt I was on the right track: when I thought to use the phrase "the sickness of our time." I loathe that phrase and tried to put it into perspective.

BROWN: Since you are now involved in long poems, what do you think are their possibilities and limitations at this stage of American poetry? I assume that epic is out of the question. You seem to like the theme and variations best.

MERRILL: Well, everybody has agreed that psychological action is more interesting than epic. One mainly wants a form where one thing leads to another—it needn't, but it can.

BROWN: I keep thinking that *The Prelude* could still be used as a model of some sort. It was very bold of Wordsworth, don't you agree, to write a poem of epic length that departed from the inherited tradition of mythology that almost everybody had depended on? It *is* somewhat ruminative, but it has a real unity.

MERRILL: You will have imagined (and come close to the truth) that I fell asleep on the seventh page of *The Prelude* and woke only the next morning. It's not me, I'm afraid!

BROWN: In "The Thousand and Second Night" the writing of the poem itself is part of the subject—the "immediate reality" as you were saying about *The (Diblos) Notebook*. Would you care to comment on this?

MERRILL: I don't know what the main subject is—the poem is flirtatious in that sense. Writing poems about the act of writing both attracts and repulses me—like "the sickness of our time." The idea is usually more interesting than the execution, as in Mallarmé's "Un Coup de Dés." Some people balked at the name-dropping in the poem, but this was only the representational plane. And I meant the comedy of the surface to sugar the pill. I don't think it's like the *serious* name-dropping of the Beats— Ferlinghetti is the worst offender there.

BROWN: "From the Cupola" is your most ambitious work so far—you stretch your form to the limit. Could you talk about the inception of the poem? Why did you elaborate it in the way that you did?

MERRILL: I had no sense of the extent to which I would take it when I began it. At first it was just a little poem in the first person. It was involved with a curious experience—receiving letters from somebody I never met, who seemed to know everything about me. I'm not paranoiac, but it was rather unsettling. After a while I became engrossed with this interior experience. I didn't want to meet the writer of the letters; I wanted to detach myself from the experience to write about it. The poem from the beginning needed "body," and I gave it this by way of landscape—what I can see from this window. And then I thought of Psyche. Psyche, you know, is a Hellenistic myth. I also liked the "montage" of Hellenistic Alexandria and Stonington, which likewise has a lighthouse and a library. Well, it *is* ambitious, but the first and the last parts, I think, tone it down—I frame it in "my own voice." A friend of mine, Benjamin DeMott, was very helpful in urging me to make this framework as explicit as possible. I did the best I could!

BROWN: You seem very confident about the state of poetry today—you were saying earlier that prose feeds it more than the reverse.

MERRILL: Oh, yes! But there are still things to be learned from prose. What I value more than anything else is the fluid seamless narrative of Stendhal. But I read so quickly. I even have to read novels twice, and my attitude toward writing is probably affected by that. In *(Diblos)* I tried to slow down the reader—make him see the sentences, as it were, by leaving some of them unfinished. Make him pause to complete them.

BROWN: We do seem to be going through a major shift in the arts. The period of Eliot and Stravinsky and Joyce is being succeeded by something else, the era of the "dithyrambic spectator." The only absolute for some people now is change. Do you feel involved in this?

MERRILL: I think that under the circumstances I'm lucky to be a poet rather than a painter or sculptor—they have to think of something new every year. I don't worry about it. What else can one do except grow old gracefully? I've yet to see a poem that I can't relate to something at least fifty years old if not two hundred. I think one should try in what one does to charm the reader. I still like Stevens' idea about the imagination "pressing back against the pressure of reality."

An Interview
with Helen Vendler

VENDLER: When you called your last book *Divine Comedies*, did you mean by that allusion to Dante that you were planning a trilogy?

MERRILL: Not consciously. I'd convinced myself that "The Book of Ephraim" told everything I had to say about the "other world." Because of its length and looniness I'd taken to calling *it* the Divine Comedy—not of course a usable title, until David Jackson thought of making it plural. Dante, subtler as always, let posterity affix the adjective.

VENDLER: In your new book, *Mirabell: Books of Number*, you say there will be one more volume in this vein; after that you will be permitted to return to your "chronicles of love and loss." These three books have all been based on Ouija board material. Is there anything else that unites them, in general, and that separates them from your earlier poetry?

MERRILL: Chiefly, I think, the—to me—unprecedented way in which the material came. Not through flashes of insight, wordplay, trains of thought. More like what a friend, or stranger, might say over a telephone. DJ and I never knew until it had been spelled out letter by letter. What I felt about the material became a natural part of the poem, corresponding to those earlier poems written "all by myself."

VENDLER: In "The Book of Ephraim," the first book, we heard the voices of the dead; but in *Mirabell* nonhuman voices are added, telling a complicated tale of evolutionary history, molecular biology, and subatomic behavior. Would you like to talk about the books you read before

Published as "James Merrill's Myth: An Interview" in *The New York Review of Books*, vol. 26, no. 7 (May 3, 1979). "The questions it occurred to me to ask Merrill," wrote Vendler, "are those of a reader confronting a poem [*Mirabell: Books of Number*] unquestionably beautiful, but also baffling."

49

creating your phantasmagoria of "science"? (You mention *The Lives of a Cell*, and looking at a model of the double helix.)

MERRILL: They weren't many. The simplest science book is over my head. At college I'd seen my dead frog's limbs twitch under some applied stimulus or other—seen, but hadn't believed. Didn't dream of thinking beyond or around what I saw. Oh, I picked up a two-volume *Guide to Science* by Asimov—very useful still, each time I forget how the carbon atom is put together, or need to shake my head over periodic tables. A book on the black holes. Arthur Young's *Reflexive Universe*—fascinating but too schematic to fit into *my* scheme. The most I could hope for was a sense of the vocabulary and some possible images.

VENDLER: Do you think the vocabulary, models, and concepts of science—cloning, DNA, carbon bonds, the ozone layer, protons, etc.—offer real new resources to poetry? So far, poets haven't seemed inclined to see poetry and science as compatible, even though Wordsworth thought they should.

MERRILL: The vocabulary can be perfectly ghastly ("polymerization," "kink instability") or unconsciously beautiful, like things a child says ("red shift," "spectral lines"). Knowing some Greek helped defuse forbidding words—not that I counted much on using them. You'll find only trace elements of this language in the poem. The images, the concepts? Professor Baird at Amherst gave a course in "Science and Literature" which showed how much the "ideas" depended on metaphor, ways of talking. And while Science may have grown more "imaginative"—or at least more "apocalyptic"—in the decades since I left school, how many writers in that, or any, field are really wise to the ways of the word? Lewis Thomas is an exception—if only he would give us more than snippets. I'd like to think the scientists need us—but do they? Did Newton need Blake?

VENDLER: What would you especially like a reader to be caught up by in your trilogy? The density of your myths? The civilized love of conversation? The range in tone? The domesticity?

MERRILL: For me the talk and the tone—along with the elements of plot—are the candy coating. The pill itself is another matter. The reader who can't swallow it has my full sympathy. I've choked on it again and again.

VENDLER: The new mythology you've invented via the Ouija board—including the new God Biology, a universal past including Atlantis, Centaurs, and Angels, an afterlife which includes reincarnation—how real does it all seem to you?

MERRILL: Literally, not very—except in recurrent euphoric hours when it's altogether too beautiful not to be true. Imaginatively real? I would hope so, but in all modesty, for the imagination in question kept assuming proportions broader and grander than mine. Also at times sillier: Atlantis, UFOs? I climbed the wall trying to escape that sort of material. But the point remained, to be always of two minds.

VENDLER: In the past, you've written fiction as well as lyrics. Does the trilogy satisfy your narrative impulse as much as your fiction did? Or more?

MERRILL: Before trying a novel I wrote a couple of plays. (The Artists' Theater—John Myers and Herbert Machiz—put them on in the fifties.) Behind them lay one of my earliest literary thrills: to open a little Samuel French booklet, some simpleminded "play for children," and find on the page a fiction made up of stage directions more suggestive than any rendered narrative scene, and of words set down to be spoken by a real, undreamed-of mouth—my own if I wished! The effect was somehow far more naked, far less quilted, than the nicely written stories I fell asleep to. Twenty years later, I confused an exercise in dramatic form with "writing for the theater"—that royal road to megalomania. But those two plays left me on fresh terms with language. I didn't always have to speak in my own voice.

VENDLER: Does the quartet activating the poem—you and David Jackson at the Ouija board, W. H. Auden and Maria Mitsotáki on the other side—make up a family constellation? Why do you think the poem needed a ghostly father and ghostly mother?

MERRILL: Strange about parents. We have such easy access to them and such daunting problems of communication. Over the Ouija board it was just the other way. A certain apparatus was needed to get in touch—but then! Affection, understanding, tact, surprises, laughter, tears. Why the *poem* needed Wystan and Maria I'm not sure. Without being Dante, can I think of them as Virgil and Beatrice?

VENDLER: The intense affection that binds you to your familiar spirit Ephraim, to dead friends, and even to the inhuman Bat-Angel you talk to in the new book, seems the quality celebrated and even venerated in the poem. Do you see this as a change from your earlier poems about your family and about love?

MERRILL: In life, there are no perfect affections. Estrangements among the living reek of unfinished business. Poems get written *to* the person no longer reachable. Yet, once dead, overnight the shrewish wife becomes "a saint," frustrations vanish at cockcrow, and from the once fallible human mouth come words of blessed reassurance. Your question looks down into smoking chasms and up into innocent blankness. Given the power—without being Orpheus, either—would I bring any of these figures back to earth?

VENDLER: If it's true that every poem, besides saying something about life, says something about poetry, what is this new form saying about itself?

MERRILL: Something possibly to do with the doubleness of its source, spelled out on every page by the interplay between the spirits' capitals and our own lowercase responses. Julian Jaynes' book on the "bicameral mind" came out last year. Don't ask me to paraphrase his thesis—but, reading Jaynes as I was finishing *Mirabell*, I rather goggled. Because the poem is set by and large in two adjacent rooms: a domed red one where we took down the messages, and a blue one, dominated by an outsize mirror, where we reflected upon them.

VENDLER: The predecessors you have in mind seem to be Dante, Yeats, and Auden. Do you think of yourself as in any way distinctively American? Or of this poem as in any active relation to American literature and American culture?

MERRILL: I feel American in Europe and exotic at home—and haven't we our own "expatriate" tradition for that? I was about to suggest—until I recalled "The Anathemata" and John Heath-Stubbs' wonderful "Artorius"—that the long, "impossible" poem was an American phenomenon in our day. The thought didn't comfort me. How many of us get out of our cars when we hit the badlands in the *Cantos*, or take that detour through downtown *Paterson*? In such a context, "foreignness" would be the storyteller's rather than the missionary's concern for his reader's soul.

VENDLER: How did the poem get transcribed and composed? The work of transcription alone must have been enormous.

MERRILL: The board goes along at a smart clip, perhaps six hundred words an hour. Sometimes it was hard to reconstruct *our* words—"What was the question?" as Miss Stein put it. Then what to cut? What to paraphrase? What to add? Plus the danger of flatness when putting into verse a passage already coherent in prose. I could have left it in prose, but it would have been too sensational—like Castaneda, or Gwendolyn's diary in *The Importance of Being Earnest*.

An Interview
with Fred Bornhauser

BORNHAUSER: I don't know anything about the origin of the Ouija principle, or its name—except that it is a double affirmative. And yet I notice that you use the YES/NO found at the upper corners of the standard board, along with an interpolated ampersand, as rubrics for the three sections of *Scripts for the Pageant*. How does this figure?

MERRILL: I think what you have on the board are the raw materials of language—of thought itself. The YES and NO came to be especially telling, the more I realized how important it was—not only for the poem but for my own mental balance—to remain of two minds about everything that was happening. One didn't want to be merely skeptical or merely credulous. Either way would have left us in reduced circumstances. It's true that in the glow of some of the later messages, when all the themes began to connect, and every least detail added its touch to the whole, there was no question of *not* assenting to what we were being shown. But the glow fades, as Yeats knew when he compared his system to the stylization of a Wyndham Lewis drawing. What's being conveyed is essentially beyond words, and every artist will have to draw on his own temperament, or way with words, in order to render this.

BORNHAUSER: Did you have any idea when you wrote "Voices of the Other World" [Merrill's first occult poem in *The Country of a Thousand Years of Peace*, 1959] that you were on to something that would lead to prophetic poetry on so grand a scale?

MERRILL: No, and thank goodness! For one thing, the prospect of any

Published in *Contemporary Authors*, New Revision Series, vol. 10 (Detroit: Gale Research Company, 1983). Eight of the questions-and-answers have been deleted, and four others from the original set (conducted by correspondence in October 1981) that were not included in the published interview have been restored.

very demanding piece of work would have sent me into a dither. My ideal poem was less than a page long, with all its connections visible, its overtones audible, and no loose ends. For another thing, I felt it would be "cheating" to use any of the Ouija material—except, as in that poem you mention, in an account of our experience of the board. The prejudice lasted for decades, and probably explains why our own reactions and circumstances loom so large in the finished trilogy.

BORNHAUSER: You spoke somewhere about your surprise at the final length of "From the Cupola"—the Psyche poem and a different kind of poem from what was to follow. Could you generalize about the need for increasing scope and scale in your development as a poet?

MERRILL: I think of it ruefully as a sort of "middle-age spread." Perhaps the general drift is to greater talkativeness, if not garrulity. Ideas, which in youth set out on their quests and find themselves at once in an allegorical wood, in middle life must first cross rivers infested with razor-toothed memories, or be obliged to stop for weeks at a time with a tribe of digressions, naked and giggling . . . I don't know. I still like short poems best, when other people write them!

BORNHAUSER: With the possible exception of Pound's *Cantos*, I can think of no poetic work of the twentieth century longer than your trilogy. Most of us, brought up on Cleanth Brooks and Robert Penn Warren, are used to close meticulous reading of even the simplest lyrics. Clearly, that kind of analysis does not always work. What guidelines or warnings would you give the reader of the long poem?

MERRILL: I too was teethed on Brooks and Warren. I learned to read, and to write, with as much care as possible. Before them, Keats had spoken of loading every rift with ore. And isn't "God lurks in the details" the motto of the Warburg Institute? The best I could hope for from a reader is that he keep one eye on the ever-emerging (and self-revising) whole, and another on the details. A lot of the talk sounds like badinage, casual if not frivolous, but something serious is usually going on under the surface.

BORNHAUSER: One cannot help noticing that eight years passed between your first and second books of poetry, then three or four years between the appearance of the next four; finally, only two years have elapsed between these most recent really big ones. Given the complexity and importance of your latest work, one would almost expect the length of interims to be reversed. Would you comment on this?

MERRILL: I was writing novels and plays along with some of those early books. But you're right, my early poems took longer to finish. I wanted it that way. Those poems were undertaken, by and large, without my knowing what I wanted them to say. They were occasions for self-discovery, experiments not only in technical matters, rhymes and phrasing and all that, but in attitudes and feelings and beliefs, in the uses of obscurity—everything! Later on, by the time of *Nights and Days*, I knew my mind a touch better than I had at first. Those novels and plays, also, had shown me things I could use, effects of narrative and contrasting voices. Much of the trilogy, of course, was written "for" me, at the board, and what remained to say was in a sense dictated by the need to provide a context for those transcripts. So that it all went like the wind!—at least by comparison with the languorous doodling I'd relied on twenty-odd years earlier.

BORNHAUSER: *The Oxford Dictionary of English Christian Names* gives the meaning of Ephraim as "double fruitfulness," from the Hebrew. Were you conscious of this? The Bible tells us (Jer. 31:20) that Ephraim, the son of Joseph, was called by God His son. Then in *Mirabell*, we find posited the notion that Ephraim was Mirabell's pupil; Mirabell then speaks of "MY TEACHER'S VOICE," one also heard by Dante. Presumably the voice of God? By divine succession, according to DJ, Ephraim could be "a composite/Voice, a formula thought up by [Mirabell]." Clearly you are a student of the Old Testament. How much of the biblical account of Ephraim were you aware of when you first began to establish contact with a spirit of this name? What about the name Mirabell?

MERRILL: Mirabell's name is from Congreve. I don't think his TEACHER'S VOICE is the same as God's. Dante, we learn, received instruction from a mendicant ex-priest who turns out to be one of Mirabell's bat-legions in disguise. *Their* senior officer, as I call him, is a voice identified only as OO, who very much prostrates himself before the Angels. Isn't it funny how uncomfortable all these hierarchies make us; yet we read the Table of the Elements with no embarrassment whatever. I'm not at all a Bible person, by the way. I've started the Old Testament again and again, but never get much beyond Abraham and Sarah—though I've peeked, I confess, at some of the later high points. It looks like an utterly fascinating book—if only I knew how to read it. (I have the same problem with *Moby Dick*.) Other people have had to tell me about the biblical Ephraim—there was also apparently a *Saint* Ephraim who wrote poetry—but I never knew what to make of either connection until the poem's epilogue makes it for me, by the revelation that Ephraim and Michael are—how to say it?—aspects of the same power. The ultimate composite voice. Training in word-play might have alerted me much earlier. Five out of seven letters in those two names are the same. Well, that dictionary says it all: double fruit-fulness.

BORNHAUSER: You are bravely mythopoeic in these matter-of-fact days. With a cast including God B[iology], the Archangels, Jesus, and Mo-hammed, do you conceive what you are doing as in any way within the province of Polyhymnia, the Muse of Sacred Poetry?

MERRILL: You'll notice that Polyhymnia doesn't figure among *our* nine Muses—that's just one of a long list of revisions the poem puts us through. It's not so much a visionary poem as a revisionary one, I often fear. I don't want to talk—I'm not equipped to talk—about the nonviability of sacred poetry nowadays. Seen at a certain distance, the issue of profane versus divine comes to be that of the self versus the selfless. This isn't something one has any control over; one can't evidently *will* it, much as one might long to get beyond some of those barriers of the self. They're represented, I suppose, by that "hedge" at Sandover, which we overlook from the schoolroom.

BORNHAUSER: Whatever the case, you have not at the same time shied from the looming theories and threats of the atomic age, from the coils and throes of time and history, from the impenetrabilities of psychology. How much learning do you expect from your reader?

MERRILL: Most poetry written today expects none, and I get rather fed up with that diet of nuts and wheat germ. On the other hand I don't—how could I?—expect a reader to have picked up exactly the same odds and ends that have stuck in my mind over the last forty years or so. Ideally a reader might happen to know, let's say, about a third of these things, might have read Proust but not Dante or E. F. Benson—enough to feel partly at home. And he might have on his own shelves books that I've never read, by whose light he might see implications and dimensions undreamed of in *my* corner of the library. I'd especially like this to be the case where Science and History are concerned. My "learning" in these fields is paltry, to say the least. Yet this doesn't prevent (it may even have allowed) a broad *view* of Science from being set forth in the trilogy. This view might conceivably interest a trained scientist more than it does me—someone who couldn't otherwise see the forest for the trees. Or is that just wishful thinking?

BORNHAUSER: How would you respond to scholarly annotation of your recent work? Or would you laugh this off as unnecessary and inflationary?

MERRILL: No, certainly not. Annotation's probably inevitable. I've made some lists already of things that either needed explaining or the little leaden weight of a reference to keep a passage from seeming merely vapid. I do a certain amount of this in the poem; the classroom format allows for it. Certain other connections get made only much later. *Mirabell* had been published, for instance, when a friend sent me a clipping from that day's paper, with the headline: "Rare Metal Linked to Death of Dinosaurs." Frankly I keep rereading the poem, leafing the pages to see what's there, and *where*. Another friend, Robert Polito, is at work right now on an index—a little pamphlet to be published separately—which I expect to find very useful in tracking down a mislaid line or reference.

BORNHAUSER: Are you afraid of ingenious creative criticism? Or are you more like Eliot, who said he was pleased to see, if for the first time, what responsible critical readers might discover in his poems?

MERRILL: Probably more like Eliot. I've always been oddly comforted by the notion that, no matter how well I think I know what I've said in a poem, it might have a whole dimension that's hidden from me—by the very nature of art. The way one can't ever see one's own face, except in a mirror. Naturally one would like the mirror to be both "responsible" and "creative," like the mirror that painters once used to see properly, for the first time, what they'd done.

BORNHAUSER: You give the lie to C. P. Snow's once famous theory of the two worlds, the conflict and uncommunicativeness between science and the humanities. You do this by the novelistic intensity of your portrayal of the human experience of confronting difficult, elusive, and often abstract concepts. Yet a person like myself is still intimidated by science. What have you assimilated, and what, in order to follow you, must I?

MERRILL: I've assimilated nothing! The tiny bit I learned about science in order to write a few pages of the poem—pages meant to reassure a reader that something *could* be learned and wouldn't be irrelevant to all the "mythology" behind us and ahead of us—came out of books, and sank back into them as soon as I was done. Beginner's books mostly: I relied a lot on Asimov's two-volume *Guide to Science*. So don't imagine that I know. I like your knowing that I imagined. The only lifeline to science, for idiots like ourselves who find the very vocabulary impenetrable, has to be the imagination. Hence the constant drive to *personify* throughout the transcripts—and throughout history. No average person is going to feel comfortable with the idea of solar energy. So a figure slowly takes shape, takes human, or superhuman, form, and is named Apollo or the Archangel Michael, and his words, which *we* put into his mouth, become part of the vast system whereby the universe reveals itself to us. What can you and I profitably learn from a neutrino? Yet give it a human mask and it will, as Oscar Wilde said, tell the truth. Read science *this* way.

BORNHAUSER: Have you read Thomas Pynchon's *V* or *Gravity's Rainbow*? Is there anything there that corresponds to your conceptions? Pynchon, of course, was trained at Cornell as a scientist.

MERRILL: Pynchon's enthralling. He's ten times brighter than I am, yet I can recognize, in his centripetal paranoia, a lot of the same energy—the same quality of energy—that shaped the trilogy. We've both made spider webs on a rather grand scale. Something fairly sinister is sitting at the heart of his. Is that because he knows things I don't? Or purely a matter of temperament? I'm not sure I want those questions answered.

BORNHAUSER: You report in *Mirabell* that it was "twenty / Years in a cool dark place that Ephraim took / In order to be palatable wine. / This book by contrast, immature, supine, / Still kicks against its archetypal cradle." Are we to take this as ironic, or is there some chance that the book will undergo revision, which is to say that *Mirabell* may retap your word bank?

MERRILL: Oh no, there's to be next to no revision of *Mirabell* or *Scripts*. I've made perhaps a half dozen very slight changes. One of them involved resurrecting, from the transcript, a distinction between "matter" and "substance." I just couldn't face introducing a new term, then realized that not to do so left a nasty smudge. Throughout those last two volumes, it's true, my nose is very close to the page. I can only hope that what I lost of "aesthetic distance" I gained in "immediacy." In any case, they were too compelling for me to wait till I was seventy to write them.

BORNHAUSER: Are you ever very conscious of your readership—beyond, of course, the critics who write about your work? How much do you think it matters for any writer?

MERRILL: It's madness to think of an audience. It's madness also not to think of one. Who would write on a desert island—beyond making notches for the passing days? With the trilogy, I've begun to get letters—never very many, thank goodness—from people who are, well, let's say, more interested in spiritualism than in literature. Those are usually fun to answer. An intelligent review, whether good or bad, is stimulating. But I like best of all the feeling that *lots* of people are writing, not about me, though they may dimly know that I exist; just as I dimly know that they do. That sense, however dim, of mutual endeavor is the indispensable thing.

BORNHAUSER: It has been said that at the present time there are more really competent, respectable poets, in sheer number, than have ever lived before at any one time. Do you believe it?

MERRILL: Well, poetry has become a fairly loose term, one that often doesn't exceed the epigram, the diary jotting, the scholarly note. You just break these up into a few lines, and there you are. If you include all the people who write *this* stuff, then I'm sure it's true that there are more poets than readers nowadays. They're all "respectable." Poetry, even at that level, is a civilizing force, a kind of compost. There are a very few poets I wish would *stop* writing, and perhaps exactly the same number that I wish would never stop.

BORNHAUSER: Why have almost all nondramatic poets in England and America, from the eighteenth century on, attempted at least one play? Even such disparate and unlikely ones as Hopkins (the fragmentary *St. Winifred's Well*), Longfellow (the book-length *Christus*), and Stevens (*Three Travellers Watch a Sunrise*).

MERRILL: It can't have been, in those three instances—though I haven't even heard of the Longfellow play—a wish to try out different voices. Perhaps it's that a play, even a play you read to yourself, appeals to your credulity on a more naive level than a poem does. You begin imagining scenery, gestures for the actors, tones of voice, in a way that you simply don't when you read, oh, Browning or Frost—their narrative or "dramatic" poems, that is. With them, you're still conscious of being in the hands of the artful author. But the dramatic format puts you in the hands of the characters. It's an illusion, but how liberating!

BORNHAUSER: Would it be fair to ask you to comment on your own diction, which has been justly praised as one of your chief virtues? I would have to say I notice in your poetry an absolutely astonishing range—from the arcane and rarefied to the technical, the commonplace, and even the cliché—all of which you manage to endow with a rightness and richness and freshness. And of course a naturalness. Behind the scenes, how hard do you have to struggle for *le mot juste* and the right tone?

MERRILL: The range is nothing I'm aware of striving for. We *have* all these languages—technical terms, clichés, polite circumlocutions, as you say—so why not use them? If you know some French words, use *them*, too. Poets don't write first of all in "English" or "American" so much as each in an idiom peculiar to himself. Naturalness is always becoming. I'm not sure, though, that many poets know what it is. They're haunted by bugaboos like "natural word order," which teaches them to write "See Jane run," when the truly *natural* way of putting it would be something closer to "Where on earth can that child be racing off to? Why, it's little—you know, the neighbor's brat—Jane!" It can take me dozens of drafts to get something right, which often turns out to be a perfect commonplace. What joy when it works—like fighting one's way through cobwebs to an open window. I don't mean that the more work you put into something, the better it turns out. Often you can feel the life ebbing away at the hands of a Mad Embalmer.

BORNHAUSER: Do a dictionary and thesaurus play an active role in the process of your writing?

MERRILL: Indeed they do. So does a rhyming dictionary, though not as regularly. I used to be furious with the *OED* for never taking the etymologies back far enough. But now that I've found the *American Heritage Dictionary* with that splendid appendix of Indo-European roots a serene sort of ménage à trois has been set up. I expect it will go on for years.

BORNHAUSER: Auden, whose poetry could be quite political and topical, said that the poet could never change the world, but that his function was to preserve and purify the language. How do you feel about this?

MERRILL: I don't know. Auden was changed by his reading of poets like Hardy and Eliot, Rilke and Cavafy, and he was part of the world. Writing his or her poems changes a poet, over the years, in ways that perhaps time or society by themselves couldn't. Perhaps he meant that these changes hardly count against the great coarsening drift of things. One doesn't particularly notice that the language *is* being preserved or purified, no matter how busily the poets function. I know one thing: worrying about it helps not at all.

BORNHAUSER: Commentators on your work, especially the late work, quite often mention Dante, Milton, Pope, and Yeats. And I suppose Blake and Goethe (in the second part of *Faust*). The writer I would like to ask about is Hawthorne, who in the introductions to his romances (*not* novels) cumulatively and persistently defines romance as what is familiar by sunlight seen in the transforming moonlight. Would you say that in some sense you are turning both lights, together or successively, on your subject? Can the trilogy be profitably approached as a romance?

An Interview with Fred Bornhauser

MERRILL: A line kept recurring as I wrote my little Greek novel—"the sun and moon together in the sky." I meant that I was drawn to both sides of things: masculine and feminine, rational and fanciful, passionate and ironic. With the trilogy, as I said just now, remaining of two minds seemed the essential thing. I didn't read Julian Jaynes' book on the bicameral mind until I'd finished *Mirabell*, and was all the more struck by how the entire action of that volume took place in two adjacent rooms of the Stonington house: the red dining room where we took down the messages, and the blue parlor where we thought about them afterwards. So, yes, both lights were vital to the poem. I'm rather shaky as to genres and modes, but it does seem to be a romance in certain ways—and perhaps a mock-romance in others? Frye says that in a romance "a ghost as a rule is merely one more character." Actually, I suspect that the trilogy touches on a variety of modes, and the one thing that holds it together, if anything does, is that it all truly happened to us, came to us in these various ways.

BORNHAUSER: What about received ideas of "received forms"?

MERRILL: Unfortunately there's a lot of defensiveness on both sides. And self-indulgence—both the formal and the experimental poet too often use their gifts as an easy way out. For myself, I by and large put my faith in forms. The attention they require at once frees and channels the unconscious, as Auden kept reminding us. Even if your poem turns out badly, you've learned something about proportion and concision and self-lessness. And at best the form "received" by the next poet to use it will have taken on a new aspect because of what you learned there.

An Interview
with J. D. McClatchy

MCCLATCHY: You've left your house in Athens for good now, right?

MERRILL: It looks that way.

MCCLATCHY: And your original decision to settle there—was that just an accumulation of accidents?

MERRILL: Oh, there's no accident. I went first to Greece to visit Kimon Friar in 1950. Between then and 1959, when I went back with David, we'd gone to a great number of other places too—to the Orient and, either together or separately, all over Europe, except Greece. And suddenly here was a place—I can't tell you how much we liked it. We liked Stonington, too, but didn't want to stay there all year round. It had slowly dawned on us, as it continues to dawn on young people in Stonington, that it's a community of older people by and large. Nearly all our friends were five to *fifty* years older than we were. And in Greece we began seeing, for a change, people our own age, or younger.

MCCLATCHY: I presume you came to Stonington to get away from New York. If, by analogy, you went to Athens to get away from things in America, what was it you found there?

MERRILL: Things that have mostly disappeared, I'm afraid. The dazzling air, the drowsy waterfronts. Our own ignorance, even: a language we didn't understand two words of at first. That *was* a holiday! You could imagine that others were saying extraordinarily fascinating things—the point was to invent, if not what they were saying, at least its implications, its overtones. Also, in those days foreign tourists were both rare and welcome, and the delighted surprise with which the Greeks acknowledged our ability to put two words together, you know, was irresistible.

Published in *The Paris Review*, no. 84 (Summer 1982), as 31 in the series "The Art of Poetry."

MCCLATCHY: What sort of people did you find yourselves falling in with? Other Americans?

MERRILL: No, certainly not. In fact, even Greeks who spoke English or French had to be extremely charming for us to want to see them more than once. We wanted to learn Greek and we also wanted to learn *Greece*, and the turn of mind that made a Greek.

MCCLATCHY: It can't be accidental, then, that your leaving Greece co-incides with the completion of your trilogy—

MERRILL: Probably not. A coincidence over which I had no control was that, within a year of my finishing the trilogy, David had come to see that Athens was no longer a livable place. We'd both seen this day coming, I'm afraid, but for one reason or another neither of us wanted to believe his eyes. If he'd stayed on, I'd still be going back and forth. Maria might have been another reason for staying. Even after her death—or especially after her death, as her role in the poem grew clearer—I couldn't have faced, right away, cutting ourselves off from the friends we'd had in common, friends also in their own right, who made all the difference.

MCCLATCHY: That's Maria Mitsotáki? Was she really—

MERRILL: Everything I say she was in the trilogy? Oh yes, and more. Her father had indeed been prime minister, three times, I think—but under which king? Constantine I or George II, or both? I'm vague about things like that. I'm vague too about her husband, who died long before our time. They'd lived in South Africa, in London. . . . Maria went home for a visit and was stranded in Athens during the whole German occupation. Horrible stories—and wonderful ones: dashing young cousins in the underground, hidden for weeks in bedroom closets. Literary men fell in love with her, quite understandably—aside from being an enchantment to look at, she *never missed a thing you said*.

MCCLATCHY: Your trilogy attests to a warm, intimate relationship with Maria Mitsotáki and W. H. Auden. Did working on the poem *change* your feelings about them?

MERRILL: In a way, yes. The friendships, which had been merely "real" on earth—subject to interruption, mutual convenience, states of health, like events that have to be scheduled "weather permitting"—became ideal. Nothing was hazed over by reticence or put off by a cold snap. Whenever we needed them, there they were; and a large part of *that* wonder was to feel how deeply they needed *us*. I can't pretend to have known Wystan terribly well in *this* world. He liked me, I think, and approved of my work,

63

and liked the reassurance of David's and my being in Athens to stand by Chester Kallman [Auden's friend and collaborator] when emergencies arose. But he was twenty years older and had been famous while I was still in boarding school, and—well, it took the poem, and the almost jubilant youthfulness he recovers after death, to get me over my shyness. With Maria it was different. In the years we knew her she saw very few people, but we were part of that happy few. Many of her old friends whom she no longer saw couldn't imagine what had come over her—"she's given us up for those *Americans!*" We simply adored her. It seemed like the perfection of intimacy, light, airy, without confessions or possessiveness—yet one would have to be Jung or Dante to foresee her role in the poem.

MCCLATCHY: You hadn't even an inkling of that role when you began the poem?

MERRILL: Oh, no. It's true, I began "Ephraim" within days of hearing that she'd died—and felt, I suppose, enough of a coincidence to list her among the characters. There's only one mention of her in the whole "Book of Ephraim," yet I kept her in, and look what happened! The cassia shrub on the terrace—how could the poem have ended without it? I couldn't bring *it* home to America, though I did the next best thing and sneaked some seedpods through customs. They've given rise to that rather promising affair out there on the deck.

MCCLATCHY: Panning the Ouija board transcripts for poetic gold—*that* must have been a daunting project. How did you go about it?

MERRILL: The problem changed from volume to volume. With "Ephraim," many of the transcripts I had made from Ouija board sessions had vanished, or hadn't been saved. So I mainly used whatever came to hand, except for the high points which I'd copied out over the years into a special notebook. Those years—time itself—did my winnowing for me. With *Mirabell* it was, to put it mildly, harder. The transcript was enormous. What you see in the poem might be half, or two-fifths, of the original. Most of the cuts were repetitions: things said a second or third time, in new ways often, to make sure we'd understood. Or further, unnecessary illustrations of a point. I haven't looked at them for several years now, and can only hope that nothing too vital got left out. Getting it onto the page seemed really beyond me at first, perhaps because I'd begun imagining a poem the same length as "Ephraim." By the time the fourteen-syllable line occurred to me (that exchange with Wystan is largely contrived) I'd also decided where to divide it into books, so it all got under way at last.

With *Scripts*, there was no shaping to be done. Except for the minutest changes and deciding about line breaks and so forth, the Lessons you see on the page appear just as we took them down. The doggerel at the fêtes, everything. In between the Lessons—our chats with Wystan or Robert [Morse] or Uni [the trilogy's resident unicorn]—I still felt free to pick and choose; but even there, the design of the book just swept me along.

MCCLATCHY: You don't feel that too much was sacrificed for the sake of shapeliness?

MERRILL: If so, perhaps no accident? I came upon the pages of one of our very earliest evenings with Ephraim. He's giving us a lecture about the senses: POLISH THE WINDOWS OF YOUR EYES, etc., each sense in turn. That obviously prefigures, by over twenty years, one of the themes crucial to Volume 3—but isn't it nicer and less daunting somehow to have it emerge casually, without pedantry?

Then there were things outside the transcript—things in "life" that kept staring me in the face, only I couldn't see them, as if I'd been hypnotized, until the danger was past. Only this year I was in my study, playing the perhaps ten thousandth game of Patience since beginning "Ephraim." I'm using my old, nearly effaced Greek cards with their strange neoclassical royalties, and I do a little superstitious trick when I'm through. I reassemble the deck so that the Queen of Hearts is at the bottom, facing up. Now on those old-style Greek cards the queens are all marked K, for Kyria—Lady. It's what George calls Mother Nature, and I'd simply never made the connection. Furthermore, the kings are all marked B, for Basileus. God B of Hearts? "You're nothing but a pack of cards!" You can be sure I'd have dragged all that in if I'd thought of it in time. Plus another clever but expendable allusion to the graveyard scene of the *Rake*, where Tom calls upon the Queen of Hearts and is saved. Driven out of his wits, but saved.

Other things that in retrospect seem indispensable came to hand just when they were needed, as if by magic. Stephen Yenser explaining the Golden Section when I was halfway through "Ephraim." Marilyn Lavin telling me about the X-rayed Giorgione—I'd already written V and W—and hunting up the relevant article. Stephen Orgel's book on the masque, which he sent me not a moment too soon. A friend of my nephew's, Michael Beard, writing me a letter on the metaphysical implications of Arabic calligraphy. A month or so later I would simply need to versify some of his phrases in order to make that little lyric about the Bismillah formula. Then

RECITATIVE

Alfred Corn's joke about E—Ephraim—equalling any emcee squared. I felt like a perfect magpie.

MCCLATCHY: What do the Ouija transcripts look like?

MERRILL: Like first-grade compositions. Drunken lines of capitals lurching across the page, gibberish until they're divided into words and sentences. It depends on the pace. Sometimes the powers take pity on us and slow down.

MCCLATCHY: The Ouija board, now. I gather you use a homemade one, but that doesn't exactly help me to imagine it or its workings. An overturned teacup is your pointer?

MERRILL: Yes. The commercial boards come with a funny see-through planchette on legs. I find them too cramped. Besides, it's so easy to make your own—just write out the alphabet and the numbers and your YES and NO (punctuation marks too, if you're going all out) on a big sheet of cardboard. Or use brown paper—it travels better. On our Grand Tour, whenever we felt lonely in the hotel room, David and I could just unfold our instant company. He puts his right hand lightly on the cup, I put my left, leaving the right free to transcribe, and away we go. We get, oh, five hundred to six hundred words an hour. Better than gasoline.

MCCLATCHY: What *is* your fuel, would you say? With all the other disciplines available to a poet, why this one?

MERRILL: Well, don't you think there comes a time when everyone, not just a poet, wants to get beyond the self? To reach, if you like, the "god" within you? The board, in however clumsy or absurd a way, allows for precisely that. Or if it's still *yourself* that you're drawing upon, then that self is much stranger and freer and more farseeing than the one you thought you knew. Of course there are disciplines with grander pedigrees and similar goals. The board happens to be ours. I've stopped, by the way, recommending it to inquisitive friends.

MCCLATCHY: When did you start using a Ouija board?

MERRILL: Frederick Buechner gave me one as birthday present in 1953. As I recall, we sat down then and there to try it, and got a touching little story from a fairly simple soul—that engineer "dead of cholera in Cairo," who'd met Goethe. I used it in the first thing I ever wrote about the Ouija board (a poem called "Voices from the Other World"), although by that time the *experiences* behind this poem were mine and David's. We started in the summer of 1955. But the spirit *we* contacted—Ephraim—was anything but simple. So much so that for a long time I felt that the material he dictated really couldn't be used—then or perhaps ever. I felt it would be

66

like cheating, or plagiarizing from some unidentifiable source. Oh, I put a few snippets of it into *The Seraglio*, but that was just a novel, and didn't count. Twenty years later, though, I was yet again trying to tell the whole story as fiction, through a set of characters bearing little resemblance to David or me. I'd got about fifty pages done, hating every bit of it. I'm not a novelist, and never was. No accident, then, that I simply "forgot" the manuscript in a taxi in Atlanta and never recovered it—well, all that's described in "The Book of Ephraim." But I went on, I didn't take the hint. I put together all the drafts and notes for those lost pages and proceeded to forget *these* in a hotel room in Frankfurt! By now I was down to just two pages of an opening draft. As I sat glaring at them, the prose began to dissolve into verse. I marked the line breaks with a pencil, fiddled a bit, typed it up, and showed the two versions to a friend who said quite firmly, "You must never write prose again." At that point "The Book of Ephraim" crystalized, and got written without any particular trouble.

MCCLATCHY: Throughout the trilogy you have many "voices"—Wallace Stevens, Gertrude Stein, Pythagoras, Nefertiti. How does this work? Do they simply break in, or do you ask specifically for them?

MERRILL: Either way. Most of the time, we never knew what to expect. Last summer, for instance, we were about to sit down at the board—no, I was already in my chair—when David called from the kitchen. He can never keep abreast of the rising postal rates, and wanted to know which stamp to put on his letter. I called back, "Put on an Edna St. Vincent Millay"—I'd bought a sheet of her commemoratives just that week. And when we started at the board, there she was. Very embarrassing on both sides, as it dawned on the poor creature that we hadn't meant to talk to *her* at all.

MCCLATCHY: Does what Auden tells you via the Ouija board remind you of him? Are there distinctive phrases or sentiments that could only be his?

MERRILL: Some of his best-known sentiments get revised—his Christian views, for instance—but the turns of phrase sound very like him, to my ears. Remember, though, that we never knew each other well, not in *this* world.

MCCLATCHY: Would the Ouija board be your instrument—like a keyboard on which a musician composes or improvises?

MERRILL: Not a bit! If anything, the keyboard was us. And our one obligation, at any given session, was to be as "well tempered" as possible.

MCCLATCHY: So the Ouija board is by no means a mnemonic device—it is not something to get you going.

MERRILL: No. At least, not something to start me *writing*. In other ways, evidently, it did start us "going"—thinking, puzzling, resisting, testing the messages against everything we knew or thought possible.

MCCLATCHY: What is David's function when you use the Ouija board?

MERRILL: That's a good question. According to Mirabell, David is the subconscious shaper of the message itself, the "Hand," as they call him. Of the two of us, he's the spokesman for human nature, while I'm the "Scribe," the one in whose words and images the message gets expressed. This would be a fairly rough distinction, but enough to show that the transcripts as they stand could never have come into being without him. I wonder if the trilogy shouldn't have been signed with both our names—or simply "by DJ, as told to JM"?

MCCLATCHY: Could not the "they" who move the teacup around the board be considered the authors of the poems?

MERRILL: Well, yes and no. As "they" keep saying throughout, language is the human medium. It doesn't exist—except perhaps as vast mathematical or chemical formulas—in that realm of, oh, cosmic forces, elemental processes, which *we* then personify, or tame if you like, through the imagination. So, in a sense, all these figures are our creation, or mankind's. The powers they represent are real—as, say, gravity is "real"—but they'd be invisible, inconceivable, if they'd never passed through our heads and clothed themselves out of the costume box they found there. *How* they appear depends on us, on the imaginer, and would have to vary wildly from culture to culture, or even temperament to temperament. A process that Einstein could entertain as a formula might be described by an African witch doctor as a crocodile. What's tiresome is when people exclusively insist on the forms they've imagined. Those powers don't need churches in order to be sacred. What they do need are fresh ways of being seen.

MCCLATCHY: Does the idea of the Ouija board ever embarrass you—I mean that you have this curious collaborator?

MERRILL: From what I've just said, you see how pompous I can get. The mechanics of the board—this absurd, flimsy contraption, creaking along—serves wonderfully as a hedge against inflation. I think it does embarrass the sort of reader who can't bear to face the random or trivial elements that coalesce, among others, to produce an "elevated" thought. That doesn't bother me *at all*.

MCCLATCHY: Does the Ouija board ever manifest maniacal tendencies? Do you ever feel yourself lost in its grip?

MERRILL: Thanks perhaps to a certain ongoing resistance, we seem to have held our own. We kept it as a parlor game for the first twenty years. Those early voices in *Mirabell* gave us, I admit, a nasty turn. Looking back, though, I've the sense that we *agreed* to let them take us over, for the sake of the poem. Poems can do that, even when you think you're writing them all by yourself. Oh, we've been scared at times. A friend who sat with us at the board just once went on to have a pretty awful experience with some people out in Detroit. She was told to go west, and to sail on a certain freighter on a certain day, and the name of the island where she'd meet her great-grandmother reincarnated as a Polynesian teenager who would guide her to a mountain cave where in turn an old man . . . and so forth. Luckily she collapsed before she ever made it to California. I don't believe she was being manipulated by the other people. The experience sounds genuine. But she didn't have the strength to use it properly—whatever I mean by that! It would seem that David and I *have* that strength; or else, that we've been handled with kid gloves. A number of friends have been scared *for* us over the years. One of them took me to a Trappist monastery to talk to one of the more literary priests. It was a lovely couple of hours. I read from some of the transcripts, filling in as much as I could of the background. Afterwards, the priest admitted that they'd all been warned in seminary against these devilish devices, but that, frankly, I'd read nothing to him that he didn't believe himself. I suspect a lot of people use the board to guide them through life—"What's next week's winning lottery number?"—and get the answers they deserve. Our voices are often very illuminating when we bring up a dilemma or a symptom, but they never *tell* us what to do. At most they suggest the possibilities, the various consequences. Now that I think of it, our friend might have misread a hint for a command, or a metaphorical itinerary of self-discovery for a real trip to Hawaii.

MCCLATCHY: What about more conventional aids to inspiration—drugs? Drink?

MERRILL: Liquor, in my parents' world, was always your reward at the end of a hard day—or an easy day, for that matter—and I like to observe that old family tradition. But I've never drunk for inspiration. Quite the contrary—it's like the wet sponge on the blackboard. I do now and then take a puff of grass, or a crumb of Alice Toklas fudge, when I've reached the last drafts of a poem. That's when you need X-ray eyes to see what you've done, and the grass helps. Some nice touches can fall into place.

MCCLATCHY: In hindsight, do you have any general feelings about the occult, about the *use* of the occult in poetry?

MERRILL: I've never much liked hearing about it. Usually the people who write about it have such dreadful style. Yeats is almost the only exception I can think of. The first thing to do is to get rid of that awful vocabulary. It's almost acceptable once it's purged of all those fancy words—"auras" and "astral bodies."

MCCLATCHY: Has it been a kind of displaced religion for you? I take it you *have* a religious streak somewhere in you.

MERRILL: Oh, that's a very good phrase for it—"displaced religion." I never felt at home with the "pastoral" Episcopalianism I was handed. Unctuous mouthings of scripture, a system that like the courtier-shepherds and milkmaids at the Petit Trianon seemed almost willfully deluded, given the state of the world and the fears and fantasies already raging in my little head. Mademoiselle's Catholicism corresponded more to these. She taught me the Ave Maria—without which the Lord's Prayer calls up the image of dry bread in a motherless reformatory. Even her Jesus, next to the Protestant one, was all blood and magic—the face on Veronica's napkin, the ghastly little Sacred Heart hanging above her bed, like something out of a boy's book about Aztec sacrifice, or something the gardener pulled out of the earth. These images *connected*. I mean, we used napkins the size of Veronica's at every meal. As Shaw reminds us, Christ wasn't out to proselytize. He said that God was in each of us, a spark of pure potential. He held no special brief for the Family. All very sensible, but I'm afraid I've long since thrown out the baby with the churchly bathwater. The need, as you say, remained. I never cared for the pose of the atheist—though the Angels came round to that, you know, in their way, insisting on man as master of his own destiny.

MCCLATCHY: You don't describe yourself as having been a very good student, and still seem a bit self-conscious as an "intellectual."

MERRILL: Ummmh . . .

MCCLATCHY: No accident, then, that the trilogy's caps are all unrelieved meaning? A case of the return of the repressed?

MERRILL: You're probably exactly right there, at least where the "Grand Design" is concerned. Also in passages—like Mirabell on Culture or Technology—where the proliferation of crisp ideas sounds almost like a Shaw preface. Not at all the kind of page I could turn out by myself. On the other hand, a lot of what we're loosely calling "meaning" turns out, on inspection, to be metaphor, which leads one back toward language: wordplay, etymology, the "wholly human instrument" (as Wystan says) I'd used and trusted—like every poet, wouldn't you say?—to ground the lightning of ideas. We could say that the uppercase represented a *range* of metaphor, a depth of meaning, that hadn't been available to me in earlier poems. Victor Hugo described his voices as his own conscious powers multiplied by five, and *he* was probably exactly right there, too.

MCCLATCHY: Though your trilogy takes up the ultimate question of origins and destiny, you are not a poet—like Yeats or Auden or Lowell—who has taken on political issues in your work. Or is that very avoidance itself a kind of "stand"?

MERRILL: The lobbies? The candidates' rhetoric—our "commitments abroad"? The Shah as Helen of Troy launching a thousand missile carriers? One whiff of all that, and I turn purple and start kicking my cradle. I like the idea of nations, actually, and even more those pockets of genuine strangeness within nations. Yet those are being emptied, turned inside out, made to conform—in the interest of what? The friendly American smile we're told to wear in our passport photos? Oh, it's not just in America. You can go to an outdoor concert in Athens—in that brown, poisonous air the government isn't strong enough to do anything about—and there are the president and the prime minister in their natty suits, surrounded by flashbulbs, hugging and patting each other as if they hadn't met for months. God have mercy on whoever's meant to be impressed by that. Of course I can't conceive of anyone *choosing* public life, unless from some unspeakable hidden motive.

MCCLATCHY: What newspapers do you read?

MERRILL: In Europe the Paris *Herald*—I get very American over there, and it's so concise. Here, I never learned how to read a paper. My first year away at school, I watched my classmates, some of them littler than I was, frowning over the war news or the financial page. They already knew how! I realized then and there I couldn't hope to catch up. I told this to Marianne Moore before introducing her at her Amherst reading in 1956. She looked rather taken aback, as I did myself, a half hour later, when in the middle of a poem she was reading—a poem I thought I knew—I heard my name. "Now Mr. Merrill," she was saying, "tells me he doesn't read a newspaper. That's hard for me to understand. The things one would miss! Why, only last week I read that our U.S. Customs Bureau was collecting all the egret and bird-of-paradise feathers we'd confiscated during the twenties and thirties—collecting them and sending them off to Nepal, where they're *needed*. . . ." And then she went right on with her poem.

MCCLATCHY: I'll have to interrupt. Why were those feathers needed in Nepal?

MERRILL: Oh, headdresses, regalia . . . *you* must remember—the papers were full of it!

But let's be serious for a moment. If our Angels are right, every leader—president or terrorist—is responsible for keeping his ranks thinned out. Good politics would therefore encourage death in one form or another—if not actual, organized bloodshed, then the legalization of abortion or, heaven forbid, the various chemical or technological atrocities. Only this last strikes me as truly immoral, perhaps because it's a threat that hadn't existed before my own lifetime. I take it personally. That bit in "The Broken Home"—"Father Time and Mother Earth, / A marriage on the rocks"—isn't meant as a joke. History in our time *has* cut loose, *has* broken faith with Nature. But poems, even those of the most savage incandescence, can't deal frontally with such huge, urgent subjects without sounding grumpy or dated when they should still be in their prime. So my parents' divorce dramatized on a human scale a subject that couldn't have been handled otherwise. Which is what a "poetic" turn of mind allows for. You don't see eternity *except* in the grain of sand, or history except at the family dinner table.

MCCLATCHY: You had a very privileged childhood, in the normal sense of "privileged"—wealth, advantages. But the privilege also of being able to turn the pain of that childhood into art. How do you look back on it now?

MERRILL: Perhaps turning it into art came naturally. . . . I mean, it's hard to speak of a child having a sense of reality or unreality, because after all, what are his criteria? It strikes me now maybe that during much of my childhood I found it difficult to *believe* in the way my parents lived. They seemed so utterly taken up with engagements, obligations, ceremonies—every child must feel that, to some extent, about the grown-ups in his life. The excitement, the emotional quickening *I* felt in those years came usually through animals or nature, or through the servants in the house—Colette knew all about that—whose lives seemed by contrast to make such perfect *sense*. The gardeners had their hands in the earth. The cook was dredging things with flour, making pies. My father was merely making money, while my mother wrote names on place-cards, planned menus, and did her needlepoint. Her masterpiece—not the imaginary fire screen I describe in the poem—depicted the facade of the Southampton house. I could see how stylized it was. The designer had put these peculiar flowers all over the front lawn, and a stereotyped old black servant on either side. Once in a while my mother would let me complete a stitch. It fascinated me. It had nothing really to do with the world, yet somehow. . . . Was it the world becoming art?

MCCLATCHY: The picture your poems paint of yourself as a child is of someone who's bored. Were you?

MERRILL: We shouldn't exaggerate. There were things I enjoyed enormously, like fishing—something responding and resisting from deep, deep down. It's true, sometimes I must have been extremely bored, though never inactive. My mother remembers asking me, when I was five or six, what I wanted to do when I was grown up. Didn't I want, she asked, to go downtown and work in Daddy's office? "Oh no," I said, "I'll be too tired by then." Because, you see, everything was arranged: to so-and-so's house to play, the beach for lunch, a tennis lesson. As we know, the life of leisure doesn't give us a moment's rest. I didn't care for the games or the playmates. I don't recall there being anyone I really liked, my own age, until I went away to school.

MCCLATCHY: There may be links between that boredom and an impulse to write, to make up a life of your own. I suppose you were a great reader as a child?

MERRILL: Was I? I loved stories, but can't remember being very curious about the books in the library. Once, all by myself, I opened a copy of Barrie's *Dear Brutus* to the following unforgettable bit of dialogue: "Where is your husband, Alice?" "In the library, sampling the port." Now I knew what port was: it was where ships went. And I knew what a sample was because even *I* had been consulted as to new wallpaper and upholstery. Suddenly a surrealist bit of language! But generally I read what I was told to read, not always liking it. My mother gave me *Mrs. Wiggs and the Cabbage Patch* and I remember throwing it out the window. By then I was . . . eight? A couple of years later I read *Gone with the Wind*. No one told me there were any other novels, *grown-up* novels. I must have read it six or seven times in succession; I thought it was one of a kind. As for *good* literature—one got a bit of it at school, but not at home.

MCCLATCHY: You began writing at that age too?

MERRILL: I had written at least one poem when I was seven or eight. It was a poem about going with the Irish setter into my mother's room—an episode that ended up in "The Broken Home." The Irish setter *was* named Michael and I think the poem began: "One day while she lay sleeping, / Michael and I went peeping." My first publication was in the *St. Nicholas* magazine, a quatrain: "Pushing slowly every day / Autumn finally makes its way. / Now when the days are cool, / We children go to school." They wanted a drawing to illustrate your verses. And that gave me my first *severe* aesthetic lesson, because when the poem and sketch were printed—the sketch showed a little boy on the crest of a hill heading for a schoolhouse far below—I saw to my consternation that, although I'd drawn the windows of the schoolhouse very carefully with a ruler, the editors had made them crooked, as befitted a child's drawing. Of course they were right. But the lesson sank in : one must act one's age and give people what they expect.

MCCLATCHY : A ballroom, empty of all but ghostly presences, is an image, or *scene* of instruction, that recurs in key poems during your career. I'm thinking of "A Tenancy" in *Water Street*, "The Broken Home" in *Nights and Days*, the Epilogue to the trilogy. It is a haunting image, and seems a haunted one as well. What associations and significance does that room have for you?

MERRILL : The original, the primal ballroom—in Southampton—would have made even a grown-up gasp. My brother once heard a Mrs. Jaeckel say, "Stanford White put his *heart* into this room." Four families could have lived in it. Two pianos *did*, and an organ, with pipes that covered the whole upper half of a wall, and a huge spiral column of gilded wood in each corner. And a monster stone fireplace with a buffalo head above it. At night it was often dark; people drank before dinner in the library. So that, after being sent to bed, I'd have to make my way through the ballroom in order to get upstairs. Once I didn't—I sat clutching my knees on one of the window seats, hidden by the twenty-foot-high red damask curtain, for hours it seemed, listening to my name being called throughout the house. Once I was allowed to stay up, before a party, long enough to see the chandeliers lit—hundreds of candles. It must have answered beautifully to my father's Gatsby side. It's a room I remember *him* in, not my mother. He took me aside there, one evening, to warn me—with tears in his eyes—against the drink in his hand. We didn't *call* it the ballroom—it was the music room. Some afternoons my grandmother played the organ, rather shyly. One morning a houseguest, a woman who later gave me piano lessons in New York, played through the whole score of *Pag-*

liacci for me, singing and explaining. That was my first "opera." Looking back, even going back to visit while my father still had that house, I could see how much grander the room was than any of the uses we'd put it to, so maybe the ghostly presences appeared in order to make up for a thousand unrealized possibilities. That same sense probably accounts for my "redecoration" in the Epilogue—making the room conform to an ideal much sunnier, much more silvery, that I began to trust only as an adult, while keeping carefully out of my mind (until that passage had been written) the story of how Cronus cuts off the scrotum, or "ballroom," of his father Uranus and throws it into the sea, where it begins to foam and shine, and the goddess of Love and Beauty is born.

MCCLATCHY: As a young poet starting out in the fifties, what did you look forward to? What did you imagine yourself writing in, say, 1975?

MERRILL: I was a perhaps fairly typical mixture of aspiration and diffidence. Certainly I could never see beyond the poem I was at work on. And since weeks or months could go by between poems, I tried to make each one "last" as long as possible, to let its meanings ever so slowly rise to the surface I peered into—enchanted and a touch bored. I looked forward, not without apprehension, to a lifetime of this.

MCCLATCHY: How would you now characterize the author of *The Black Swan*?

MERRILL: This will contradict my last answer about "starting out in the fifties." By then I'd come to see what hard work it was, writing a poem. But *The Black Swan*—those poems written in 1945 and 1946 had simply bubbled up. Each took an afternoon, a day or two at most. Their author had been recently dazzled by all kinds of things whose existence he'd never suspected, poets he'd never read before, like Stevens or Crane; techniques and forms that could be recovered or reinvented from the past without their having to sound old-fashioned, thanks to any number of stylish "modern" touches like slant rhyme or surrealist imagery or some tentative approach to the conversational ("Love, keep your eye peeled"). There were effects in Stevens, in the *Notes*, which I read before anything else— his great ease in combining abstract words with gaudy visual or sound effects: "That alien, point-blank, green and actual Guatemala," or those "angular anonymids" in their blue and yellow stream. You didn't have to be exclusively decorative *or* in deadly earnest. You could be grand *and* playful. The astringent abstract word was always there to bring your little impressionist picture to its senses.

MCCLATCHY: But he—that is, the author of *The Black Swan*—is someone you now see as a kind of happy emulation of literary models?

MERRILL: No, not a bit. It seems to me, reading those poems over—and I've begun to rework a number of them—that the only limitation imposed upon them was my own youth and limited skill; whereas looking back on the poems in *The Country of a Thousand Years of Peace*, it seems to me that each of at least the shorter ones bites off much less than those early lyrics did. They seem the product of a more competent, but in a way smaller, spirit. Returning to those early poems *now*, obviously in the light of the completed trilogy, I've had to marvel a bit at the resemblances. It's as though after a long lapse or, as you put it, displacement of faith, I'd finally, with the trilogy, reentered the church of those original themes. The colors, the elements, the magical emblems: they were the first subjects I'd found again at last.

MCCLATCHY: About the progress of a poem, a typical poem—one, say, you've never written—is it a *problem* that you feel nagging you and try to solve by writing? Are you led on by a subject, or by chance phrases?

MERRILL: Often it's some chance phrases, usually attached but not always—not even always attached to a subject, though if the poem is to go anywhere it has somehow to develop a subject fairly quickly, even if that subject is a blank shape. A poem like "About the Phoenix"—I don't know where any of it came from, but it kept drawing particles of phrases and images to itself.

MCCLATCHY: But by "subject" you mean essentially an event, a person . . .

MERRILL: . . . a scene . . .

MCCLATCHY: . . . a landscape?

MERRILL: A kind of action . . .

MCCLATCHY: . . . that has not necessarily happened to you?

MERRILL: Hmmm. And then I think one problem that has presented itself over and over, usually in the case of a poem of a certain length, is that you've got to end up saying the right thing. A poem like "Scenes of Childhood" made for a terrible impasse because at the point where my "I" is waking up the next morning, after a bad night, I had him say that *dawn was worse*. It took me a couple of weeks to realize that this was something that couldn't be said under nearly any circumstances without being dishonest. Dawn is not worse; the sacred sun rises and things look up. Once I reversed myself, the poem ended easily enough. I had the same problem with "An Urban Convalescence" before writing those concluding quatrains. It broke off at the lowest point: "The heavy volume of the world / Closes again." But then something affirmative had to be made out of it.

MCCLATCHY: You're so self-conscious about *not* striking attitudes that the word "affirmative" makes me wonder. . . .

MERRILL: No, think of music. I mean, you don't *end* pieces with a dissonance.

MCCLATCHY: When you write a poem, do you imagine an immediate audience for it?

MERRILL: Oh, over the years I've collected a little anthology of ideal readers.

MCCLATCHY: Living and dead?

MERRILL: Now, now . . . But *yes*, why not? Living, dead, imaginary. Is this diction crisp enough for Herbert? Is this stanza's tessitura too high for Maggie Teyte? The danger with your close friends is that they're apt to take on faith what you *meant* to do in a poem, not what you've done. But who else has their patience? Three or four friends read the trilogy as it came out, a few pages at a time. I don't see how I could have kept going without their often very detailed responses.

MCCLATCHY: Are these reactions ever of any practical help? Would they lead you to change a line?

MERRILL: That's the point! Ideally you'd think of everything yourself, but in practice. . . . There were two lines in "Ephraim" about a stream reflecting aspen. The word "aspen" ended one sentence, and "Boulders" began the next. Madison Morrison, out in Oklahoma, sent me this little note on that section: "Aspen. Boulders . . . Colorado Springs?" I'd never have seen that by myself. Nine times out of ten, of course, I use those misgivings to confirm what I've done. So-and-so thinks a passage is obscure? *Good*—it stays obscure: that'll teach him! No wonder that the most loyal reader gets lost along the way—feels disappointed by a turn you've taken, and simply gives up.

MCCLATCHY: Yet one of your strengths as a poet is so to disarm your reader, often by including his possible objections.

MERRILL: That might even be the placating gesture of a child who is inevitably going to disappoint his parents before he fulfills the expectations they haven't yet learned to have. I was always very good at seeming to accede to what my father or mother wanted of me—and then going ahead to do as I pleased.

MCCLATCHY: You say in "The Book of Ephraim" that you've read Proust for the last time. Is that true?

MERRILL: I thought so when I said it, but in fact—just before starting to write the party scene which ends the Epilogue—I took a quick look at *Le Temps retrouvé*.

MCCLATCHY: In a sense, Proust has been the greatest influence on your career, wouldn't you agree?

MERRILL: I would.

MCCLATCHY: Odd for a poet to have a novelist over his shoulder.

MERRILL: Why? I certainly didn't feel his influence when I was writing novels. My attention span when writing or "observing" is so much shorter than his, that it's only in a poem—in miniature as it were—that something of his flavor might be felt.

MCCLATCHY: Speaking of influences, one could mention Stevens, Auden, Bishop, a few others. What have you sought to learn from other poets, and how in general have you adapted their example to your practice?

MERRILL: Oh, I suppose I've learned things about writing, technical things, from each of them. Auden's penultimate rhyming, Elizabeth's way of contradicting something she's just said, Stevens' odd glamorizing of philosophical terms. Aside from all that, what I think I *really* wanted was some evidence that one didn't have to lead a "literary" life—belong to a ghetto of "creativity." That one could live as one pleased, and not be shamefaced in the glare of renown (if it ever came) at being an insurance man or a woman who'd moved to Brazil and played samba records instead of discussing X's latest volume. It was heartening that the *best* poets had this freedom. Auden did lead a life that looked literary from a distance, though actually I thought it was more a re-creation of school and university days: much instruction, much giggling, much untidiness. Perhaps because my own school years were unhappy for extracurricular reasons, I didn't feel completely at ease with all that. So much was routine—and often wildly entertaining of course. Once, a long lunchtime discussion with Chester Kallman about whether three nineteen- or twenty-year-old guests who were expected for dinner should be offered *real drinks* culminated that evening in Wystan's removing three tiny, tiny glasses from the big hearts-and-flowers cupboard and asking *me* to "make vodka and tonics for our young friends." (I gave them straight vodka, of course.) The point's not that Wystan was stingy—or if he was, who cares?—but that his conflicting principles (Don't Waste Good Liquor on the Young versus *Gas-*

trecht, or the Sacred Duty of a Host) arrived at a solution that would have made Da Ponte smile. Soon everyone was having a good time. One of the young Englishmen proposed—this was late in the sixties—that poems should appear in common, everyday places: on books of matches, beer cans, toilet paper. "I sense the need," said Chester rolling his eyes, "for applied criticism."

It was *du côté de chez* Elizabeth, though, that I saw the daily life that took my fancy even more, with its kind of random, Chekhovian surface, open to trivia and funny surprises, or even painful ones, today a fit of weeping, tomorrow a picnic. I could see how close that life was to her poems, how much the life and the poems gave to one another. I don't mean I've "achieved" anything of the sort in *my* life or poems, only that Elizabeth had more of a talent for life—and for poetry—than anyone else I've known, and this has served me as an ideal.

MCCLATCHY: When you read someone else's poem, what do you read *for*? What kind of pleasure do you take? What kind of hesitations do you have?

MERRILL: Well, I'm always open to what another poet might do with *the line*, or with a stanza. I don't know what particular turn of phrase I look for, but it's always very important, the phrasing of the lines. Elizabeth's elegy for Lowell struck me as such a masterpiece because you read the poem a couple of times and felt you knew it by heart. Every line fell in the most wonderful way, which is perhaps something she learned from Herbert. You find it *there*. I think you find it very often in French poetry.

MCCLATCHY: You're drawn, then, primarily to technical matters?

MERRILL: To the extent that the phrasing leads to the content. I don't really know how to separate those. The poems I most love are so perfectly phrased that they seem to say something extraordinary, whether they do or not.

MCCLATCHY: Increasingly, your work has exhibited a striking range in what would once have been called its poetic diction. Conversational stops and starts alternate with stanza-long sentences bristling with subordinate clauses. Scientific jargon lies down with slang. What guides these choices?

MERRILL: Taste, instinct, temperament . . . Too much poetry sounds like side after side of modern music, the same serial twitterings, the same barnyard grunts. Just as I love multiple meanings, I try for contrasts and disruptions of tone. Am I wrong—in the old days didn't the various meters imply different modes or situations, like madness, love, war? It's too late, in any event, to rely very much on meter—look at those gorgeous but imbecile antistrophes and semichoruses in Swinburne or Shelley or whoever. I'm talking from a reader's point of view, you understand. Poets will rediscover as many techniques as they need in order to help them write better. But for a reader who can hardly be trusted to hear the iambics when he opens *The Rape of the Lock*, if anything can fill the void left by these obsolete resources, I'd imagine it would have to be diction or "voice." Voice in its fullest tonal range—not just bel canto or passionate speech. From my own point of view, this range would be utterly unattainable without meter and rhyme and those forms we are talking about.

Of course, they breed echoes. There's always a lurking air of pastiche that, consciously or unconsciously, gets into your diction. That doesn't much bother me, does it you? No voice is as individual as the poet would like to think. In the long run I'd rather have what I write remind people of Pope or Yeats or Byron than of the other students in that year's workshop.

MCCLATCHY: The hallmark of your poetry is its *tone*, the way its concerns are observed and presented. And much of its effect depends on your fondness for paradox. Is that a cultivated habit of mind with you? A deliberate way into, and out of, the world and the poem?

MERRILL: It's hard to know. "Cultivated" certainly in the gardening sense of the word—which doesn't explain the mystery of the seed. I suppose that early on I began to understand the relativity, even the reversibility, of truths. At the same time as I was being given a good education I could feel, not so much from my parents, but from the world they moved in, that kind of easygoing contempt rich people have for art and scholarship—"these things are all right *in their place*, and their place is to ornament a life rather than to nourish or to shape it." Or when it came to sex, I had to face it that the worst iniquity my parents (and many of my friends) could imagine was for me a blessed source of pleasure and security—as well as suffering, to be sure. There was truth on both sides. And maybe having arrived at *that* explained my delight in setting down a phrase like, oh, "the pillow's dense white dark" or "Au fond each summit is a cul-de-sac," but the explanation as such neither delights nor convinces me. I believe the secret lies primarily in the nature of poetry—and of science too, for that matter—and that the ability to see both ways at once isn't merely an idiosyncrasy but corresponds to how the world needs to be seen: cheerful *and* awful, opaque *and* transparent. The plus and minus signs of a vast, evolving formula.

MCCLATCHY: I want to come back to a phrase you just used—"pleasure and security." Would those twinned feelings also account for your affectionate and bracing reliance on traditional forms?

MERRILL: Yes, why not? Now and then one enjoys a little moonwalk, some little departure from tradition. And the forms themselves seem to invite this, in our age of "breakthroughs." Take the villanelle, which didn't really change from "Your eyen two wol slay me sodenly" until, say, 1950. (Of course the Chaucer isn't quite a villanelle, but let's say it is to make my point.) With Empson's famous ones, rigor mortis had set in, for any purposes beyond those of *vers de société*. Still, there were tiny signs. People began repunctuating the key lines so that each time they recurred, the meaning would be slightly different. Was that just an extension of certain cute effects in Austin Dobson? In any case, "sodenly" Elizabeth's ravishing poem "One Art" came along, where the key lines seem merely to approximate themselves, and the form, awakened by a kiss, simply toddles off to a new stage in its life, under the proud eye of Mother, or the Muse. One doesn't, I mean, have to be just a stolid "formalist." The forms, the meters and rhyme-sounds, are far too liberating for that.

MCCLATCHY: Liberating?

MERRILL: From one's own smudged images and anxiety about "having something to say." *Into* the dynamics of—well, the craft itself.

MCCLATCHY: Few words can make contemporary poets cringe more than "great"—I mean, when applied to poems or poets. That's something that certainly doesn't hold for other arts, say, painting. Why do you suppose this is so? Is the whole category outdated?

MERRILL: I hope not. Just because "great" is now a talk-show word meaning competent or agreeable, it doesn't follow that we have to take this lying down. It's really the bombast, the sunless pedantry—waste products of ideas—that make us cringe. They form on a text like mildew. Straining for exaltation, coasting off into complacency. . . . Words keep going bankrupt and ringing false, and as you say, this wouldn't be true in painting. A "new" Revlon color doesn't invalidate a Matisse that used it fifty years earlier. Subjects date more quickly; you don't see many weeping Magdalens or meadows full of cows in the galleries nowadays, and I can't think of much celestial machinery in poetry between *The Rape of the Lock* and "Ephraim." But painters still go to museums, don't they? They've *seen* great paintings and even survived the shock. Now surely *some* of our hundred thousand living American poets have read the great poems of the Western world and kept their minds open to the possibilities.

MCCLATCHY: Is "heroism" or "high tone" the word I want to pinpoint what's been missing from American literature these past decades? Or do those terms mean anything to you?

MERRILL: Oh, heroism's possible, all right, and the high tone hasn't deserted some of us. Trouble is, our heroes more and more turn up as artists or invalids or both—the sort that won't be accepted as heroic except by fellow artists (or fellow sufferers). Sir Edmund Hillary will "do" of course, but I don't gasp at his achievement the way I do at Proust's. Must this leave the healthy, uncreative reader at a loss, not being sick or special enough to identify? Does he need to, after all? It's not as though only people in superb physical shape were thrilled by the conquest of Everest. And Proust is subtle enough to persuade us that the real feat has been one not of style but of memory, therefore within even the common man's power to duplicate. It's not the prevailing low tone so much as the imaginative laziness. We don't see life as an adventure. We know that our lives are in our hands; and far from freeing us, this knowledge has become a paralyzing weight.

MCCLATCHY: An adventure without obvious dragons and princesses, composed merely of the flat circumstances of a given life—that's not always apparent to the naked eye.

MERRILL: No. Yet your life, and that means people and places and history along with *la vie intérieure*, does keep growing and blossoming, and is always *there* as potential subject matter. But the blossom needs to be fertilized—you don't just versify your engagement book—and when that bee comes can't ever be predicted or willed.

MCCLATCHY: You'd disagree, then, with Auden, who said he was a poet *only* when actually writing a poem.

MERRILL: Lucky him. What was he the rest of the time?

MCCLATCHY: A citizen, I believe he said.

MERRILL: Oh. Well, that citizen must have heard a lot of funny sounds from the poet pigeonhole next door. I certainly do. Whether you're at your desk or not when a poem's underway, isn't there that constant eddy in your mind? If it's strong enough all sorts of random flotsam gets drawn into it, how selectively it's hopeless to decide at the time. I try to break off, get away from the page, into the kitchen for a spell of mixing and marinating, which gives the words a chance to sort themselves out behind my back. But there's really no escape, except perhaps the third drink. On "ordinary" days, days when you've nothing on the burner, it might be safe to say that you're not a poet at all: more like a doctor at a dinner party, just another guest until his hostess slumps to the floor or his little beeper goes off. Most

of those signals are false alarms—only they're not. Language *is* your medium. You can be talking or writing a letter, and out comes an observation, a "sentence-sound" you rather like. It needn't be your own. And
it's not going to make a poem, or even fit into one. But the *twinge* it gives
you—and it's this, I daresay, that distinguishes you from the "citizen"—
reminds you you've got to be careful, that you've a condition that needs
watching. . . .

MCCLATCHY: Sounds like that doctor's turning into a patient.

MERRILL: Doesn't it! How about lunch?

II.
WRITERS

Divine Poem

Many readers of these columns will have encountered, as I did, their first Dante in the "Prufrock" epigraph. We learned to smile at the juxtaposition of ineffectual daydreamer and damned soul speaking from the fire. "For this is hell, nor are we out of it," we innocently marveled, peering forth from our own gemlike flames at worktable and bookshelf, sunset and dozing cat. Purgatory and paradise awaited us too, in the guise of the next love affair. In a single elegant stroke Eliot had shown us one way to approach *l'altissimo poeta*: Dante's passionate faith and our intrepid doubts could be reconciled by triangulation with the text itself.

To believe, however, that Dante had in any real sense seen God threatened both the poem and us. Who wanted song to curdle overnight into mere scripture, or himself to be trivialized in the glare of too much truth? Yet we must—or so I begin to think, decades later—allow that something distinct from mere "inspiration" came to Dante. It had come to others; he is not after all our only mystic, just more literary and more fortunate than many. In an age that discouraged the heretic, his vision reached him through the highest, most unexceptional channels. Its cast included saints, philosophers, emperors, angels, monsters, Adam and Ulysses, Satan and God. To these he added a poet he revered, a woman he adored, plus a host of friends and enemies whose names we should otherwise never have heard; and garbed them in patterns of breathtakingly symmetrical lights-and-darks woven from a belief everybody shared. Even the pre-Christian souls in hell know pretty much what they are damned for not having known in time. No question ever of an arcane, Blakean anti-mythology. Dante's conceptual innovations—as when he lifts purgatory to the surface of the earth, or reveals his lady as an agent from highest heaven—refigure rather than refute the thought that preceded them. As for his verbal ones, he was in the historical position to consolidate, vir-

A review of Allen Mandelbaum's translation of Dante's *Inferno*, published by the University of California Press. A slightly different version of the review was published in *The New Republic*, vol. 183, no. 22 (November 29, 1980).

tually to invent, for purposes beyond those of the lyric, a living Italian idiom. No poet could ask for more; yet more was given him.

Revelation can take many forms. St. Paul was "caught up into paradise, and heard unspeakable words"—a one-shot trip. Milton, on the other hand, dreamed each night the next day's installment of his poem. Blake kept open house, through much of his life, for spirits with whom he conversed wide awake. Yeats, married to a medium, took down the voices that spoke through her. A lay visionary—where poetry is at issue, someone whose powers of language and allusion aren't up to the demands made upon them—reports a complex, joyous wonder compressed into a few poor human moments and verging dangerously upon the unutterable. Much as it may change his life, the experience defeats his telling of it. Dante imagined this to be his case; it was not.

For he was already a poet. He had completed his apprenticeship in lyrics of high perfection. As for allusion, he had read widely and seriously if, to us, eccentrically. Homer lay beyond his ken, but he knew Paulus Orosius and the *Voyage of St. Brendan*, and may well have come across this sentence from the Sufi Ibn Arabi (found by me heading the chapter on Beatrice in Irma Brandeis' *The Ladder of Vision*): "When she kills with her glances, her speech restores to life as though she, in giving life, were thereby Jesus."

The *Comedy*'s energy and splendor suggest that Dante indeed "saw the light" in a timeless moment. Its prophetic spleen and resonant particulars hint at something not quite the same, that like Milton or Yeats he had mediumistic powers—a sustaining divinatory intelligence which spoke to him, if only (as Julian Jaynes would have it) from that center of the brain's right hemisphere which corresponds to Weinecke's area on the left. This much granted, it would still remain to be amazed in the usual fashion when faced by a masterpiece: How on earth was it brought safely into being and onto the page?

Poets nowadays are praised for performing without a net. "These poems take risks!" gloat the blurbs. Akhmatova saddles Dante with a cold and implacable Muse. I wonder. One does not wince *for* him the way one does for Rimbaud. He is spared even the mortification of a system that dates. The electronic marvels of paradise—stars clustering into eagles, and all that—have according to Beatrice been devised to suit the seer: a laser show of supreme illusion projected through Dante's human senses and image banks. (Do hell and purgatory keep being modernized to extract the maximum pain and penance from the new arrival? I suppose they do.) Page after page the Powers overwhelm the pilgrim, while treating the poet—the textures of his verse affirm it—with kid gloves.

A reader whose experience of terza rima is limited to Shelley can but faintly imagine its force and variety in the hands of its inventor. At the humblest level it serves as a No Trespassing sign, protecting the text. A copyist's pious interpolation or unthinking lapse would at once set off the alarm. No verse form *moves* so wonderfully. Each tercet's first and third line rhyme with the middle one of the preceding set and enclose the new rhyme-sound of the next, the way a scull outstrips the twin, already dissolving oarstrokes that propel it. As rhymes interlock throughout a canto, so do incidents and images throughout the poem. Thus any given tercet reflects in microcosm the triple structures explored by the whole, and the progress of the verse, which allows for closure only when (and because) a canto ends, becomes a version "without tears" of the pilgrim's own. Rendering here some lightning insight or action, there some laborious downward or upward clambering, the terza rima can as well sweeten the pill of dogmatic longueurs ("This keeps moving, it will therefore end") and frame with aching fleetness those glimpses of earth denied now to the damned and the blest alike.

We feel everywhere Dante's great concision. He has so *much* to tell. Self-limited to these bare hundred cantos averaging a scant 140 lines apiece, he can't afford to pad—he is likelier to break off, pleading no more room—let alone spell out connections for a torpid reader. This *we* must do, helped by centuries of commentary. And what a shock it is, opening the *Comedy*, to leave today's plush avant-garde screening room with its risk-laden images and scrambled sound track and use our muscles to actually get somewhere. For Dante's other great virtue is his matter-of-factness. Zodiacal signposts, "humble" similes, glosses from philosophy and myth—there is nothing he won't use to locate and focus his action as sharply as possible.

A random example. Sun is climbing toward noon above the Ganges as we enter a smoke "dark as night" on the slopes of purgatory; meanwhile, these moles that come and go in a passing phrase are kin, surely, to Miss Moore's real toads:

> Ricorditi, lettor, se mai ne l'alpe
> ti colse nebbia per la qual vedesti
> non altrimenti che per pelle talpe. . . .

Singleton renders this: "Recall, reader, if ever in the mountains a mist has caught you, through which you could not see except as moles do through skin. . . ." Helpful; but was the mole in Dante's day thought to see through its *skin*? A note explains what is made clear enough in Longfellow's version, where alliteration, moreover, brings a certain music to *"pelle talpe,"* that tiny consonantal lozenge we have paused, I trust, to savor:

> Remember, Reader, if e'er in the Alps
> A mist o'ertook thee, through which thou couldst see
> Not otherwise than through its membrane mole. . . .

It is the merest instance of that matter-of-fact concision I have in mind, and makes a small plea for translation into verse such as this which deftly evokes, as prose or indeed rhymed versions so rarely can, the diction and emphasis of the original. (Why, oh, why is the Longfellow *Comedy* not in print? Comparing it with the latest prose version, by Charles Singleton, and allowing for pains rightly taken by the latter to *sound* like prose, one is struck by how often he has had apparently no choice but to hit on that good gray poet's very phrase. There is also Longfellow's delectable nineteenth-century apparatus, including essays by Ruskin and Lamartine—"Dante a fait la gazette florentine de la postérité"; Boccaccio's account of the dead Dante guiding his son to the missing final cantos of the *Paradiso*; and James Russell Lowell on the poet's monument in Ravenna: "It is a little shrine covered with a dome, not unlike the tomb of a Mohammedan saint. . . . The *valet de place* says that Dante is not buried under it, but beneath the pavement of the street in front of it, where also, he says, he saw my Lord Byron kneel and weep.")

Those moles, to resume, are just one filament in a web whose circumference is everywhere. They presently mesh with an apostrophe to the imagination, which also sees without using its eyes. A case made in passing for divine inspiration ("A light moves you which takes form in heaven, of itself. . . .") gives way to three trancelike visions—Procne, Haman, Amata—appropriate to this level of the mountain Dante climbs. The center of the web is still far off, almost half the poem away, but we may as well glance at it now.

The passage in question, long a commentators' favorite, has lately begun to engage the scientists as well. Mark A. Peterson proposes (*American Journal of Physics*, Dec. 1979) that Dante's universe "is not as simple geometrically as it at first appears, but actually seems to be a so-called 'closed' universe, the 3-sphere, a universe which also emerges as a cosmological solution of Einstein's equations in general relativity theory." Let who can, experience for themselves the full complexity and symmetry of the resulting figure. Roughly, two spheres are joined *at every point* through their "equator," itself a third sphere of sheer connectivity, and the whole suspended within a fourth dimension. The figure has finite volume but no boundary: "every point is interior."

On the threshold of the Empyrean, Dante is given his first glimpse of God, an infinitesimally small, intensely brilliant point reflected, before he turns to gaze at it directly, in Beatrice's eyes. Around it spin concentric rings or haloes gaining in brightness and speed in proportion to their closeness to it. These represent the angelic orders, from inmost seraphim to furthest messengers, and compose one of the two interconnected "semi-universes" of Peterson's figure. The other, also composed of nine rings, has at its center the little "threshing-floor" of earth far down at which Dante has just been peering, and extends through the geocentric levels to his present vantage in the Primum Mobile. What he is looking at *now*, explains Beatrice, is the "point" on which "the heavens and all nature are dependent." All nature: the mole and the mountain, the sinner and the sun.

That her words paraphrase Aquinas in a commentary on Aristotle cannot account for the hallucinatory wonder of this little point. We may picture it partly as a model of electrons whirling round the atomic nucleus—in our day, the point on which all nature and its destruction depend; partly as an abstracted solar system—only with the relative planetary speeds reversed, since these Intelligences turn physics inside out. According to Peterson, however, this is exactly what they do *not* do. For the fourth dimension here is speed of rotation, or in Dante's view the dimension of divine precedence. The inmost ring moves fastest, as does the Primum Mobile outermost among the other set, because both are nearest to God. The two universes, heavenly and natural, are alike governed by that tiny point. The vision as reported sets the mind reeling. What must it have been to experience?

Here too we understand, not for the first time, how Dante is helped by Beatrice. Seeing this light through her eyes will enable him to put it into words, to translate into his poem's measures those that depend upon this timeless and dimensionless point, to receive what he may of the mystery and not be struck mad or dumb by it. A further, more profound glimpse will indeed be largely wiped from his mind by the uncanny image of the Argo's shadow passing over amazed Neptune.

RECITATIVE

Concise and exact, Dante is naturally partial to points. We have come across others before this one: the "point" in the tale at which Paolo and Francesca read no further; the high "point" of the sun's meridian over Jerusalem; the "point" where all times are present, into which Cacciaguida gazes to read Dante's future. A children's book comes to mind—"Adventures of a Hole" or whatever—where the small round "hero" piercing the volume from front to back serves as focus to the picture on every page. It would be in some such fashion that each episode or passing image in Dante connects with absolute Good—or Evil. For there is finally the very terrible point in the last canto of the *Inferno*. At the moral and physical universes' nether pole, it is the other center required by Peterson's scheme.

Here also are angelic spheres, those of the fallen angels. Satan, who as Lucifer belonged to that halo nearest the point of light, now towers waist-deep in ice, "constrained by all the weights of the universe," and at first glance oddly unthreatening. Nine rings narrow downward to this figure of raging entropy. From one to the next we have felt the movement decelerating. Wind-driven souls (Francesca) give way to runners (Brunetto), to the painfully walking hypocrites cloaked in gilded lead, to the frozen, impacted souls of Cocytus. This is "natural" movement; unlike those angels of the Empyrean, it obeys the second law of thermodynamics. W. D. Snodgrass has traced (*In Radical Pursuit*) the pilgrim Dante's regression, as he faces the murderers of parents and children, through the traumatic phases of early childhood, infancy, and birth. Last comes this nadir, this "point" he must pass in order to be reborn. It lies at the exact center of earth, of gravity, of the entire Ptolemaic universe. As the pilgrims skirt it, everything abruptly turns upside down, psychological time once again flows forward, and their ascent begins toward the starlight of earth's further side.

To my knowledge no one appears to have defined this point much beyond the account of it above. "Here all is dark and mysterious," says Singleton. Dante himself, as he clambers down between the deep floor of ice and Satan's shaggy thigh—there "where the thigh curves out to form the haunches"—averts his eyes and language: "Let gross minds conceive my trouble, who cannot see the point I had passed." He means, as we know, earth's center, but he would hardly be Dante to leave it at that. Hell, reads the inscription on its gate, was made by "the divine Power, the supreme Wisdom, and the primal Love"—the trinity in action. In Satan's figure, to which we've been led by a parodied Latin hymn, we see these reversed.

Power becomes impotence; wisdom, a matter of mechanical gnawing and flapping; love, a congealing wind. As counterpoise to that radiant, all-engendering point in heaven, we may expect something more graphically awful than a fictive locus. "The sacred number *three* is symbolic of the whole male genitalia," writes Freud in the *Introductory Lectures*; it is the source of endless jokes in Greece today. Satan, as an angel, would lack genitals—a touch appropriate to the nullity Dante wishes to convey. For surely this point in hell is where they would have been and are not: a frozen, ungenerative, nonexistent trinity. And it is hardly from squeamishness or to spare his reader that Dante contrives to "miss the point" in hell. He has come a long way since Virgil's own hands prevented a stolen glance at the Medusa. His wiser reticence here implies a risk to the spirit, which might have vanished at a closer look, as into a black hole.

The point—my point and everyone's by now, not these of Dante—is that the *Comedy* throughout sustains the equilibrium we have been told to look for in a haiku by Basho. There is no rift, as in conventional allegory, between action and interpretation, physical and moral, "low" and "high." All is of a piece. It is a mystic's view of the world, if you like. It is also a scientist's. And to have it tally with Einstein? For the year 1300, that's seeing the light in spades.

What diction, then, is even faintly suited to divine grace when it illuminates all things great and small? The answer must lie in the entire range, from the courtly metaphysics of the love poems, on which Dante would draw for his highest flights in paradise, to the broad innuendo of those sonnets to Forese. These also served him, as a farting devil in the Malebolge reminds us. Like the Jongleur de Notre-Dame in the pureness of his heart doing *what he can*, Dante will run through his whole bag of tricks, and the performance will be rewarded by an extraordinary universal Smile.

This wealth of diction and detail gave the *Comedy* its long reputation for a grotesque farrago flawed by "the bad taste of the century." The mature Milton asked *his* Muse to help him soar "with no middle flight"—a costly decision. Whatever its glories, the diction of *Paradise Lost* labors under its moral regalia, its relentless pre-Augustan triumphs over precisely this eclectic middle style which allows Dante his touching, first-person particularity, moles and all. It also suggests why he is continually being rediscovered by poets—now by Hugo, now by Pound—and why translations, especially into verse, keep appearing.

93

RECITATIVE

Having been asked to write a "general piece" leaves me, I fear, with little space for its occasion—the publication of the *Inferno*, Volume I of *The California Dante*: three volumes of text and three of commentary under the editorship of its translator, Allen Mandelbaum.

It is first of all a noble work of typography. The face was designed by the great modern printer Mardersteig and named for our poet. The text is set in spacious 42-line pages with, properly for once, the original on the host's, or reader's, right. Touches of red hint that no expense was spared. The book's co-designer, with Czeslaw Jan Grycz, is also its illustrator, Barry Moser. For my taste, used to the groupings and vistas of Blake or Doré, his drawings are too often close-ups; perhaps we may expect a wider lens upon leaving this hell of unleavened selfhood. They are in any case at best fearfully expressive, always beautifully reproduced, and placed so as not to intrude upon a reader who would rather picture things for himself.

The translation, into iambic pentameter with a rich orchestration that includes sporadic rhyme, is lucid and strong. Everyone knows the poem's opening lines in Italian; here they are as done by Mr. Mandelbaum:

> When I had journeyed half of our life's way,
> I found myself within a shadowed forest,
> for I had lost the path that does not stray.
> Ah, it is hard to speak of what it was,
> that savage forest, dense and difficult,
> which even in recall renews my fear:
> so bitter—death is hardly more severe.

I should probably have tried—tried and failed, rhymed couplets being a weakness of my own—to avoid them in rendering terza rima. The great success of this passage is, however, its third line. Here at the outset making for luck his ritual gesture toward the original form, Mandelbaum solves *"la diretta via"* in a free, brilliant, utterly Dantesque stroke. Countless more turn up in even a cursory reading—Francesca's "Love that releases no beloved from loving," for instance. "Love that exempts no one beloved from loving," Longfellow has it; but the verb unwizened in our time by the tax collector is surely to be preferred. Mandelbaum is especially good whenever Dante imitates the pains and anxieties that beset him as a pilgrim:

> Of course I wept, leaning against a rock
> along that rugged ridge. . . .

Some impudent alliteration by Auden comes to mind ("Round the ram-
pant rugged rocks / Rude and ragged rascals run"). Here, though, the device enacts rather than mocks the poet's plight, like a fist struck despon-
dently into a palm as the memory overwhelms him. English, obviously,
permits immense variety of diction—whereas a single good French translation of the *Comedy* might suffice for centuries—and Mandelbaum takes
full advantage of this. Now and then he gives me pause: at his antiquated
"reboantic fracas" or his hostessy "Do tell me" addressed to some poor
souls neck-deep in ice. But such pauses are lost in the overall sweep and
felicity. A faint note of self-congratulation in Mandelbaum's elegant, up-
to-date introduction is more than justified by what follows. This version
will not displace Longfellow's, or Binyon's, or Sinclair's; nor do I imagine
it was designed to. Rather it joins a very small company of renderings that
stand both on their own as English poetry and to the *Comedy* as disciples
round a master grown, thanks to their attention, ever more complex and
less obscure.

Unreal Citizen

Mr. Liddell's is the first life in English of the Greek poet Cavafy. A sensitive and informed chronicler, he also quotes generously from Greek sources, Cavafy's diaries and scholia, as well as recollections of people close to him. His treatment of Cavafy's social and sexual life is entirely plausible. Mr. Liddell knows Egypt, too, and guides his reader blindfolded through the Alexandrian genealogical maze, as through the smart or infamous quarters of the city.

Born there (in 1863) into a world of forms and frivolities, Cavafy was to be anchored firmly beyond its shallows, less by impoverishment—for in "le grand cérémonial du tralala" a good family like his would still have a part to play—than by his vocation and his sexuality. He was seven when his father died. There followed years of displacement from one Unreal City to another. His closest ties were to his mother Haricleia, "one of the most beautiful women in Alexandria" and one of the most idle—"her son affectionately addressed her (in English) as 'Fat One'"; and to his two immediately older brothers, the dependable John who worshiped him, who even translated him, and the unhappy Paul who drank and ran up debts. The latter and Cavafy, both over forty, still shared a flat and "a 'phaeton' in which they drove about. Mention is made of their rings and their ties; one is afraid they may have been rather 'flashy,' trying to prolong youth into middle age." Paul finally went to the Riviera and made ends meet as a kind of Jamesian companion-guide. "To the last he sighed for the great days in Alexandria. . . . Constantine never mentioned him to his younger literary friends."

The prevailing idea of culture cannot have gone much beyond salon music, *vers de société*, and lip service to the illustrious dead. Half Cavafy's life was over before he met, in Athens, any real authors. One of them noted

A review of *Cavafy, a Critical Biography* by Robert Liddell and *C. P. Cavafy: Collected Poems*, translated by Edmund Keeley and Philip Sherrard. Published under the title "Marvelous Poet" in *The New York Review of Books*, vol. 22, no. 12 (July 17, 1975).

his smart clothes, "slight English accent" in Greek, and how "all his ceremonies and politenesses strike an Athenian used to . . . the shy naïveté and
simple awkwardness of our men of letters."

The difficulty of being Cavafy's kind of homosexual in Alexandria in those
years must have been staggering: how to choose among a thousand daily
opportunities. Cavafy by and large stuck to Greeks, young men of the
working class. "We do not know whether his emotions were in any way involved," writes Mr. Liddell, meaning by emotions "genuine affection"
rather than the mere desire, compassion, and regret that fill the poems.
But he makes the essential observation that

> out of the mess and squalor that occupied part of his life he has created
> a unique order and beauty. Homosexuality was no doubt a disadvan-
> tage to Paul Cavafy, who was *mondain*, and at one time hoped to make
> a marriage of convenience; but it made Constantine what he was.

As Constantine knew very well:

> My younger days, my sensual life—
> how clearly I see their meaning now.
> What needless, futile regret. . . .
> In the loose living of my early years
> the impulses of my poetry were shaped.
> the boundaries of my art were plotted

At thirty Cavafy settled down in Alexandria's Ministry of Public Works,
as a clerk in the Dantesque "Third Circle of Irrigation." Here he stayed
(he was also a broker on the Egyptian stock exchange) until his retirement
thirty years later. He would not hit his stride as a poet, in fact, until after
the office routine had provided the foil his ever livelier imagination
needed. His successor, then a young employee, recalls:

> On very rare occasions he locked himself into his room. [Cavafy was
> by then a "subdirector."] Sometimes my colleague and I looked
> through the keyhole. We saw him lift up his hands like an actor, and
> put on a strange expression as if in ecstasy, then he would bend down
> to write something. It was the moment of inspiration. Naturally we
> found it funny and we giggled. How were we to imagine that one day
> Mr. Cavafy would be famous!

RECITATIVE

After the Fat One's death and Paul's removal to Europe, Cavafy spent his last twenty-five years alone in a flat on rue Lepsius—"rue Clapsius" as it was known to some, a neighborhood of brothels and shops gradually overtaking some nice old houses. Indoors one found a high concentration of the usual period junk, inlaid tables, carpets, mirrors, shabby divans, fringes of society, photographs, a servant bringing drinks and appetizers cheap or not, depending on who was there; the lighting constantly adjusted—an extra candle lit "if a beautiful face appeared in the room." The company seems to have been predominantly younger men of letters; but one may bear in mind that the guest from a higher or lower world seldom troubles to write memoirs.

Cavafy is that rare poet whose essential quality comes through even in translation. One sees why Auden thought so. By limiting his subject to human deeds and desires, and his mode to statement, Cavafy makes the rest of us seem to be reading ourselves laboriously backward in a cipher of likenesses and generalizations. He writes without metaphor. Of the natural world we see nothing. The Nile?—an agreeable site for a villa. Flowers?—appropriate to grave or banquet table. Not for Cavafy to presume upon his kinship with sunset and octopus. Having once and for all given the lie to the nonhuman picturesque in eight appalling lines ("Morning Sea"), he is free to travel light and fast and far. His reader looks through brilliantly focused vignettes to the tonic ironies beyond.

What ironies? Well, take "The Mirror in the Front Hall." The handsome delivery boy gets that far and no further into the house, whose rich privacies would in any case be lost on him. Nor is Cavafy about to pretend interest in anything so conventional, so conjectural, as one more young man's inner life. Is there to be no "understanding," then, beyond that which brings him and his boys together in some anonymous room with its bed and its ceiling fixture? Ignorance is bliss, he might answer—or would he? For it is not ignorance so much as a willed narrowing of frame; and it is not bliss but something drier and longer-lasting, which radiates its own accumulated knowledge. Always, in Cavafy, what one poem withholds, another explains. This coldness of his comes through elsewhere as reticence imposed by an encounter with a god,

> his hair black and perfumed—
> the people going by would gaze at him.
> and one would ask the other if he knew him.

98

if he was a Greek from Syria, or a stranger.
But some who looked more carefully
would understand and step aside. . . .

Indeed, one way to sidestep any real perception of others is to make gods of them. But the ironic wind blows back and forth. The gods appeared to characters in Homer disguised as a mortal friend or stranger. Put in terms acceptable nowadays, that was a stylized handling of those moments familiar to us all when the stranger's idle word or the friend's sudden presence happens to strike deeply into our spirits. Moments at the opposite pole from indifference: though on that single pole Cavafy's world revolves.

The unity of divine and human, or past and present, is as real to him as their disparity. Between the poor, unlettered, present-day young men and the well-to-do, educated ones in his historical poems ("Myris . . . reciting verses / with his perfect feeling for Greek rhythm"), there is an unbroken bond of type and disposition: what Gongora called "centuries of beauty in a few years of age." This bond is at the marrow of Cavafy's feeling. It reflects his situation as a Greek, the dynamics of his language—indeed the whole legacy of Hellenism—and incidentally distinguishes him from, say, that German baron who spent his adult life in Taormina photographing urchins draped in sheets and wreathed in artificial roses.

The first verb to learn in Ancient Greek was παιδεύω. Pronounced pie-dew-o, it meant "I teach." In Modern Greek the same verb, spelled as before, is pronounced pe-dhe-vo, and means "I torment." The old word ἀγαθός (good) has come to mean "simpleminded." These shifts are revealing, and their slightness reassures. I have heard my host in a remote farmhouse tell Aesop's fables as if he had made them up; that they had made *him* up was closer to the truth. I have heard a mother advise her child to tell its bad dream to the lighted bulb hanging from a kitchen ceiling, and for the same reason that Clytemnestra, in one of the old plays, tells hers to the sun. For while the ancient glory may have grown dim and prosaic, many forms of it are still intact. (One feels it less in Italy than in Greece where, thanks first to Byzantium and then to the Turks, the famous Rebirth of Learning had no opportunity to sweep away just this kind of dusty, half-understood wisdom.)

So, in Cavafy, the Greek—or Hellenized—character shines forth: scheming, deluded, gifted, noble, weak. The language survives the reversals of faith and empire, and sharpens the dull wits of the barbarian.

RECITATIVE

The glory dwindles and persists. The overtly historical poems illustrate this great theme in a manner which certain Plutarchian moments in Shakespeare—Casca's deadpan account of a crown refused—read like early attempts to get right. Cavafy himself draws on Plutarch, Herodotus, Gibbon, and a host of "Byzantine historians" whom he praised for writing "a kind of history that had never been written before. They wrote history dramatically." So did he.

Unexpected strands interconnect these historical pieces. A Syrian "Craftsman of Wine Bowls," at work fifteen years after Antiochus in 190 B.C. is overheard while decorating a silver bowl with the remembered figure of a friend killed in that battle. "The Battle of Magnesia" itself reminds Philip of Macedonia of his own defeat by the Romans; with scant pity to waste on Antiochus, he calls for roses, music, lights. We see elsewhere ("To Antiochos Epiphanis") a grandson of the defeated king greeting with prudent silence, thirty years later, his favorite's plea for the liberation of Macedonia—*that* would be worth, to the boy, "the coral Pan . . . the gardens of Tyre / and everything else you've given me." (The issue is still alive in our time.) This very favorite, or another, becomes the ostensible subject of some erotic verses by "Temethos, Antiochian, A.D. 400"—a flashback from far in the future, the date referring us to poems about the last stages of Hellenism in the Middle East.

In one of these ("Theatre of Sidon") the speaker confesses: "I sometimes write highly audacious verses in Greek / and these I circulate—surreptitiously," much as Cavafy did his own, neither wanting to offend the prevailing Christian morality. Back to Antiochus the Great's lineage, a second grandson ("Of Dimitrios Sotir, 162–50 B.C.) next occupies the Syrian throne with Roman recognition. This idealistic young king was raised as a hostage in Rome. At last where he belongs, he cannot recognize the Syria of his dreams in exile. It has become "the land of Valas and Herakleidis." Valas is the adventurer who, bribed by a Ptolemy whom Dimitrios Sotir once tried to help ("The Displeasure of Selefkidis"), is presently to overcome Dimitrios. In "The Favor of Alexander Valas," its fatuous object will be found exulting, briefly we may assume, "Antioch is all mine." And the Satrap Herakleidis is none other than he who, years earlier as Antiochus Epiphanis' treasurer, commissions a wine bowl from the melancholy but uncomplaining silversmith.

Thus, fixed to earth at these several points (I have omitted a few), the tent of an entire lost world can be felt to swell and ripple in the air above them. It is not Cavafy's concern to occupy—by spelling out every connection, or cramming with detail—this historical, no, this emotional space. He does something more skillful yet by suggesting it, by manipulating it.

As a reader of Cavafy, Mr. Liddell—while providing helpful glosses and fine insights (he introduces "The God Abandons Antony" as a poem which "seems to take farewell of symbolism")—prefers to let the work speak for itself. But not always. I can't help wishing that he had been able, in a single sweeping period, to express his disagreement with the novelist and critic Stratis Tsirkas—whose continuing studies of Cavafy can at present be appraised only by readers of Greek—instead of paraphrasing his interpretations, nine times out of ten for the sole purpose of disputing them. Thus Tsirkas' reading of the short poem "Thermopylae" (1901) comes off as preposterously topical. Leonidas and the traitor Ephialtes are thinly overlaid upon figures in Alexandria's Greek community in the 1880s—the Persians are the British, etc. Liddell's "ethical" reading raises problems he is the first to admit.

Neither interpretation is particularly absorbing; nor for that matter is the poem itself, except where one feels it come to life through the suggestive interplay of its three proper nouns. Ephialtes (one of those names like Quisling?) happens to mean "nightmare." "Οἱ Μῆδοι"—the Medes—can be heard as a dream-pun allusion to words like μή (not, don't), μηδέν (zero), μηδενιστής (nihilist), etc. At this level "Thermopylae" has little to do with either history or ethics, but implies that a subconscious horror is forever about to betray the self's "warm gates" to a host of negative powers, and that to be truthful or "generous in small ways" is honorable but vain in the face of the recurrent onslaught. Here is Cavafy (under "Table Talk" in Liddell's appendix): "We must study our language since we don't know it. What hidden treasures it contains, what treasures! Our thought ought to be how we are to enrich it, how to bring to light what it has hidden in it."

Liddell and Tsirkas go on to read "the next poem in the canon," "Che Fece . . . il Gran Rifiuto" (1899), according to their lights. The latter has it alluding to the career of an Alexandrian Patriarch fifteen years earlier (Dante's phrase, used as title, refers to Pope Celestine V). The former calls it "a generalized reflection with no bearing on any refusal that we know of in Cavafy's own life . . . an unsuccessful work." Uncharacteristic perhaps, in its bald lack of particulars:

> For some people the day comes
> when they have to declare the great Yes
> or the great No. It's clear at once who has the Yes
> ready within him; and saying it,
>
> he goes from honor to honor, strong in his conviction.
> He who refuses does not repent. Asked again,
> he'd still say no. Yet that no—the right no—
> drags him down all his life.

But surely we know—and know now more vividly than before, thanks to Mr. Liddell—of many refusals in Cavafy's life: the refusal to be a husband and father, an enterprising merchant, a popular poet, or to frequent exclusively the world of "the Salvago balls." This little poem remains a schoolboy exercise unless it is taken personally. (Also, it is an early poem. The quarrel with Tsirkas dies down when Liddell comes to the mature work, whose possible meanings no longer roam freely outside the poem, but are controlled, as it were, from within.)

In fact, as Marguerite Yourcenar says, all the historical poems are intimate, just as all the intimate poems are historical—hence, in the latter, the dwelling upon dates and the exact number of years gone by. We do not know whom any given love poem is for; there is no Agostinelli in Cavafy's life. Nor will most readers know the fuller context of the historical pieces. But we know what happens in history, to ideas and nations. And we know what happens when a loved one is struck down in youth, or disfigured by age, or leaves us for somebody else, or for Australia. To Cavafy's moments of truth are appended consequences so implicit in the nature of things as hardly having to be uttered. One of his notes on Ruskin hints at the turn of mind that made for such far-reaching yet discreet authority:

> When we say "Time" we mean ourselves. Most abstractions are simply our pseudonyms. It is superfluous to say "Time is scytheless and toothless." We know it. We are time.

A reader without Greek will finally, or first of all, respond to the earmark of nearly every Cavafy poem. Like all experienced raconteurs he knows how to repeat himself. Key words—often whole lines—get said over, re-iteration serving, since no detail's value can be assured until it "comes to rest in this poetry," to woo it back, fix it more lastingly in the mind. The overall brevity and compression lend relief to these touches, by turns poignant, wry, haunted. Cavafy's economies are lavish. The old gentleman living on a shoestring still tips well for the good services of the telling phrase.

Messrs. Keeley and Sherrard print the Greek *en face* (warning: but not in the paperback edition) and have given it a thoroughly serviceable English version, the best we are likely to see for some time. A few examples may indicate their success and limitations.

CHANDELIER

In a room—empty, small, four walls only,
covered with green cloth—
a beautiful chandelier burns, all fire;
and each of its flames kindles
a sensual fever, a lascivious urge.

In the small room, radiantly lit
by the chandelier's hot fire,
no ordinary light breaks out.
Not for timid bodies
the lust of this heat.

The original (1895) is in two rhymed stanzas. (Notes at the back supply Cavafy's metrical and rhyme schemes whenever relevant. This is most helpful, as far as it goes, though the reader faced with "*ababcdbbef aghbi-bibjb agklmbbc*" might feel that he is studying nothing so much as the transliteration of an Arabic curse.) "Chandelier," however, is a symbolist poem. In a space scaled to the small room, it presents its glowing image—presents it twice, on the replay spelling out more clearly the erotic message. One cannot greatly mourn the loss of some rather ordinary music. In fact, the translators, by reducing 133 syllables in Greek to 78 in English, actually enhance the poem's dramatic brevity. Many unrhymed, loosely metered poems are equally well served by this approach.

But the mature Cavafy writes a subtle, flexible Greek whose elements—classic, purist, regional, demotic—come together, as Kimon Friar observes, in "an artifice suited to and made integral by his temperament." A comparison to the shifts of manner in a Pound canto would be to the point if, in Cavafy, the unity of temperament weren't everything. Still, this English often reads more dryly and simply than it needs to. The crucial literary note in "Comes to Rest" (1918)—an erotic memory "the vision of which / has crossed twenty-six years and now / comes to rest within this poetry"—is soft-pedaled. The phrase "ἐπύρωνε θεῖος Ἰούλιος μῆνας" requires something on the order of "the fires of divine July were lit" or "divine July had brought us to white heat." Instead we are given "it was a beautiful hot July." This turns Cavafy into a nicer guy, but misses the point he is making about artifice. No great harm done. Cavafy himself prevents any misunderstanding in a poem written later that year, "Melancholy of Jason Kleander, Poet in Kommagini, A.D. 595":

> The aging of my body and my beauty
> is a wound from a merciless knife.
> I'm not resigned to it at all. . . .
>
> Bring your drugs. Art of Poetry—
> they do relieve the pain at least for a while.

(I should have thought the third line meant: "I do not bear up under it at all." Mavrogordato's version sounds almost chipper: "I have no long-suffering of any sort.")

In other poems, the formal effects, unlike those of "Chandelier," are indispensable to meaning. The famous "Walls," for instance, with its homophonic rhymes. "They," other people, unnoticed by him, have immured the poet—so *he* says. Yet these rhymes, stifling, narcissistic, arrogantly accomplished, tell the inside story—the walls are of his own making—without which the poem is an exercise in self-pity. An effect unrenderable in English? Cavafy's brother John (see a group of his English versions introduced by Keeley, *St. Andrews Review*, Fall–Winter 1974) does nobly by the homophonic rhymes in "For the Shop," but at the cost of clarity and pace.

Formality in the later work appears, so to speak, informally. When it does, it is usually of one fabric with the meaning. Here is the Keeley-Sherrard "Days of 1909, '10, and '11":

> He was the son of a misused, poverty-stricken sailor
> (from an island in the Aegean Sea).
> He worked for an ironmonger: his clothes shabby,

his workshoes miserably torn,
his hands filthy with rust and oil.

In the evenings, after the shop closed,
if there was something he longed for especially,
a more or less expensive tie,
a tie for Sunday,
or if he saw and coveted
a beautiful blue shirt in some store window,
he'd sell his body for a half-crown or two.

I ask myself if the great Alexandria
of ancient times could boast of a boy
more exquisite, more perfect—thoroughly ne-
    glected though he was:
that is, we don't have a statue or painting of him;
thrust into that poor ironmonger's shop,
overworked, harassed, given to cheap debauchery,
he was soon used up.

By consulting the notes ("Loosely rhymed *abcde ffffcfc gfhdhdf*") we notice rum doings in the second stanza. The effect is in fact magical. One
foot, then two, are subtracted from the opening's basic seven-foot line.
Suddenly, where no rhymes had been come four consecutive ones, each an
end-stopped *ee*. (This is now the most common sound in Greek, repre-
sentable on the page by no fewer than six vowels and diphthongs each of
which had its own value in classical times.) Line five moves past another
stressed *ee* (the word "saw") to the poem's most passionate verb (λαχτα-
ρούσε, "coveted"), which two lines later will rhyme with "sell." The seven-
foot line, as central to Greek prosody as the pentameter to ours, returns,
closing this stanza and governing the next. The barrel-organ interlude is
over, though two further *ee* rhymes echo it in the final stanza. The Greek
attains the ease and freshness of a jingle learned in childhood:

> Τὸ βραδυνό, σὰν ἔκλειε τὸ μαγαζί,
> ἂν ἦταν τίποτε νὰ ἐπιθυμεῖ πολύ,
> καμιὰ κραβάτα κάπως ἀκριβή,
> καμιὰ κραβάτα γιὰ τὴν Κυριακή. . . .

Cavafy's aim here can only have been to imitate, through that poorest,
commonest of rhyme sounds, the quality of pleasure available to the young
man with his pitiful needs and by-the-numbers behavior. To meet the

same rhyme further on, as Cavafy's "own" voice is winding up the story, sheds light both on his lasting compassion, at its best without pity, and on the means whereby he remade it into poetry.

Of course a rhymed English version is possible:

> But when the shop closed down at night,
> if there was something he'd delight
> in having, a necktie somewhat dear,
> tie that on Sundays he might wear,
> or in some showcase saw and loved on sight
> a lovely shirt of deepest blue,
> he'd sell his body for a dollar or two.

Or:

> As dusk fell, and the shop closed, had there been
> something he longed for, something seen—
> a Sunday tie, a tie beyond his means,
> or shirt of beautiful dark blue
> coveted in this or that vitrine—
> he'd go and sell his body for a dollar or two.

These, alas, are barely adequate (the first is Kimon Friar's, the second my own). "This or that vitrine" smacks of fussiness; "delight" and "loved on sight," of gush. Mainly one misses Cavafy's polysyllabic rhyme words, and their expert division among different parts of speech, which keep the passage from sounding like baby talk.

The last poem in the "Days" series, "Days of 1908," begins with twenty-four lines of which nineteen end with assorted masculine rhymes. This time the protagonist is "reasonably educated," feels entitled to better employment than he has yet found. So he gambles, wins, loses, borrows— dressed always in the same wretched "cinnamon-brown suit." The poem ends with an idealized view of him at the beach on summer mornings. The final seven lines, where the boy sheds, along with his clothes, his circumstances and responsibilities, are unrhymed, with fluid, feminine endings. We breathe something of the unconstricted freshness here evoked.

If nothing else, the feminine and masculine endings could have been managed in English without great trouble. A nagging voice in me wants to say that these sound effects—like the more complex ones in "Days of 1909, '10, and '11"—are such a poem's secret power, and that a translation which fails to suggest them is hardly worth making. Having said so, I retract the statement at once. It is too grumpy and too unfair to Messrs. Keeley and Sherrard who, whether or not they have the skill, certainly do not have the time, the lifetime they would need to achieve the—in any case—impossible. On their own terms they have done admirably. Readers who once preferred to existing English versions Marguerite Yourcenar's elegant French prose ones must now admit that these have been surpassed, with respect at least to accuracy and completeness.

Single-handed in our century, Cavafy showed the Greek poets who followed him what could be done with their language. In that quarter, he has had the greatest conceivable influence. Yet these later men, with their often superior lyric or epic gifts, their reverence for Earth, their virtuoso talent for metaphor, next to him strike me as loud and provincial (Kazantzakis) or curiously featureless (Seferis and Elytis), through overlong immersion in the new international waters of Eliot, Perse, the surrealists. They have, of course, claimed huge territories for Greek letters; but how gladly, having surveyed those shifting contours, one reenters the relative security of Cavafy's shabby flat with its view of the street and of the ages. I should add that my reading in (and of) Greek is insufficient to justify this kind of pronouncement.

A few years ago, as the Brindisi-Patras ferry was docking, a young Belgian needing a ride to Athens asked if there was room for him in the car. En route he said that he had left Brussels weeks earlier with fifty francs in his pocket, of which nearly half remained. I praised his economy. Ah, he said, he made friends easily; kept up old friendships, too. Would he be staying, then, with friends in Athens? Just so. Night had fallen, we drove on, now silent, now talking a bit. He may have suspected some wraith of education behind my words, for presently he asked if I knew the Greek poet Cavafy. When I said yes, he lit up: "Well, it's with *him* that I shall be staying these next days in Athens."

The lively interest I expressed was rewarded by a description of a man in late middle age, charming, clever, fluent in French, and living on a street quite near to where I stayed. Who knows?—if *I* had been charming and clever I might have played my cards so as to drink coffee later that week with my companion and his host. Instead—it had been a long day—I cut things short by disclosing that the real Cavafy had died of throat cancer on his seventieth birthday, in 1933, having never, aside from brief visits, lived in Greece at all. The Belgian took it badly. He'd seen books, been shown poems done into French, English, Italian, plus hundreds of clippings and critical articles. "At home my friends all know his name. They say: Cavafy, *c'est un monument* !" "How right they are," I agreed sadly; "a monument is all he is, now."

I would have liked to drive my passenger to this Mr. Cavafy's door, but he asked to be dropped downtown, near a telephone. Home at last, tired as I was, I went straight to the directory—where no Cavafy is listed. But it remains a comfort to think that in my very neighborhood a civilized old humbug is still misrepresenting himself to seasonal waves of good-looking if imperfectly educated visitors. Whoever he is, I take off my hat to him, as well as to the marvelous poet he is evidently translating, for once not into some other language, but boldly into life itself.

Object Lessons

"Printanier et merveilleux," René Char called him. Ponge himself can imagine being ranked with Chardin and Rameau. He is seventy-three. The two books under review are selections from his writings, which fill a dozen volumes. While practising "pure and simple abstention from themes imposed by ideologies of the time," Ponge has been embraced by the existentialists in their time, and by the structuralists in theirs. Only human, and French, he too has devoted his requisite pages to the Absurd. Still the bloom does not wear off. This genial life's-work will outlast the ideas by which it is judged.

> If ideas disappoint me, give me no pleasure, it is because I offer them my approval too easily, seeing how they solicit it, are only made for that. . . . This offering, this consent, produces no pleasure in me but rather a kind of queasiness, a nausea.

How one agrees.

No thoughts, then, but in things? True enough, so long as the notorious phrase argues not for the suppression of thought but for its oneness with whatever in the world—pine woods, spider, cigarette—gave rise to it. Turn the phrase around, you arrive no less at truth: no things but in thoughts. Was the apricot any more *real* without a mind to consider it, whether this poet's or that starving goat's? We'll never know.

> What is more engaging than blue sky if not a cloud, in docile clarity? This is why I prefer any theory whatever to silence, and even more than a white page some writing that passes as insignificant.

So Ponge, in 1924, restores *l'azur* and *le vide papier que la blancheur défend*, all that rare, magnetic emptiness so prized by Mallarmé and Valéry, to a backdrop for something common, modest, real.

A review of two books by Francis Ponge: *The Voice of Things*, translated by Beth Archer Brombert, and *Things*, translated and selected by Cid Corman. Published in *The New York Review of Books*, vol. 19, no. 9 (November 30, 1972).

RECITATIVE

And elsewhere: "It's a question of the object as notion. Of the object in the French language (an item, really, in a French dictionary)."

For a thought is after all a thing of sorts. Its density, color, weight, etc., vary according to the thinker, to the symbols at his command, or at whose command he thinks. One would hardly care so much for language if this were not the case.

One of the ideas that most solicit a poet's approval is that of meter. Ponge naturally distrusts it. His prose arrives now and then at a diffident *mise en page* resembling verse, but only very seldom, as in "The Mimosa," at overt numbers. Unlike Valéry, who could instruct and no doubt surprise himself by recasting his decasyllabic "Cimetière Marin" into alexandrines, Ponge is not absorbed by conventional formal problems. Which of course only helps him again and again, since he is Ponge, to achieve a form, a movement, a kind of poem enchantingly, unmistakably his own.

A tone first of all. Of moss he writes: "Patrols of vegetation once halted on stupefied rocks. Then thousands of tiny velvet rods sat themselves down cross-legged." In a related key Gautier describes the interior of a coach in Spain, and Michaux the actions of a Chinese prostitute. With Ponge, the object being closer to home, the result is more importantly light, more detachedly involved.

THE CRATE

Halfway between *cage* and *cachot* (prison) the French language has *cageot*, a simple openwork case for the transport of those fruits that invariably fall sick over the slightest suffocation.

Put together in such a way that at the end of its use it can be easily wrecked, it does not serve twice. Thus it is even less lasting than the melting or murky produce it encloses.

On all street corners leading to the market, it shines with the modest gleam of whitewood. Still brand new, and somewhat taken aback at being tossed on the trash pile in an awkward pose with no hope of return, this is a most likable object all considered—on whose fate it is perhaps wiser not to dwell too long.

(1932–1934)

The frailty of the crate induces *un faible* in the poet, a weakness for—the weakness of—his subject. Where certain later poems will expose the elaborate nervous system beneath their transparent phrasing, here the form remains suitably minimal, a simple openwork conceit. To read something else into these lines—some lament for untimely death, or statement about form's adaptation to content—would be excessive. Not to read it into them would be no less so. The sacrifice of overtones, whether for the sake of a more concrete image or of a more purified idea, is distasteful to Ponge, unhealthy, inhumane. Thoughts and things need to be the best of friends.

A more explicit poem ("Blackberries," 1934–1937) begins and ends:

> On the typographical bushes constituted by the poem, along a road leading neither away from things nor to the mind, certain fruits are formed of an agglomeration of spheres filled by a drop of ink. . . .
> . . . With few other qualities—blackberries (*mûres*) made perfectly ripe (*mûres*)—just as this poem was made.

That first sentence, with its provocative sidelong glances (at thoughts, at things) contained by words that stress their place in a black-and-white, two-dimensional composition the more vibrant for not aspiring much beyond design, can stand for what is best in French art old and new and suggest the extent of Ponge's lifelong debt to Braque. Consciousness of his trade saturates the work. The snail exudes a "proud drivel." The dinner plate is manufactured in quantity by "that benevolent juggler who now and then stealthily replaces the somber old man who grudgingly throws us one sun per day." The *y* of "Gymnast" "dresses on the left." The *è* of *chèvre* becomes the note of the bleating goat. Meadows "surge up from the page. And furthermore the page should be brown." And man? He too is "one of nature's decisions." He secretes language.

In the closing sentence of "Blackberries" we glimpse a most suspect device, the pun.

A pity about that lowest form of humor. It is suffered, by and large, with groans of aversion, as though one had done an unseemly thing in adult society, like slipping a hand up the hostess's dress. Indeed, the punster has touched, and knows it if only for being so promptly shamed, upon a secret, fecund place in language herself. The pun's objet trouvé aspect cheapens it further—why? A Freudian slip is taken seriously: it betrays its maker's hidden wish. The pun (or the rhyme, for that matter) "merely" betrays the hidden wish of words.

RECITATIVE

It betrays also a historical dilemma. If World War I snapped, as we hear tell, the thread of civilization except where it continued briefly to baste the memories of men like Valéry and Joyce, the next generation's problem was to create works whose resonance lasted more than a season. A culture without Greek or Latin or Anglo-Saxon goes off the gold standard. How to draw upon the treasure? At once representing and parodying our vital wealth, the lightweight crackle of wordplay would retain no little transactional power in the right hands. But was it—had the gold itself been— moral? Didn't all that smack of ill-gotten gains? Even today, how many poets choose the holy poverty of some secondhand diction, pure dull content in translation from a never-to-be-known original. "There is no wing like meaning," said Stevens. Two are needed to get off the ground.

Ponge, to be sure, forfeits no resource of language, natural or unnatural. He positively dines upon the etymological root, seasoning it with fantastic gaiety and invention:

> You will note . . . to what tools, what procedures, what rubrics one should or can appeal. To the dictionary, the encyclopedia, imagination, dreams, telescope, microscope, to both ends of the lorgnette, bifocals, puns, rhyme, contemplation, forgetfulness, volubility, silence, sleep, etc., etc. . . .

This preamble, complete with disclaimers about the "poetry" that will follow, and reading like the afterthought it may well be, introduces "L'Oeillet" (The Carnation), a particularly attractive kind of Ponge poem. The text proper takes off from a glossary, words that may or may not figure later on. He looks up *déchirer, jabot, festons,* connects *dents* with *dentelles. Bouton* (bud) needn't, he observes, be used together with *bout* (end, butt), *bouton* (button), or *déboutonner* (unbutton), since each stems from *bouter* (to push or butt). Scruples like these discourage banality. Ponge makes one fleeting, never repeated, allusion to the boutonniere, and knows better than to spell out even once the second meaning of *oeillet*: eyelet, little eye. With words, then, at his fingertips, the writing can begin. Has begun—already we've been given: "At stem's end, out of an olive . . . comes unbuttoned the marvelous luxury of linen." And: "Inhaling them you experience the pleasure whose reverse would be the sneeze." Now to consolidate the findings of "these first six pieces, night of the 12th and 13th of June 1941, amidst the white carnations in Madame Dugourd's garden."

Ponge may be the first poet ever to expose so openly the machinery of a poem, to present his revisions, blind alleys, critical asides, and accidental felicities as part of a text perfected, as it were, without "finish." (No other serious poet asks less to be reread; this work is done for us by the number of alternate readings left standing. The technique will be put to narrative use by Robbe-Grillet.) One meets a mind desiring and deferring, both, according to the laws of baroque music, solution and resolution, the final breaking of an enchantment that may already have lasted weeks, years.

The next day he begins again:

> At stem's end comes unbuttoned from a supple olive of leaves a marvelous frill of cold satin with hollows of virid snow-shadow where a little chlorophyll still resides, and whose perfume excites within the nose a pleasure just on the verge of the sneeze.

Which doesn't wholly satisfy him, not to *be* satisfied being the point. Whereupon he sets about disheveling phrases, breaking up lines:

> Deluxe cold satin duster
> Deluxe beautifully toothed rag
> Frizzed duster of cold satin. . . .
> At stem's end bamboo green. . . .
> Multiple fragrant sachets
> From which the whipped robe spurts

—a quickened pace, a heightened foreplay, reminding us that the sneeze is a minor ejaculation. Some one hundred lines, over the next two days, repeat, vary, modulate, improvise upon these and other motifs (the sneeze presently elicits "trumpets of linen") with the self-reflexive energy of Bach. When this toccata of conceits reaches a crescendo, the subject is sounded again, note by note, letter by letter:

> O split into OE
> O! Bud of an energetic haulm
> split into OEILLET! . . .
> ELLE O youthful vigor
> with symmetrical apostrophes
> O the olive supple and pointed

unfolded in OE, I, two Ls, E, T
Little tongues torn
By the violence of their talk
Wet satin raw satin

—yielding precisely here to an organ point:

Wet satin raw satin

etc.

(My carnation should not be too much of a thing; one should be able
to hold it between two fingers.)

Then silence. A silence that lasts more than two years, during which the
poem's fate hangs in the balance. Other subjects have come to hand, one
of them, "Le Savon," allowing for a far more elaborate treatment. That
finished text (Jonathan Cape/Grossman published [1969] an English version by Lane Dunlop, Ponge's best translator) will run to 128 pages. Presented as an (imaginary?) radio broadcast to a German audience, it is a
complex account—hymn, analysis, charade—of the "*toilette intellec-
tuelle*," the mind's ebullient autocatharsis, typically embodied in the humble cake of soap that, whenever obtainable during the Occupation, was of
some ersatz variety that *made no suds* (Ponge's italics). One small passage
(July 1943) illustrates, without bearing on "The Carnation," the turn of
mind that helped Ponge to resolve the shorter poem:

THEME (dry and modest in its saucer) AND VARIATIONS
(voluminous and nacreous) upon
SOAP (followed by a paragraph of rinsing in plain water)

And indeed, when Ponge returns to "The Carnation" in 1944, his concern is for some rinsing of his hands in a plainer idiom. "Though you
should invent," he had written on that distant evening at Mme. Dugourd's, "a pill to dissolve in the vase's water, to make the carnation eter-
nal"—*éternel* with its echo of *éternuer*, to sneeze—"it would still not sur-
vive long as a flower." Neither, perhaps, would it have survived long as a
poem had Ponge been content to leave it tossing in a high rhetorical fever.
But now, to end it, he sets down a few pages describing the carnation's root
system:

. . . horizontally underlining the ground, a long, very stubborn will-
ing of resistance . . . a kind of very resistant string which baffles the
extractor, forces him to alter the direction of his effort. . . .

In France of 1944 these were charged words. (Ponge himself had underground contacts during the war.) Yet "resistance" is no more the buried issue here than "faith" is, or "style," or the relation between what one knows deep down and what one utters—all mildly, glancingly apparent through Ponge's own altered effort in these concluding paragraphs. The poem ends with one last, abstracted, decasyllabic blossoming:

> Let us emerge from earth at this choice spot. . . .
> So, here is the tone found, where indifference is attained.
> It was indeed the main point. Everything thereafter will
> flow from the source . . . another time
>
> And I too can rightly be silent.

The covenant between maker and carnation has been observed.

Words and silence, things and thoughts, excitation and detumescence: no opposites but brought into peaceful coexistence. One remembers those two fingers between which the flower must be held.

Ponge keeps insisting that he does not write poetry. "I need the poetic magma, but only to rid myself of it." He means "demonstrative outbursts," "beauty . . . all dolled up in an illusion of destiny," "gods and heroes." His Athena is a shrimp with "weapons now wilted and transformed into organs of circumspection." His pine woods are "Venus' beauty parlor with Phoebus the bulb inserted into the wall of mirrors." Such imagery, he remarks, would please a poet minor or epic. "But we are something other than a poet and we have something else to say." Whether this other thing ever really gets said, or said so memorably as in the ravishing passages Ponge shrugs off, is for each reader to decide according to his lights. Those who wonder if the "poetic abcess" doesn't leave less of a scar than the programmatic one will have to gauge, from the major and minor triumphs that come through unscathed, how close to life and how essential to art the entire process is.

By major triumphs I mean (to mention only pieces available in the two selections under review) poems too novel and rich to be patronized by any brief account of them—poems such as "The Meadow," "The New Spider," "The Pebble," "The Goat." Mme. Brombert provides for the last of these a helpful context in which "god and heroes" abound, and starry shapes. Among them, not identified as such by her, we can make out that absolute cogitator who in Mallarmé wore "the lucid and lordly aigrette of vertigo on his invisible brow," and in Ponge becomes a characteristically verifiable emblem of himself:

> Magnificent knucklehead, this dreamer . . . whose thoughts, formulated as weapons on his head, for motives of high civility curve backwards ornamentally.

Well and good; but Ponge remains—it is one of his strengths—open to understanding without apparatus. His words are "conductors of thought, as one says conductors of heat or electricity." One understands, at every blessed turning, why he turned, why he wrote, for what delight, for what beautifully envisionable end. "The poem is an object of *jouissance* (enjoyment, gratification, use) offered to man," he says; and elsewhere, "to nourish the spirit of man by giving him the cosmos to suckle"—item by item, in a lifelong application of sure, brilliant touches (cosmos and cosmetic sharing a single root). And yet again, with simple justice, "I have given pleasure to the human mind."

Ponge, one discovers soon enough, is very hard to translate. Bless him also for that. (And may I not be damned for somewhat tampering with Mme. Brombert's and Mr. Corman's English in my quotations. To refrain, in most cases, would have been to leave well enough alone.) I prefer Mme. Brombert's clear, unobtrusive versions. Mr. Corman, out of long practice, does more with the "line," but his lines, in turn, are more apt to err and omit. (Why does he leave out the phrase about resistance in "The Carnation"?) Or else he will follow the original syntax so doggedly that I had the eerie impression of reading an actual French text, not necessarily Ponge's. Both selections are worth owning. If Mme. Brombert's seems a shade more generous and representative, no one who cares should miss "The Notebook of the Pine Woods," "The Wasp," and "The New Spider" in Mr. Corman's.

On Wallace Stevens'
Centenary

I was introduced to Wallace Stevens' work at a time when it had begun to be taken very seriously indeed by people whose opinions mattered. Mine didn't—I was nineteen—but let me tell you how I felt about it anyhow. The first of his books to come my way was not *Harmonium* but the lovely Cummington Press edition of *Notes Toward a Supreme Fiction*. In it I discovered a vocabulary by turns irresistibly gaudy and irresistibly abstract. Without presuming to guess what the poem or any stanza of it meant, I found myself basking in a climate that Proust might have called one of "involuntary philosophy." A world of painterly particulars—interiors, necklaces, elephants in Ceylon—became, upon little more than a single leafing-through of pages, charged with novel meanings; or potentially charged with them; or alternately charged with thought and (by the enchantment of language) absolved from thought as well. I at once set about writing poems in which colorful scenery gave rise to questions about the nature of reality. Let me read you one of these.

THE GREEN EYE

Come, child, and with your sunbeam gaze assign
Green to the orchard as a metaphor

On April 18, 1979, Merrill gave a poetry reading at the University of Connecticut at Storrs as part of its Stevens centennial celebration. He was asked to open with some words about what the example of Stevens had meant to his own work. "The Green Eye" originally appeared in *First Poems* (1951); "Charles on Fire" in *Nights and Days* (1966). On October 2, 1954—Stevens' seventy-fifth birthday and the publication day of his *Collected Poems*—Alfred Knopf held a luncheon for seventy-five guests to celebrate the occasion. One of those guests was Merrill, then the house's promising young poet. He was seated at the head table with the guest of honor. A couple of months later Stevens wrote to his old friend Witter Bynner about the party: "There were a lot of people there whom you would have enjoyed quite as much as I did, including young James Merrill, who is about the age which you and I were when we were in New York."

RECITATIVE

For contemplation, seeking to declare
Whether by green you specify the green
Of orchard sunlight, blossom, bark, or leaf,
Or green of an imaginary life.

A mosaic of all possible greens becomes
A premise in your eye, whereby the limes
Are green as limes faintly by midnight known,
As foliage in a thunderstorm, as dreams
Of fruit in barren countries; claims
The orchard as a metaphor of green.

Aware of change as no barometer
You may determine climates at your will;
Spectrums of feeling are accessible
If orchards in the mind will persevere
On their hillsides original with joy.
Enter the orchard differently today:

When here you bring your earliest tragedy,
Your goldfish, upside-down and rigidly
Floating on weeds in the aquarium,
Green is no panorama for your grief
Whose raindrop smile, dissolving and aloof,
Ordains an unusual brightness as you come:

The brightness of a change outside the eye,
A question on the brim of what may be,
Attended by a new, impersonal green.
The goldfish dead where limes hang yellowing
Is metaphor for more incredible things,
Things you shall live among, things seen, things known.

In Stevens' hands this manner came to seem wonderfully civilized. With the vivid parasol of language to balance the reader, there was less risk of falling, as in Eliot, off any high tightrope of argument. And a greater likelihood than in Pound—or at least in many of the *Cantos*—of being spared the gritty documentary arena for the sake of a grander perspective. Neither Pound nor Eliot promised very much by way of *people* in their poems. You had on the one hand figures like poor Fräulein von Kulp, frozen forever in a single, telling gesture, and on the other, oh, John Adams wound like a mummy in a thousand ticker tape statistics. To use people as Frost did was something else again. A young poet could easily have been cowed by the sheer human experience needed in order to render "real life" with even minimal authority. Thanks to the example of Stevens, this pressure could be postponed until the time came. His people were unlike any others. Airily emblematic, yet blessed with idiosyncrasy, they fitted snugly into their poems, like figures in Vuillard. Ideas entered and left their minds easily, words came to their lips, giving point to a passage without overwhelming it or reducing it to mere vignette. They served their poet and departed undetained by him. I kept on trying my hand.

CHARLES ON FIRE

Another evening we sprawled about discussing
Appearances. And it was the consensus
That while uncommon physical good looks
Continued to launch one, as before, in life
(Among its vaporous eddies and false calms),
Still, as one of us said into his beard,
"Without your intellectual and spiritual
Values, man, you are sunk." No one but squared
The shoulders of his own unloveliness.
Long-suffering Charles, having cooked and served the meal,
Now brought out little tumblers finely etched
He filled with amber liquor and then passed.
"Say," said the same young man, "in Paris, France,
They do it this way"—bounding to his feet
And touching a lit match to our host's full glass.
A blue flame, gentle, beautiful, came, went
Above the surface. In a hush that fell
We heard the vessel crack. The contents drained
As who should step down from a crystal coach.
Steward of spirits, Charles's glistening hand
All at once gloved itself in eeriness.
The moment passed. He made two quick sweeps and
Was flesh again. "It couldn't matter less,"
He said, but with a shocked, unconscious glance
Into the mirror. Finding nothing changed,
He filled a fresh glass and sank down among us.

Finally I was struck, even then in 1945, by how naturally Stevens handled his references to art and poetry, the aesthetic performance, the "theatre of trope." Without embarrassment—without the concomitant cigarettes and whiskeys and women that in those days accompanied any

RECITATIVE

American account of the artist-as-novelist—he seemed to trust his text to hold its own against the world it evoked, as part of that world. And when we read in a little poem that the moon follows the sun across the sky "like a French translation of a Russian poet" we nod in recognition of a creation myth in which both gods and poets conspire. In a word, he pointed and still points higher than anyone in our century. The candle lit by his interior paramour often as not shines *down*, it seems to me, upon Eliot's "culture" and Pound's "history" and even, now and then, upon Frost's common touch. And all this was accomplished affably, without undue intimidation, so that the young practitioner could seek out his own faith, in his own time, and arrive (with any luck) at his own humanity.

Elizabeth Bishop
(1911–1979)

She disliked being photographed and usually hated the result. The whitening hair grew thick above a face each year somehow rounder and softer, like a bemused, blue-lidded planet, a touch too large, in any case, for a body that seemed never quite to have reached maturity. In early life the proportions would have been just right. A 1941 snapshot (printed in last winter's Vassar Bulletin) shows her at Key West, with bicycle, in black French beach togs, beaming straight at the camera: a living doll.

The bicycle may have been the same one she pedaled to the local electric company with her monthly bill *and* Charles Olson's, who one season rented her house but felt that "a Poet mustn't be asked to do prosaic things like pay bills." The story was told not at the Poet's expense but rather as fingers are crossed for luck—another of her own instinctive, modest, lifelong impersonations of an ordinary woman, someone who during the day did errands, went to the beach, would perhaps that evening jot a phrase or two inside the nightclub matchbook before returning to the dance floor.

Thus the later glimpses of her playing—was it poker?—with Neruda in a Mexican hotel, or pingpong with Octavio Paz in Cambridge, or getting Robert Duncan high on grass—"for the first time!"—in San Francisco, or teaching Frank Bidart the wildflowers in Maine. Why talk *letters* with one's gifted colleagues? They too would want, surely, to put aside work in favor of a new baby to examine, a dinner to shop for and cook, sambas, vignettes: Here's what I heard this afternoon (or saw twenty years ago)—imagine! Poetry was a life both shaped by and distinct from the lived one, like that sleet storm's second tree "of glassy veins" in "Five Flights Up." She was never unwilling to talk about hers, but managed to make it sound

Published in *The New York Review of Books*, vol. 26, no. 19 (December 6, 1979).

agreeably beside the point. As in her "Miracle for Breakfast" she tended to identify not with the magician on his dawn balcony but with the onlookers huddled and skeptical in the bread-line below.

This need for relief from what must have been an at times painful singularity was coupled with "the gift to be simple" under whatever circumstances. Once, after days of chilly drizzle in Ouro Preto, the sun came out and Elizabeth proposed a jaunt to the next town. There would be a handsome church and, better yet, a jail opposite whose murderers and wifebeaters wove the prettiest little bracelets and boxes out of empty cigarette packages, which they sold through the grille. Next a taxi was jouncing through sparkling red-and-green country, downhill, uphill, then, suddenly, *under* a rainbow! Elizabeth said some words in Portuguese; the driver began to shake with laughter. "In the north of Brazil," she explained, "they have this superstition, if you pass underneath a rainbow you change sex." (We were to pass more than once under this one.) On our arrival the prisoners had nothing to show us. They were mourning a comrade dead that week—six or eight men in their cavernous half-basement a narrow trench of water flowed through. They talked with Elizabeth quietly, like an old friend who would understand. It brought to mind that early prose piece where she imagines, with anything but distaste, being confined for life to a small stone cell. Leaving, she gave them a few coins; she had touched another secret base.

In Ouro Preto, literary visitors were often a matter of poets from other parts of Brazil—weren't there fifteen thousand in Belem alone? These would arrive, two or three a week during the "season," to present her with their pamphlets, receiving in turn an inscribed *Complete Poems* from a stack on the floor beside her. The transaction, including coffee, took perhaps a quarter of an hour, at whose end we were once more by ourselves. The room was large, irregular in shape, the high beams painted. Instead of a picture or mirror, one white wall framed a neat rectangular excavation: the plaster removed to show timbers lashed together by thongs. This style of construction dated the house before 1740. Across the room burned the cast-iron stove, American, the only one in town. More echoes, this time from "Sestina."

I was her first compatriot to visit in several months. She found it uncanny to be speaking English again. Her other guest, a young Brazilian painter, in town for the summer arts festival and worn out by long teaching hours, merely slept in the house. Late one evening, over old-fashioneds by the stove, a too recent sorrow had come to the surface; Elizabeth, uninsistent and articulate, was in tears. The young painter, returning, called out, entered—and stopped short on the threshold. His hostess almost blithely made him at home. Switching to Portuguese, "Don't be upset, José Alberto," I understood her to say, "I'm only crying in English."

The next year, before leaving Brazil for good, she went on a two-week excursion up the Rio Negro. One day the rattletrap white river-steamer was accosted by a wooden melon-rind barely afloat, containing a man, a child of perhaps six, and a battered but ornate armchair which they were hoping to sell. Nothing doing. However, a "famous eye" among the passengers was caught by the boatman's paddle—a splendidly sanded and varnished affair painted with the flags of Brazil and the United States; it would hang on her wall in Boston. When the riverman understood that the eccentric foreign Senhora was offering, for this implement on which his poor livelihood depended, more money (six dollars, if memory serves) than he could dream of refusing, his perplexity knew no bounds. Then the little boy spoke up: "Sell it Papá, we still have *my* paddle!"—waving one no bigger than a toy. Which in any event, the bargain struck, would slowly, comically, precariously ply them and their unsold throne back across the treacherous water.

Will it serve as momentary emblem of her charm as a woman and her wisdom as a poet? The adult, in charge of the craft, keeping it balanced, richer for a loss; the child coming up with means that, however slow, quirky, humble, would nevertheless—

Nevertheless, with or without emblems, and hard as it is to accept that there will be no more of them, her poems remain. One has to blush, faced with poems some of us feel to be more wryly radiant, more touching, more unaffectedly intelligent than any written in our lifetime, to come up with such few blurred snapshots of their maker. It is not her writings—even to those magically chatty letters—whose loss is my subject here. Those miracles outlast their performer; but for her the sun has set, and for us the balcony is dark.

The Transparent Eye

It is a sad pleasure to take up this book. Of all the splendid and curious work belonging to my time, these are the poems (the earliest appeared when I was a year old) that I love best and tire of least. And there will be no others.

Elizabeth Bishop was born in 1911 in Worcester, Massachusetts, and raised largely by her Nova Scotian grandmother and various scattered aunts. Her friends at Vassar included Mary McCarthy and Eleanor Clark. After graduation she lived in New York, Paris, and Key West; then, in 1952, on her way to an Orient blithely renounced, settled for the better part of eighteen years in Brazil. It was there that word of her Pulitzer Prize drew this exuberant response from the local butcher: "All my customers are lucky—just last week Senhora X. won the lottery!" Living at such a remove from the literary world brought compensations only a writer can fully appreciate. Still, she came home—"wherever that may be"—to teach for a while at Harvard. She died suddenly in 1979, on the point of leaving her apartment above Boston's harbor for a dinner with friends.

Her original *Complete Poems* (1969) is here expanded to include *Geography III* (1976), a few hitherto uncollected treasures, all her verse translations, plus some juvenilia and occasional pieces. One could conceivably have lived without certain odds and ends in the latter categories. Yet it is touching to see her at work under influences (like Millay and Hopkins) soon to be outgrown. And after all, in the case of a poet like Bishop, less is *never* more. The book as it stands deserves only grateful praise.

The watercolor on the jacket, a view of a Mexican town done by the poet in 1942, serves nicely as introduction. It's a cheerful scene, in no way traditionally "picturesque." Beyond a balustrade flanked on one side by an

A review of *The Complete Poems, 1927–1979* by Elizabeth Bishop. Published under the title "The Clear Eye of Elizabeth Bishop" in *The Washington Post Book World*, vol. 13, no. 8 (February 20, 1983). A brief discussion of Bishop's poem "Exchanging Hats" has been deleted from this review because it is substantially repeated in "A Class Day Talk."

absurd ornamental urn (so much for Art?) and on the other by flourishing palm fronds, we see some little, run-down, brilliantly colored houses. Above these, near and far, quite upstaging the few church-spires lost among them, perhaps fifty windmills crowd the horizon—so that, like the mysterious flooded dreamscape in "Sunday, 4 A.M.," it appears to be "cross- and wheel-studded / like a tick-tack-toe." The picture illustrates at once Bishop's delight in foreign parts, her gratitude for the givens of a scene, and her typical way with systems. These tend to fade beside her faith in natural powers—here, those jaunty cockades turning in wind to draw water, compared to which the Christian temples, though neatly delineated, look a touch feeble and evanescent.

For systems exhaust themselves; the elements remain numinous. In "Sunday, 4 A.M." the jetsam of a great story—instruments of the Passion, organ music, altarcloth and donor, some unidentifiable "Mary"—litters the waking dreamer's world with useless, cryptic detail. Not until "a bird arranges / two notes at right angles" does life once more make sense. (That bird, we may safely assume, is not a dove.) Or if the Christmas trees in "At the Fishhouses" are, as David Kalstone has remarked, "behind us" in both senses of the phrase, they leave that poem free to conclude with seawater, fire, and stone, together performing a grave alchemical masque:

> If you should dip your hand in,
> your wrist would ache immediately,
> your bones would begin to ache and your hand would burn
> as if the water were a transmutation of fire
> that feeds on stones and burns with a dark gray flame.
> If you tasted it, it would first taste bitter,
> then briny, then surely burn your tongue.
> It is like what we imagine knowledge to be:
> dark, salt, clear, moving, utterly free . . .

Robert Lowell, among many, praised her "famous," farsighted eye. In her elegy for him, she acknowledges it herself:

> *I can make out the rigging of a schooner*
> *a mile off; I can count*
> *the new cones on the spruce. . . .*

But the marvels that appear on every page are as much acts of imagining as of seeing. Here is fog in Nova Scotia:

Its cold, round crystals
form and slide and settle
in the white hens' feathers,
in gray glazed cabbages,
on the cabbage roses
and lupins like apostles.

And here in New York City at daybreak through a window

Where it has slowly grown
in skies of water-glass

from fused beads of iron and copper crystals,
the little chemical "garden" in a jar
trembles and stands again,
pale blue, blue-green, and brick.

More telling even than her image-making is Bishop's way with tone and overtone. "Arrival at Santos" sounds at moments like a sixth-grader's report—rich in pathetic fallacy, trivial detail, and complacent generalization ("Ports are necessities, like postage stamps, or soap"). Technically, and this is part of her strategy, the somewhat amateurish rhymes and meters could be the work of a clever twelve-year-old: the mental and emotional age, after all, of her fellow tourists with their

. . . immodest demands for a different world
and a better life, and complete comprehension
of both at last, and immediately,
after eighteen days of suspension.

The poem ends, "we are driving to the interior." Precisely. Only a few pages further on comes a poem like "The Riverman" in which her eye, still clear as a child's, penetrates a world unimaginable to the innocents lined up at Customs. Here all is primal, animistic—and touchingly matter-of-fact. "It stands to reason," the young witch-doctor insists, "that everything we need / can be obtained from the river." Yet his world has already been grazed by the cinema and mass production that will destroy it, and so is linked to the earlier poem's tourists in ways Bishop wouldn't dream of spelling out. She shows us that fragile culture. Whatever conclusions we may draw belong outside the poem.

In "12 O'Clock News" she constructs a minithriller whose narrator is both criminal and victim. Thanks to clues in the margin, *we* know that the eerie, war-torn, enemy landscape is no more than the writer's lamplit desk. But here the tone, that of a media analyst pathetically conjecturing under his pretended omniscience, opens up ironies that reach from the Ivory Tower to the Oval Office. As part of a generation that included Lowell, Berryman, and Roethke, she had glimpsed the megalomania lying in wait for the solitary maker—or indeed for anyone "in power"—and her account of it here is all the more unnerving for her superficially playful sleights of scale.

These sleights figure with a difference in "Visits to St. Elizabeths"—the Washington hospital where Ezra Pound, so as not to be tried for treason, was detained in the early 1950s. Bishop (then poetry consultant at the Library of Congress) went regularly to see him. As her title hints, however, it was not only the irascible great poet but aspects of herself that she was curious to face. With her own mother in a mental hospital since Bishop's early childhood, she must have known the threat of insanity firsthand. Not that she would ever have been prey to either of those (male?) drives, the one that produced the *Cantos'* huge unruly text, the other that made its bid to change the map of Europe. More than anything she cared to keep her work and her wits, in the phrase of her beloved George Herbert, "new, tender, quick." To define *and* disarm, then, this figure of Pound—while sympathizing with his predicament if not with his politics—she modeled her St. Elizabeths poem upon "The House That Jack Built." In her hands the painful subject with all its vast overtones (anti-Semitism, the war) takes on a bittersweet, singsong shapelessness, as if a young self were gazing back through time at the formidable, by then half-cracked titan he had become:

> These are the years and the walls and the door
> that shut on a boy that pats the floor
> to feel if the world is there and flat.
> This is a Jew in a newspaper hat
> that dances joyfully down the ward
> into the parting seas of board
> past the staring sailor
> that shakes his watch
> that tells the time
> of the poet, the man
> that lies in the house of Bedlam.

RECITATIVE

Last month a young Bishop fan told me that his favorite was "The Shampoo." I wonder if it isn't mine as well. Two of its three short stanzas play with notions of time. On one hand it is cyclical, as unobservably slow as the "gray, concentric shocks" whereby the lichens grow in order "to meet the rings around the moon." On the other hand, time is linear, moves at "precipitate" human speed, is "nothing if not amenable." The phrase is exact: without us to feel it, time would not exist. In stanza three, "shooting" and "flocking" echo those "shocks" at the beginning, which now in the denouement we hear as shocks of hair. Otherwise the language is supremely plain, and the everyday gesture it clothes, supremely tender:

> The shooting stars in your black hair
> in bright formation
> are flocking where,
> so straight, so soon?
> —Come, let me wash it in this big tin basin,
> battered and shiny like the moon.

It is as unexpected and convincing a love poem as I know.

Finally, "The End of March" recounts a walk with friends down the beach on a sunless day of numbing wind. All is "withdrawn as far as possible / indrawn. . . ." The receding tide worries "a thick white snarl, man-size, awash," of string: "A kite string? —But no kite." As they follow "a track of big dog-prints (so big / they were more like lion-prints)" a bizarre structure comes into view. In this "crypto-dream-house" Bishop images a solitary existence, more like an afterlife, where she too might withdraw and "do *nothing*, / or nothing much, forever, in two bare rooms." Before turning back, she remarks a chimney, infers a stove

> and electricity, possibly
> —at least, at the back another wire
> limply leashes the whole affair
> to something off behind the dunes.
> A light to read by—perfect! But—impossible.

In short, another system, its attractions recognized and foregone in favor of the elements. (Besides, "of course the house was boarded up.") Turning back brings its own reward, as the sun briefly, marvelously appears:

> For just a minute, set in their bezels of sand,
> the drab, damp, scattered stones
> were multi-colored,

and all those high enough threw out long shadows,
individual shadows, then pulled them in again.
They could have been teasing the lion sun . . .
who perhaps had batted a kite out of the sky to play with.

The stones behave oddly like souls in Dante, and for something not too
unlike the same reason: the quickening of their relation to a glowing creative source. "The ancients said poetry is a staircase to God," wrote Montale. Bishop shows how this can still be so in a world relieved of theological
apparatus. Her conclusion is both playful and lofty. Best of all, the poet
does not feel obliged to tell us what the experience did for *her*.

This is characteristic. Most of Bishop's poems are in the first person,
singular or plural. Sometimes she speaks as the Riverman, or Robinson
Crusoe, more often "simply" as herself. The voice can be idiosyncratic
("Heavens, I recognize the place, I know it!"). Yet because she is to no least
degree concerned with making herself any more remarkable than, as the
author of these poems, she already is, hers is a purified, transparent "I,"
which readers may take as their virtual own. Whether this voice says hard
and disabused things or humorous and gentle ones, its emotional pitch remains so true, and its intelligence so unaffected, that we hear in it the
"touch of nature" which makes the whole world kin. Is this an obsolete way
to judge poetry? I cannot envy anyone who thinks so.

Robert Bagg:
A Postscript

In dealing with his experiences Mr. Bagg is helped by a sense of form which candidates to graduate schools as well as to the various colleges of hard knocks would do well to cultivate. For instance, the final section of his book is prefaced by Yeats' stanza beginning, "Does the imagination dwell the most / Upon a woman won or a woman lost?" Mr. Bagg's answer is nicely implied by the *kinds* of imagination at work in the two poems that follow. The first and longer, "The Tandem Ride," celebrates a girl who refused the poet. She is an undergraduate at Smith, all airs and poses. Mr. Bagg gallantly rises to her level. Yeats and Keats appear in the first of his thirty-five Spenserian stanzas, Zelda Fitzgerald in the last; between them he drops the names of Blanche Dubois, Belafonte, Emily Dickinson, Donne, Zeus, etc. The poem glimmers with indulgent echoes. The fraternity brothers set out on their "wild swan chase" riding

> A phosphorescent Bike of the Baskervilles
> Which soon struck bony terror through the Pelham Hills.

The characters see themselves in extravagant mirrors, narcissistically:

> ". . . I go on long walks and show off at Proms."
> Her look flicked at me from a Hitchcock thriller
> Where the stunned eyes of dead nudes photograph their killer.

The second poem, "The Madonna of the Cello," is by contrast mysteriously open—no tags, no argument, a "free-form" sequence of tender, brimming vistas:

A response to an unfavorable review by Ralph J. Mills, Jr. of *The Madonna of the Cello* by Robert Bagg, who was an undergraduate at Amherst while Merrill was teaching there. The two articles appeared in the same issue of *Poetry*, vol. 98, no. 4 (July 1961).

> Sliding tears drew out of her eyes
>   The things she saw:
> Her mother staring into the whorls
>   Of the washing machine,
> Her father's eyes receding,
> Her own body growing beyond her control.
>   . . . .
> Silence, after music, awakens the child.
>   Her lover opens his palm
> Over her turbulent belly, where the child
> Troubles it with his footprints, turning
>   Against the flesh.

Clearly, where the woman won is concerned, the poet can unbuckle, discard the entanglements that kept him from getting lost in Yeats' "vast labyrinth." One does not need Yeats, furthermore, to admire the instinctive rightness of conception and execution in these two poems.

    The same rightness shows in many another: in the elegy "Ronald Wyn" where the classical scenery and costumes that numb a few slighter pieces truly become the poem, and show the poet what can honestly be made of his friend's death; in the remarkable "Adventures" whose "blank verse" is forever swelling with extra stresses or faltering into decasyllabics, attuned to the young hero's tentative arrogance; in the haunting "Soft Answers." Before reading this one, only twelve lines long, it is wiser not to have decided that the erotic comes through awkwardly in our language, that, for the last three hundred years or so, the French have done these things better. (I am thinking less of Donne's roving hands than of an emotion more passive and fatalistic, as in Baudelaire's "La douceur qui fascine et le plaisir qui tue," and whose closest English counterpart would be, conceivably, the "Ode on Melancholy.") Here is how Mr. Bagg's poem ends:

> Lazy as her love is, I have my hands full
>
> With her, letting every beauty she owns
>   Slip through my tongue and fingers, still hoping
> For the whole of her, soon closing and opening
>   Like a giant heart toying with my bones.

What "works" here is an illusion of unpremeditated, languorous movement; one feels that the poet, in his availability to what he is feeling, does not entirely comprehend it.

RECITATIVE

He sees to it that *we* comprehend, however. It is their clear hold on the commonplace, the shared and shareable, that distinguishes the best of these poems. Mr. Bagg has worn neither handcuffs nor straitjacket. His "Adventures" are those that may be supposed to have befallen any red-blooded American boy. Whether through chance or artistry (a good deal of each, I should think) they present, in exuberant detail, a first person at once engaging, credible, and oddly larger than life, almost a paradigm of Youth here and now, with its bewildering privileges, raptures, flaws. Indeed a young man can easily offend, if seen to go his way accompanied by no particular view of life, or by a "suburban and collegiate" one, flashy, gum-chewing, too smart for anyone's good. What is forgotten, and inevitable, is that the Muse matures with her poet. Another few years may find her lunching on crudities dressed with vinegar—*tout pour la ligne*—and denying she ever accepted three sundaes in an afternoon from him. She will teach him some of Mr. Dugan's "dark, harsh humor." But I should not think he would belittle those early hours of companionship. The "life" Robert Bagg renders in his first book has been vividly lived. He has had lighthearted experiences and painful ones, and, what is seldom enough done, has set these down without bitterness, making one glad that he has had them.

The Relic,
Promises, and Poems

Robert Hillyer's new collection holds no surprises for his readers. There is the usual dependable technique, lifted now and then—as in "Cock of the Wind"—to a truly winning resourcefulness. There is also the dependable sensibility whereby poem after poem evolves at the pace of the pantoufle and with the complacency of the peignoir. It is not my wish to run down light, agreeable verse. Mr. Hillyer himself is quite aware that to preserve the lyric impulse during the middle years is no easy matter. In "One Kind of Colloquy" the older poet keeps silent while his young colleague

> . . . floats through flowers that yesterday
> Were treated with manure and spray,
> And sees them vaguely as pale gems
> Suspended without roots or stems.

What is hard to swallow here is the falsification, for whatever innocent purpose. I cannot call to mind a single young poet—unless he writes only for Mr. Hillyer's eye—who looks at nature in this fashion. Indeed, it is far more Mr. Hillyer's own view of things that he attributes to the young. In his revealing poem "The Bats" (chosen by the Borestone Mountain Poetry Awards as the best poem of 1953) we find bats used as images for

> our underdreams that keep
> Our secrets from ourselves,

A review of *The Relic and Other Poems* by Robert Hillyer, *Promises* by Robert Penn Warren, *Poems 1947–1957* by William Jay Smith, and *The Open Sea and Other Poems* by William Meredith. Published in *Voices: A Journal of Poetry*, no. 166 (May–August 1958). The magazine's editor, Harold ("Beauty hurts, Mister") Vinal had asked Merrill to be guest editor for this issue. Having assembled the contents and sent them to Vinal—who then refused to print a Robert Bagg poem because it used the word "urine"—Merrill demanded in protest that he be listed merely as "Editorial Assistant" on the issue's masthead.

RECITATIVE

The lark becomes half rodent in that dark
Wherein his downward mountain climber delves.

This is dexterous enough, but the poem ends on a nervous, warning note:

Seal all, before.
In ragged panic driven
These nightwings pour to heaven
And seal us from our natural sun.
Of two forbidden trees, there's one
Untampered with till now. . . .

The subconscious—seal it off! The repulsiveness of Mr. Hillyer's bat image does the work of argument, tells us what horrors to expect from psychiatry and leaves it at that. But are we persuaded? If truth were the poet's concern, mightn't he have cast about for terms that would not taint his subject from the start?—permitting the dark portions of the mind to be seen as, oh, the wings of a stage, the base of an iceberg, even perhaps the manure from which the flower grows. As it is, he ends up less a prophet than a crank.

Among the more likable poems in *The Relic* are "Light, Variable Winds," "The Magicians," "Proteus," and a number of leisurely, discursive pieces, frequently in heroic couplets. Although they lack the vitality, the spleen, and the fun that the form discovers in the hands of Pope (or, to name a living poet, Walker Gibson), these make pleasant reading. Now and then there is a heightened sparkle:

The ice puts out, beneath the frosted moon,
A tentative webbed foot on the lagoon,
And mothers, to place débutantes on view,
Sublease a duplex on Park Avenue.

Something happens here; the icy foot and the insecure matron fuse for an enchanted instant. But "frosted" is weak, the rhymes are undistinguished. . . . Felicities simply do not grow freely on Mr. Hillyer's unforbidden trees.

The more I read Robert Penn Warren's *Promises (Poems 1954–1956)*—which at first glance had seemed a powerful and glittering performance—the more disappointment I feel. The subtitle is all too telling. Mr. Warren, alas, has a virtuosity capable of turning out a volume twice as long in half that time. Most of the poems, good or bad, move at the tonic pace of an ocean breeze.

More specifically: Mr. Warren is master of a long whiplike line that is particularly effective when dealing with guilt and self-realization, as in certain earlier poems ("End of Season," "Pursuit," "Revelation," to name three) where its compulsive elongation has something in common with his heroes' doomed struggle against the poem's truth. It is a line that furthermore adapts itself in this new volume, to a graphic, humorous manner:

Their children were broadcast, like millet seed flung in a wind-flare.
Wives died, were dropped like old shirts in some corner of a country.
Said, "Mister," in bed, the child-bride; hadn't known what to find
   there;
Wept all the next morning for shame; took pleasure in silk; wore the
   keys to the pantry.

It is not, however, a line that lends itself to a transcendent vision. Consider the stanza with which a long poem closes:

For fire flames but in the heart of a colder fire.
All voice is but echo caught from a soundless voice.
Height is not deprivation of valley, nor defect of desire,
But defines, for the fortunate, that joy in which all joys should rejoice.

However simple and beautiful the opening two lines, it appears they will not do, for Mr. Warren sets about obscuring and clotting, adding here an adverbial phrase, there an auxiliary, neither essential, until the perfectly sufficient line

But defines that joy in which all joys rejoice

is lost beneath its trimmings and the rapid, jerky movement of its little feet.

The music of Marvell and Donne, which exercised a certain control over *Selected Poems*, has given way, if my ear serves, to that of Poe's "Bells":

His head in the dark air,
Gleams with the absolute and glacial purity of despair.
His head, unbared, moves with the unremitting glory of stars high
   in the night heaven there.
He moves in joy past contumely of stars or insolent indifference of
   the dark air.
May we all at last enter into the awfulness of joy he has found there.

The fault is not entirely with Mr. Warren's ear. "Country Burying (1919)" is a poem of simple, evocative imagery; the final quatrain depicts an empty church, its gloom, varnish, stacked hymnals, "And the insistent buzz of a fly lost in shadow, somewhere." What in God's name, to use a favorite phrase of Mr. Warren's, persuades him to add

Why doesn't that fly stop buzzing—stop buzzing up there!

There is no minimizing the vulgarity of such a stroke, unless the entire poem is meant as a subtle parody. Elsewhere, in the long "Ballad of a Sweet Dream of Peace," a fascinating arrangement of stock Gothic themes for the arch voice of A. A. Milne, the joke is more apparent:

What makes him go barefoot at night in God's dew?
In God's name, you idiot, so would you
If you'd suffered as he had to
When expelled from his club for the horrible hobby that taught him
   the nature of law.
They learned that he drowned his crickets in claret.
The club used cologne and so couldn't bear it.
But they drown them in claret in Buckingham Palace!
Fool, law is inscrutable, so
Barefoot in dusk and dew he must go. . . .

But at whose expense is the joke planned? The vulgarity is not that of a single ill-advised line, but of over-all proportion. The reader fidgets as the poem repeats itself again and again, harrowing irony upon mellifluous sadism, with no real heightening of effect. The game just isn't worth the candle.

The most impressive poems in the book are several composed in modest five-line stanzas, with lines kept relatively short. An easy, clear voice is heard making a number of things quite brilliantly vivid:

The springs of the bed creak now, and settle.
The overalls hang on the back of a chair
To stiffen, slow, as the sweat gets drier.
Far, under a cedar, the tractor's metal
Surrenders last heat to the night air.

In the cedar dark a white moth drifts.
The mule's head, at the barn-lot bar,
Droops sad and saurian under night's splendor.

> In the star-pale field, the propped pitchfork lifts
> Its burden, hung black, to the white star. . . .

But as fine a poem as "Summer Storm (Circa 1916), and God's Grace" falls prey to Mr. Warren's formula; to end it he must pull out all the stops and turn on the house lights:

> Oh, send then summer, one summer just right,
>> With rain well spaced, no wind or hail,
>> Let cutworm tooth falter, locust jaw fail,
> And if man wake at roof-roar at night,
>> Let that roar be the roar of God's awful Grace, and not of His flail.

It is a pity to see Mr. Warren giving way to mannerism of language and feeling alike. Conceivably he has counted on the rapid composition of these poems to keep them alive, as indeed they are, on the page and on the tongue. His *Promises* are genuinely exciting, but they remain promises. May Mr. Warren bring more judgment and patience to the next ones he makes.

The new books by William Jay Smith and William Meredith have been ten years in the making. Mr. Smith gives us a selection from his two earlier books, as well as new poems, light verse, and translations. Mr. Meredith's third volume contains forty-six poems hitherto uncollected. Both are highly artful poets in different ways. If Mr. Meredith's work has the careful depths and lights of a master of etching, Mr. Smith's shows the aplomb of a first-rate watercolorist, that air of vivid temperament, blotched arbitrarily, always very light in atmosphere and execution.

Among his choicest poems are some whose wells are ever so slightly tainted by the thirst of a gorgeous savage. Witness "American Primitive" with its mirthless refrain:

> Only my Daddy could look like that,
> And I love my Daddy like he loves his Dollar.

Or "The Ten," which begins: "Mme. Bonnet is one of the best-dressed ten: / But what of the slovenly six, the hungry five. . . ." and ends evoking "the weird, monotonous one. . ."

> who grasps your pen
> And lets the ink run slowly down your page,

Throws back her head and laughs as from a cage:
"Mme. Bonnet is one, you say? . . . And then?"

There are several debts to France in Mr. Smith's poems. "The weird, monotonous one" is surely kin to the muse of Baudelaire or Gérard de Nerval. Also, lesser Frenchmen have taught Mr. Smith the value of having, time and again, no motive other than to make a small, perfect poem— whose subject matter may even be calculated not to engage a reader overmuch; something leanly modeled, its elements composed and juxtaposed to give a sense of much ground covered in mysterious ways. For instance, from "Interior":

> Past and future, two lean panthers
> Black as coal,
> Paced out the limits of his brain,
> His life's veined ore;
> And he could see
> Gates opening before him quietly
> Upon a rose-banked carriage waiting in the rain.

A movement of terror into gentleness is achieved with an authority the more impressive for the conscious slenderness of materials. The interested reader may turn to an earlier poem, "Elegy," whose analogous theme has been enlivened and purified in the passage above.

Now and then I feel that Mr. Smith has not prepared a proper canvas; the physical or psychological donnée is too flimsy to bear the meaning he wants to draw from it. This is perhaps the price one pays for working largely in miniature: the eye tends to wander, the fancy to quicken, the ear to prompt the next line instead of the mind. Mr. Smith is at his best, accordingly, when he has either a dramatic situation so strong and simple that it needs—one fancies—only to be set down ("Light," "Death of a Jazz Musician," "Cupidon") or else a wealth of sense-impressions to be informed by moods ranging from the spare felicity of

> Waking below the level of the sea,
> You wake in peace; the gardens look
> Like roofs of palaces beneath the water,
> And into the sea the land hooks,

to the opulence, on the facing page, of "Persian Miniature":

> . . . Higher still the laden camels thread
> Their way beyond the mountains, and the clouds

Are whiter than the ivory they bear
For Death's black eunuchs. Gold, silk, furs
Cut the blood-red morning. All is vain.
I have watched the caravans through the needle's eye
As they turn, on the threshing floor, the bones of the dead,
And green as a grasshopper's leg is the evening sky.

Mr. Meredith, handily enough, has a "Miniature" from Persia. In it he becomes involved in a little tale of Eastern courtesy towards the shy:

> . . . I have not been to Persia but they tell
> How nothing is too much trouble all at once
> For irritable beaters when a shy man hunts.
> A forest bird was heard to trill for two,
> Awkward in one another's presence still—
> Two ornithologists—over and over until
> They had noted down its call in turquoise curls
> On the scrolls they paint with pictures of the fowl.
> In the spiced equivalents of cafés there
> Waiters grow civil to the ill-matched pair,
> The bald and raven-haired, the strong and halt;
> And indeed everyone is delicate
> Of their delays. . . .

Suddenly it is as though one were reading fiction; the subject is a human relationship, a scene changing with the passage of time. Mr. Meredith makes his concessions to the picturesque; he throws off "turquoise curls," he lapses wryly into a rhymed couplet or two, like a background of intermittent mandolins. The sensuous, in short, is put in its place, which is not far from where Mr. Smith himself arrives, by such a colorful route, in his own poem: "Gold, silk, furs," and finally—for, to the vision sated with these, the ultimate luxury would be that of abstract utterance—the pill beneath the sugar: "All is vain."

Their difference as poets is essentially temperamental. If Mr. Meredith is, as I feel he is, the more rewarding of the two, it may be because he adopts the more humane stance toward experiences more varied and complex, yet which—because of the dramatic sense, the restraint and compassion he brings to them—permit a very deep response from his reader. To go even a step further: Mr. Meredith's feeling for his subjects is, I suspect, directly linked with the unusual variety and resourcefulness of technique that distinguish his work. As he writes in "To a Western Bard":

> Cupped with the hands of skill
> How loud their voices ring,
> Containing passion still
> Who cared enough to sing.

There are many beautiful poems in *The Open Sea*, poems that are elevated without arrogance or sacrifice to the sound of speech, and delicate without fussiness. The tone is intimate and urbane; frequently, the rhythms of a passage, though under full control, present some pleasurable resistance to the ear, suggesting the mint condition of a book with uncut pages. In a poem as bland as "The Chinese Banyan" the following lines may be felt as a flaw:

> Teacher and bachelor,
> Hard forces both to measure.
> With Sammy, a small white cur,
> Who would dance and yap for pleasure.

The movement here seems too creaking, and one of the rhymes too emphatic, not to blemish the grisaille of the rest of the poem. But that one should be reduced to this delicate dispute points of itself to Mr. Meredith's excellence.

My own preference is for "Starlight," "A View of the Brooklyn Bridge," a half-dozen very engaging sonnets, and the amazing "On Falling Asleep by Firelight"—a poem that, with its images of heat and slumber, the poet's voice raised from within a dream, gives a sense of eerie deceleration, stanza by stanza. It is a poem that should be read entire, and I have, alas, no space in which to quote it.

III.
OCCASIONS

The Beaten Path

Here in Kyoto where the amenities reach fever pitch we have been grateful for A. who, while practising them on all eight cylinders, remains amusing and articulate. "That brazier? It's nothing at all, perhaps sixty years old. That is to say, it's the poorest of all *possible* braziers; there are others that frankly couldn't be displayed. I don't mean that this one didn't cost, oh, $200, but a *good* one will bring $10,000 at auction, even $50,000 now and then. As an American I take shocking liberties. I do a tea ceremony, for instance, serving Campbell's cream of mushroom soup instead of the *correct* soup, which takes three days to prepare. Getting back to my brazier, it formerly belonged to . . ." Every so often A. interrupts himself to call out, in petulant Japanese two octaves higher than his ordinary speech, queries or instructions to his secretary, Rev. H. This poor sweet man is struggling to complete his doctor's thesis by February. Nobody believes that he will. "When the time comes," A. chuckles, "we'll arrange for an extension; perhaps we can manage to get him sick."

David and I exchanged a glance. Each time we have seen H. he is on the run: bicycling off to purchase a "possible teabowl" from a widow; darting back to photograph an old man changing his trousers in public; there is A.'s wheelchair to push, of course, and A. himself, who looks heavy, to lift, often singlehanded. The other day, watching jugglers at Nijo Castle, David ran out of cigarettes. Before either of us had realized it, H. was heading at a trot for the nearest shop, a good half-mile away. While he was gone A. had a brainstorm. "Now tonight, what might *really* interest you," dismissing the jugglers with a shrug, "is to go with H. to his acupuncture.

Published in *Semi-Colon*, vol. 2, nos. 5 & 6 (1957). Merrill and David Jackson went to the Far East in the fall of 1956, the first leg of a nearly yearlong around-the-world trip. In lieu of travel diaries, they kept carbons of their letters home. These impressions—all but the poem—were worked up from letters at the request of the editor of *Semi-Colon*, the art dealer and critic John Bernard Myers.

Yes, he hurt his back rather badly last year, jumping off a wall, but these treatments . . ."

We went, naturally. Rev. H. led us through dark reeking streets to the clinic, a poorly lit house, inspiring no confidence. Upstairs, cushions were brought for us, the doctor took out a small metal case, H. stripped to his underdrawers and placed himself meekly facedown on the mat. Out came the needles; they are two inches long, and flexible. Each is dropped through a thin metal tube, softly, enough to penetrate the skin, then the tube is put aside and the needle guided in by hand, in, in, in, until it strikes the nerve. "But it must hurt!" exclaimed David. No, no, the patient smiled, a faint electric shock, nothing more, perhaps some trifling soreness the next day. We watch two dozen needles go in and out of the scant flesh along Rev. H.'s spine. He gave the oddest impression of basking in his treatment, there under the weak light bulb. According to A., one can turn into an acupuncture addict; there are those who crave it once or twice a week. Could it be that Rev. H. . .? But no, it is bound to be the pleasure of just lying down for a bit, needled but at rest.

We took shelter from the rain with guess who on the last lap of a trip round the world. He has carried along mescaline capsules to be swallowed at key points: one at the Prado, one at Angkor Wat, etc., and is vexed to find no occasion for the one he saved to use in Japan.

We exchanged another glance, and yet— It *is* very lonely here, with no way of sharing in anything. The language barrier is severe; that of manners, monstrous. One can endure just so long the hours spent drinking tea, or trying to get a straight answer, or holding some inscrutable ornament to the light in one's great clumsy fingers. Conceivably it is a strain upon the Japanese as well. I doubt it. They sink back into their splendidly contrived formulas as into those scalding baths, while the Westerner, in either instance, simply shrieks with pain or, if at all lucky, faints dead away.

Take their sweets. The papers are full of shocked letters about certain inferior Japanese products sold at a recent manufacturers' fair in Peking. Hollow fountain pens, watches packed with sand, *candies without flavor*. An unfair charge, I thought, seeing that no Japanese confection has any taste whatever. They are for the eye alone, and take the shape of masks, ships, autumn leaves. Here, try this specially ingenious one; it is a clam, you see, with cookie-shell ajar to reveal some chocolate-colored treat within. Ah, but bite into it!—a taste of long ago, of letters in an attic trunk;

the bean-paste center is torpid, dazed, as if having crept in for a midday snooze . . . Never again!

A chronic ethereality. Given any choice in the matter, these people would not exist physically. Neither would their rooms, their clothes, their verses. It is the *idea* of the room (or kimono or haiku), more than any embodiment of it, that has become their triumph. And it *is* a triumph, oh dear me, yes. Think of the Western writer or even the Western couturier—doesn't everything he turns out imply some bold stand taken against Chaos, conformity, tastelessness, the sluggish drift of a public whose ideas, if any, are at odds with his own and one another's? But the Japanese have laid up treasures in heaven, safe from fever, earthquakes, decay.

And yet, where else does the physical world appeal so irresistibly to the eye?

Over and over the point is reached where Art and Nature cannot be told apart. The persimmon trees, with so few leaves and so much fruit; perhaps a crow, yellow rice-fields beyond. This afternoon I saw a garden paved with fifty varieties of moss, blue-green, gold-green, rust-green, thick as plush, one or two sallow leaves floated down onto it. It had been designed to resemble somebody's description of paradise. One gets there through a grove of bamboo, innumerable hollow green tones, soaring, intersecting, like gamelan music for the eye . . .

Why not carry it a step further? Paradise is *here*, in these rocks, in that white sand! Why not say so?

No answer to such a question.

HIROSHIMA

. . . Helen was right; it is one of the most painful experiences imaginable. Oh, some of it is rebuilt, a big restless shopping section, a couple of buildings that either stood up under the Bomb or were deliberately built in the style of 1910 to look as if they had. But the rest—! Mud streets, dull empty vistas of rubble and strange, stunted trees, trunks like toothpicks. In the middle of the wilderness stand three concrete modern buildings: the New Hiroshima Hotel, the Peace Museum, and a second museum (empty as far as we could tell) with an unwisely named "Grill Room" upstairs. The Peace Museum is given over to displays relating to the Bomb, from scientific charts and diagrams all the way to the end of a child's thumb, with nail, brown, dry, cooked, which dropped off during the five days before the little boy finally died. This is displayed, bedded in cotton, along with a photograph of him in school uniform. A sickly-delicate face, great big eyes, even the picture somewhat faded. Elsewhere, melted rock, flattened bottles, scorched clothing on charred mannequins, photographs of scar tissue, a shot of Truman at the telephone—and beyond the plate glass, the filthy flat field with a man on crutches picking through a trash can. It is a favorite tourist spot. Busloads of Japanese come, gape, and, as the brochures say, "realize the mistake of their militarism." There is an Atomic Souvenir Shop where you can buy don't ask me what . . .

A VISION OF GREATNESS

Arnold Toynbee is visiting Japan. Of his arrival a reporter wrote: "His magnanimity was apparent to all who met him. Never once did he reveal his true feelings."

Tantalizing words, almost delphic. After pondering them for a full week, we had our reward at Koyasan.

Few places can match that mile-long avenue of evergreens, towering bluish above mossy tombs where sunlight turns to marble the clouds of incense and lingers upon cloths, rain-washed reds or limes, in which pilgrims have dressed certain stone dolls.

An abrupt rustling. The first snake we have seen out-of-doors in Japan (there are shops full of them; you grind them up and take them for sexual disorders), a big striped one, abulge with eggs, hurried past us, shooting cold forked looks. We quickened our pace somewhat, and so witnessed, in the holiest spot of all, the materialization of the great historian. Tall, silver and white, an angelic smile on his large sculptural mouth, he moved noiselessly in a throng of sages, black-and-white-robed, some with beards like winter waterfalls. "Maybe noble interpleters," K. whispered, "and noble pliests." We gazed and gazed.

KYOTO. AT THE DETACHED PALACE

Struck by the soft look
Of stone in rain, wet lake,
By a single evergreen
Wavering deep therein,
Reluctantly I sense

146

All that the garden wants
To have occur.
Part of me smiles, aware
That the stone is smiling
Through its tears, while
Touched by early frost
Another part turns rust-
Red, brittle, soon
To be ferried down
Past where paths end
And the unraked sand
Long after fall of night
Retains a twilight.

THE SEXES

A girl's voice is recorded at 33 1/3 RPM, then played back at 45. She becomes the mother of that strutting male child to whom, on streetcars, the aged offer their seats. She retains until death the knack of collapsing like a fan into three folds, forehead touching the floor.

The hotel maid is jolly and clean-minded, always helping you undress or feeding you like a baby. The red light district in Tokyo could be a little stage set. A hundred pretty girls in a hundred artful doorways.

(That first night in the café named Starlit Chrysanthemum Water, a drunk broke a glass. He had been sitting alone at the counter, his refreshment already before him. A few soft words. The waitress at once began to remove, one by one, the dishes she had set down, each different and delicate. He didn't try to stop her. Back went the tiny brochette, the bowl of five dead minnows, silver, staring; back went the saké bottle, the cup. He lifted a stool once, menacingly. A girl took it from his hand.)

Woman, in short, does not matter much. She has less face to lose and proportionately more "personality" than her refined husband. *He* knows that he invented her, that she is part of the Dream, and his only smile is a downward baring of gritted teeth.

K., a Buddhist novice studying Plato, explained it thus: Woman has exclusively *personal* feelings and desires; you must never discuss anything serious with her, lest she corrupt you.

(For nearly a century Buddhist priests have been permitted to marry.

Permitted? Such pressure is brought to bear upon them, if anti-Shinto circles are to be believed, that in all 500 temples at Koyasan there is but one priest strong enough to resist the trend. Formerly barred to women, the holy mountain crawls with waitresses, shopgirls, wives of abbots, daughters, granddaughters of abbots. One fancies the regime rubbing its hands. "Those Buddhists, ha! soon they'll be good for nothing . . .")

In Kabuki, to be sure, no women are allowed.

We saw Utaemon, who is probably sixty, play a virgin priestess tricked into drinking aphrodisiac wine. The hoax uncovered (a lizard is found pickled in the empty flagon), she stabs herself with a sacred arrow. An "invisible" stage attendant fixes it to her costume, at the same time deftly revealing a blood-red undergarment. She is then free to die for ten minutes of quavering speech and rapid subsidings, with hands aflutter into exquisite disarrayed postures, while three other characters, including her partner in shame, sit on their heels and study the floor.

At one time the actor of women's roles learned many a trick from geisha. But I think there must always have been geisha in the audience, white-faced, attentive, getting pointers on how to be themselves.

In the end, perhaps, even man falls short of the Dream.

The Osaka puppets fume and float, each lifted at once to a realm of pure disposition, by two or three manipulators. These wear black, with black face-veils, all but the master manipulators who have learned to veil their faces without concealing them. Like embodied passions they cluster about their creature; its eyebrows rise, its fan slams shut; it mounts a puppet horse and lurches off, howling promises, sleeves flying in no wind. It is strangely dull. To begin with, I felt weak that day, our last day in Japan. A very grown-up audience was following the text . . . What does it really mean—*to be moved*?

WHAT THEY ARE SAYING

1. At a party in San Francisco a poet accosted the decent German maidservant: "I sympathize with you." "Oh my Gott," the maid gasped, "you don't need to do that!" "Well I will," said the poet, "whether you want me to or not."

2. The *President Cleveland* has sailed; in its wake dwindles the Golden Gate. One little girl warns another to take her "last look at civilization."

3. In Yokohama harbor—Asia at last! Dr. F., an 82-year-young dentist from Oak Park, put his lips conspiratorially to my ear. "So many folks on this ship," he whispered, "wear artificial upper dentures. It spoils the whole shape of the mouth."

4. One sees Hong Kong reflected in a tailor's mirror. Everywhere, things are being fitted to the taste of somebody. But not everybody is pleased. At lunch a longtime resident brought her fist down onto the table. "The young people they send out to us nowadays!" she ranted. "Most frightfully disappointing! No conception of empire-building!"

BANGKOK

Gold leaf floats through the air. You buy it by the square inch and affix it to your favorite Buddha. The most popular are quite furry with gold; it flutters about their lips like traces of a recent meal.

The sacred buildings imitate fabulous paper lanterns not altogether unfolded. From under a roof another roof emerges. With every flight the steps grow steeper. Our climb began pleasantly enough, like the opening chapters of a society novel. By the time we had reached the top we were in the heart of a quatrain by Mallarmé.

The opium, a black bead, bubbles far, far off, along the bamboo-and-silver pipe. How to get at it? I tried too hard and was sick, but David had visions all night long of unknown charmers and moonlight on leaves. These temples were first glimpsed in such a vision.

From afar they are seen to be constructed of mauve-and-pink or green-and-yellow ceramic tiles, or of gold, sometimes purple, mosaic. Think of Istanbul, Hagia Sofia and the mosques, turned completely inside-out by a miracle, festooned with the "quaint enameled eyes" of Milton's flowers, and shining in the sun! Seen close, of course, it is only too clear that they have been put together out of chewing gum, sequins, whitewash, and broken willowware. If you still care for them after this discovery, nothing is easier than to break off a piece and carry it home.

They are akin to the works of Congreve, of Couperin, to the buildings of Borromini and Gaudí, through that air of being a trifle too chic and therefore, out of somebody's sheer ennui, wrought in dangerous, perishable mediums, ornament which the underlying structure may or may not support—mightn't the fun lie in the uncertainty?

RECITATIVE

Some Buddhas wear the smiles of brilliant hostesses, lips curled into a V, with a single beauty patch of gold. On the huge gilt toenail of the Standing Buddha a modest community subsists, day and night, made up of houses two inches high, people and animals, all of whitewashed clay, sparsely painted and half-hidden anyhow by a couple of wilting lotuses. I think you can climb up into the Buddha's head and look down onto them through his very eyes. The stair was closed today.

The Buddha's smiles are repeated on every human face. Consider that the priests here (in robes of gamboge, a color that means *Cambodia*) must renew their vows only for the month ahead. They may go back into the world whenever and as often as they please. This may account for some of the smiles, that there is nobody who hasn't gone back into the world, as we all should, over and over and over again.

A ferry navigates the tide, rapid, topaz-colored boulevard. In the long ripple of its wake the melon-rinds and almond-shells manned by old ladies, infants, priests, vanish and reappear, hardly bobbing. The seller of charcoal plies an ash-gray craft, she herself wears black and a lampshade hat. The butcher's boat is scarlet, freshly painted. Along the banks, stairs lead down into the water; the open rooms are alive with waterlight. There is nothing for a dog to do here, beyond watching somebody scrub himself in the river.

From the landing a maze of boardwalk takes us to Chew's house.

It is larger than many. Half of one whole room is occupied by the shrine—twenty Buddhas on bleachers, surrounded by flowers, photographs, extinct incense. "That fat lady is my mother," Chew says of a retreating form. Near a hole in the roof a beehive simmers.

We are seated in the parlor. It is entirely of dark wood with pale pink plastic curtains. Photographs are pointed out: Chew (aged seven) as a priest; Chew as a scout; Chew as he is now (many poses) peering up through the glass tabletop in happy consort with Elizabeth Taylor (wearing white fox), Rory Calhoun (stripped to the waist and driving a nail into something), and, inevitably, James Dean. Chew, you might say, *is* James Dean. That name at least appears on every shirttail a younger sister is ironing in the next room. When five years are up, although his teeth, his dancing, and his English are not good, Chew will go to Hollywood and be discovered.

His mother brings lunch. Ice has been procured for the visitors. We are thankful for it because there is chili in the rice.

Afterwards we each put on a sarong and take a dip in the klong with Chew and his friend Suripong.

Chew gives us his photograph, inscribed "to my best American friends. I hope you will not remember me."

Then back along the boardwalk. No wonder the Siamese are graceful! What it must be like to be always stepping on planks of varying flexibility, interminable xylophone, under banana trees, past gingerbread porches; to be always setting forth in a barque so flimsy you can feel a fish nuzzle it . . .

I rode in one, finally, down a country klong, doubled up against the knees of an American girl called Ann. The Prince paddled, confessing that he had all but forgotten how. Even so, the high overgrown ruin we had gone to see slipped behind trees and the sun beat down. Slowly, very slowly, the tiny boat filled with seepage. At the landing I turned my head. The movement sufficed. I saw the Prince's eyes narrow. These Americans, he might have cried, must they *force* their easy manners upon us? But by then we were all three waist-deep in the warm exhilarating water.

Notes on Corot

The writer will always envy the painter. Even those who write well about painting, he will envy for having learned to pay close attention to appearances. And not the writer alone; it is the rare person who can look at anything for more than a few seconds without turning to language for support, so little does he believe his eyes.

Daily the painter masters new facts about the world. But years pass, and the writer is still studying his face in the mirror, wondering at what strange tendencies lie hidden beneath a familiar surface. "Pleasant enough, but what does it *mean?*" That traditional response of the layman is one he will never contrive to repress. Making it to the oeuvre of Corot, he will feel the least bit foolish. What does *it* mean? What does *he* mean? Here are the landscapes—ruins, trees, water, cows; here are the models, both with and without clothes. What can it possibly add up to but Art? The retort, by endowing the pictures with unquestionable value, gracefully waives the little matter of their significance.

He stands before a painting by Corot. As he is not himself a painter, or even if he is—painters are forever talking nowadays—he will suffer a brief, defensive spell of verbal dizziness. Phrases to be distinguished by their incoherence—linear values, tonal purity, classical heritage—will explode between himself and the canvas. When the first smoke clears, he may look more attentively; he has routed the babbling imp. And though he will end by using the dreadful phrases, seeing at last their truth if not their beauty, an observer who is by nature oriented toward language, who in the deepest sense of the cliché requires that a picture *tell a story*, must meanwhile listen for its opening words.

Published in *Corot 1796–1875*, a catalogue to accompany the exhibition of paintings and graphic works at The Art Institute of Chicago, October 6 through November 13, 1960. Merrill's friend John Maxon had recently been appointed Curator of Paintings at The Art Institute and requested this essay.

"Once upon a time, in a far country. . . ."

The small Italian sketches are praised by those who prefer the natural to the invented, Rousseau to Chateaubriand, the early Corot to the late. They are indeed very beautiful, as well as revolutionary, with their simplifications, their early morning, open-air clarity. Let it be added, however, that they respond to a revery of the idyllic instilled in Corot by Claude and Poussin, and that, when we are moved, it is not only by their naturalism but by a revery of our own.

His rapidly brushed Rome, the Rome he transported back to France for prudent investment, is the city of our dreams: physical, somnolent, unimperially casual and even-tempered. Its domes rise from dusky washes into the sun, or by magic from the brimming, shaded fountain on the Pincio. A pane flashes. The island of S. Bartolomeo suspends its structural Gordian knot between sky and stream. The wonderful trees are everywhere, dwarfing the monuments they frame, taking the rich light upon their bulk, like placid thunderheads. Umber shadows flood the pavements of Venice, Genoa, Florence, Naples: the eye is drawn over a balustrade and down into the radiant depths of the scene, with the same sinking delight felt on the verge of sleep. All is joyously, economically accomplished, and it is an unfortunate visitor to Italy who has not, even in this day and age, enjoyed some such delusion. Over the shoulder of an old country man sitting on a trunk, beyond a crooked window frame, the sky, of a soft, blank brightness hard to mistake for any other, is enough to send one headlong down the stairs and out into that still barely retrievable world of awnings and ochres, sunstruck ruins, umbrella pines.

Italy—like youth, a simple word for a complicated, often idealized experience. No one would resist its appeal, as rendered in these little paintings. But each of us knows, in his way, what happens when it is over. Corot knew too. *A View near Volterra* (in the Chester Dale Collection) shows it happening in a scene so ravishing that it emerges unscathed from the jaws of allegory: the artist-prince, in peasant dress, heads his white horse (!) straight into the trees. Slowly it dawns on us what awaits him there, when he dismounts and sets up his easel. A change of light, a corresponding change of sensibility; in short, the paintings of Corot's maturity.

More than ever, as we look back on them, these Italian scenes take on a quality of legend. No need to people the glades with nymphs, or top the hill with crosses. The world itself is a marvelous tale. And as in all legend is found—what distinguishes it from myth—traces of the provincial, of genre, it is a happy accident, or no accident at all, that led the young painter to that already much-painted landscape where the peasant's cottage stands in relation to the aqueducts and arenas of the Giant. Taste, far more than credulity, is strained by the costumes of Corot's women. They belong to a world of story; it is well that they are a bit fussy and quaint.

". . . there lived a woman. . . ."

One woman or hundreds of women, it makes no difference. A single impulse turned a Roman girl into a sybil and a French girl into a Vermeer. What is strange is how we believe in them, for all their artifice of posture and ornament.

Who *are* they? The last of the Lamias? The first patients of Freud? From the start, they fascinate and appall us by their listlessness, their fatalism, combined with an oddly bourgeois presence. Standing by a fountain, trusting vainly to participate in all that freshness; balancing an unplucked instrument in their laps; musing without comprehension upon book or letter, upon the enigma of a nudity or a costume they would never have chosen, their faces drain of animation, a mortal tedium falls, glimmering downward from a gray sun that does its best to shine and to cheer. But alas, their painter is older now, probably indoors as well, and he will not fake a happy light either in the world or in his own eye. Thus the reader of the Metropolitan Museum's *The Letter* sits in a shuttered space at the bottom of a well. No other interpretation will do for the light that barely exposes the musty furnishings and our heroine's unlovely, heavy-skinned features. What has happened to interiors—of rooms and of people alike? One has the feeling of Venice and Delft being recreated at nightfall, on a rehearsal stage. The solitude of any Renaissance woman never bothered us; she sat at her ease on an invisible throne of philosophy and manners. In the Lowlands, there was always a music lesson, or some household matter to be dealt with, and we enjoyed looking through a door at mistress and maid, off and on during the day. The pomp and pride of one tradition, and the charming resourcefulness of the other, are lacking in Corot's women. The most they can do is *look* as if they were reading or able to pick out a tune; their minds are elsewhere, we feel anxious for them. Another *Reader* (also at the Metropolitan) has elected to sit out-of-doors in her cumbersome contadina dress; the sun beats down muggily from a mournful zenith; one guesses the strain she is under, the trickle of sweat forming beneath the silken sleeve. Behind her, a tiny figure we shall see again tries and tries to steer his boat out of the rushes.

These ladies could not say, any more than Corot, what ails them. The *maladie du temps*, to be sure. But, specifically, do they not chronically suffer from their legacy (both classical and Dutch) as surely as from a "delicate constitution"? They are the last figures that a serious painter will ever render with that particular sober "studio" look—a result of training and procedure that infect his treatment of flesh and bone in much the same way as the inbred values of an Arcadian education might have done any young person in the nineteenth century. Their postures show what art has taught them to expect of life; their faces, what life has taught them to suspect of art. And yet they cleave to it—they are timid. They have *heard* of their shameless sister, with her parrot or her paramour, but in their eyes she is worse than any chattering bird. Better to waste away, unloved, than to break faith with their creator. In the mercy of his brush salvation lies.

Arkel to Mélisande: "I have been watching you: you were there, unconcerned perhaps, but with the strange, distraught air of someone forever expecting a great misfortune, in sunlight, in a beautiful garden."

Humble, not visionary, a virgin without child, the *Reader* resists knowing herself. She would deny that the hand on which her cheek just fails to lean is constituted differently from its Raphaelesque prototype; more loosely brushed, it is nevertheless doomed to obsolescence (hence her repressive calm) by new or imminent techniques and tastes. One wants to take that hand, open those sombre eyes. Triumphs lie ahead. *She* will vanish, yes, but in her place we shall see the molecules of Pissarro, the brilliant glazes of a later reader— *L'Arlésienne*. Her nieces—she has no direct descendents—her nieces, clothed in colors as light and strokes as rapid as air, will dance all day at Bougival with bearded, floppy-hatted men. They will eat oysters! Or they will once again do *useful* things, such as bathing themselves or setting the table. If they are melancholy, it will be at their milliner's or in their music halls. (The provincial branch of the family will evidently stay on at Barbizon, ever more numerous, rich, and insufferable.)

Ah, and yet—

Lost in so much female activity will be precisely the solitary romance, the sense, however obscure, that our moments of uncomprehending loneliness are the most true; their profound dark spotlight reveals more about the human condition than any number of hours spent in dramatic relation to this or that figure or set of objects. To convey this truth, in all its narrow-

ness, the artist may have no recourse to drama. Once seen to inhabit a setting—the saint in his cell, the siren in her loge—the supreme solitude can
be shrugged off as a matter of individual preference, when it is really, as
for Corot's women, a destiny, a state of soul. Some, like the *Sybil*, are
strong, requiring almost a violence of execution; others make subtler
claims—consider the air of baleful French tenacity that envelops the
Young Woman in the Hirschland Collection, all her weakness concen-
trated into a force; others yet are merely beautiful. But even these, at their
most memorable, remain at the heart of life, which is to say, beyond any of
its resources, beyond even the methodical debauchery that sheds so cold a
light upon Lautrec's unhappy women. We must wait for Picasso to renew
the glamour of pure identity.

Seeing this far, we should not be astonished by the *Girl with a Pink
Shawl* in Boston. Flattened, simplified, positively post-impressionist in
feeling, she sits against three large, quickly done jigsaw pieces, two light,
one dark. Somehow this background escapes transformation into furni-
ture, foliage, or sky. Somehow her loose white smock escapes being fitted
or embroidered. A thin wash of mauve covers portions of her otherwise
pale strawberry-and-cream face. One hesitates to admire her, suspecting
that, if one does so, it is thanks rather to a later master than to Corot. Yet
she is his—awkward, virginal, unsmiling. The painting may be unfinished; her being is intact. Indeed, the rapid execution makes the difference. It suggests that she does not weigh too heavily on the artist's con-
science; he has not shouldered her with *his* inheritance and *his* destiny. We
are led to reflect on the degree to which these were embodied by so many
of his other women.

At times Corot's mysterious heroine is literally garbed as a muse, with
wreath and scroll; or lies nude, a gross-featured bacchante looking up,
deadpan, at the tame leopard advancing, a child astride it, to sniff politely
the lifeless bird she dangles. We may hope that such a composition is lighthearted, a spoof on certain big moments out of Titian or Poussin. But is
it? She has appeared too often in pensive, humorless guises for us to be
sure.

In one of the most suggestive—the Widener Collection's *Artist's Studio*—she sits with hound and mandolin, in Italianate finery, facing away
from us and into a small "typical" Corot landscape. Dreamily she fingers
her instrument; the dog paws her skirt in vain. She might as well be looking

into a mirror, so enraptured is she by the painter's expression of her feelings.

Though we no longer readily translate scenery into emotion, the landscape that resembled oneself or one's mistress was a widely spoken Romantic language (". . . the rocky horizon seen while approaching Arbois on the main road from Dôle, was for me a clear, live image of Métilde's inner self."—Stendhal, *The Life of Henri Brulard*). Faced with Corot's most celebrated pictures—the post-Italian landscapes—to make sense of, we must not despair. Many of them, it is true, appear to have issued, like himself, from the milieu of a small tradesman who has learned the rules of mass production. But, having identified the type of scene with his Muse, we must recognize it as one that deeply stirred Corot. He returned to it, after all, again and again, often dully, always humbly and unquestioningly.

The elements of the scene are quickly named: the little glades, pockets of poetic rurality, farmhouse, stream, a far-off figure bending over the earth not so much, one feels, to gather anything, as just vaguely to keep in touch; a white-masked cow stands by like an anesthetist. These small human or animal figures at first greatly control our responses—the nostalgia of one long pent in his hectic, Balzacian metropolis, as well as the country cynic's impatience with the too easy idyll. As we go from picture to picture, we find that we can dispense with these little guides; we are learning to "read" Corot. The Boston Museum's *Beech Tree*, in which neither man nor beast appears, nevertheless vividly suggests a human, perhaps a superhuman, presence. Attended by quiveringly erect younger trees, the strong, whitened trunk stands out against their familiar cloudy greens; this background is thinly painted and sets off a cluster of leaves, belonging to the subject, that might almost have been dribbled onto the canvas. At the foot of the tree a torn-off limb reinforces our impression of veiled narrative—we could be looking at a metamorphosed king.

The story grows more subjective.

The Ville d'Avray scenes, for example, place the sunlit building Corot had loved and learned to paint in Italy, deeper and deeper within the picture, frequently on the far side of still water. Young, white-trunked trees now grow in the foreground; they are seen less often massed from a vantage, than from a point in their midst. Even when fully grown, they rarely command the space; they filter, they intuit. Corot recreates for the eye, in two dimensions, something of the pleasurable hindrances of a winding progress through woods. We are left purer and warmer for the experience.

RECITATIVE

At the last moment a few touches of bright color are added; earlier, they would have threatened the tone of an essentially spiritual exercise. In one picture (*Ville d'Avray* at the Metropolitan) a foliage diffuse and atmospheric overlays the entire canvas, a coarsely woven veil of branches at once dark and shining. It is a perilous moment. The artist is intoxicated by the degree to which his own powers can enter the trees, can alter, withhold, make precious the clear view beyond, which they are in danger of shutting off forever.

To the trees, then, we turn, to the water and the light, for clues to the meaning of these pictures. As with the Italian sketches and the female portraits, we feel the pull of tradition. But by now, the tiny rustics and the diaphanous vegetation bring to mind Hubert Robert more than Poussin. The mood remains Corot's—passive, trustful, melancholy; let others call it unhealthy. Those stretches of water! They sustain and extend the sky; their calm shimmer overwhelms a field. Slowly, as they accumulate in scene after scene, they begin to speak of relinquishment, of escape, of an *Embarquement pour Cythère*, only ascetic, lacking the exuberant iridescence of Watteau's.

One motif recurs and recurs: the single boatman leaning over the side of his boat in what might be an effort to free it from certain reeds or bushes at the water's edge. This accomplished, he has only to cast off and glide forth across the breathless mirror. He is kept from doing so precisely by the rest of the composition, with its sum of allusions to an ideal world. The farm, the cattle, the woman and child, even the harmonious intricacy of boughs—would these not be missed, once one had given oneself up to sheer reflectiveness? Would it not, on the other hand, be braver to strike out, to dream one's own dreams for a change? Elsewhere, as before, the boatman does not need to be in sight for us to experience the delicate and crucial conflict.

The setting in motion of such insights hardly adds up to Meaning or Subject Matter (as found in, say, Millet's peasant scenes). And yet Corot's principal dilemma—loyalty to the senses or to the imagination?—does get expressed, all the more movingly for its understatement, its perverse tenuousness. There come to mind Rilke's lines:

> Were you not astonished, on Attic steles, by
> the circumspection of human gesture? were not love and farewell
> so lightly laid upon shoulders, they might have been made
> out of some other material than ourselves?

If anything can stir us in this Romantic version of classic pastoral, Corot has divined it.

His development is very subtle, hardly a development at all. We can see him applying to one period lessons learned from another: something of the convincing, pure repose of the early Italian scenes, recurs in the quite late *Venus Bathing*, and of their architectural angularity in the *Interrupted Reading* here in Chicago. But, throughout his work, his main concern was to invest places and people with the nuance of a golden or a silver age. The increasing subjectivity of his later mood can be attributed to the tarnishing of that silver in the atmosphere of his day. He was too much of an artist not to breathe it. While able, as how few dedicated painters since, to give a large contemporary public what it wanted, at the same time he could not help but reveal, particularly in his figure paintings, the inner unease of that public caught between its own sense of a way of life lost, and its imminent place at the dreamless center of the stage.

A Class Day Talk

Years ago in Paris a friend of mine was taken by her husband to have a pair of evening slippers made by the great shoemaker Roger Vivier. The gift entailed many weeks of conferences and fittings in whose course the kind of intimacy that develops between client and artist allowed my friend to ask a personal question of Monsieur Vivier. Had making shoes, she wondered, been his only drama, his only dream? Was there perhaps something else he had ever once thought of doing with his life?

"Ah *yes*," he replied. "I could have done anything! I could have made dresses, I could have made hats—!"

Very frivolous, very French. But suppose we place his remark under an X-ray beam and watch it come to mean something like this:

"True, dear lady, I may appear to give myself wholly, to take my stand if you like, upon pedestrian matters. But within my imaginative grasp is also a living body of knowledge, free and passionate and brilliantly disguisable. While above that we have the whole vast sphere of the human head and the question of how its changing contents are to be both protected and dramatized by the intellectual milliner at work within it."

So: what goes onto expresses what comes out of the head. "If they tried rhomboids, / Cones, waving lines, ellipses—/ As, for example, the ellipse of the half moon—/ Rationalists would wear sombreros." That's Wallace Stevens. Another Frenchman, Mallarmé, inferred an "aigrette of vertigo" rising from the thinker's forehead. And a final example, closer to home:

Our late President Cole, introducing a reading by Robert Frost, said what we all felt—even as he illustrated a principle the canniest among us wouldn't grasp until much later in life, namely that the limitations of an instrument can make for its most memorable effects. "The winkles," said

Delivered May 24, 1980, at Amherst College by invitation of the graduating Class of 1980. Merrill's connections with the college are close: he graduated from Amherst in 1947, he taught there in 1955–56, and was awarded an honorary degree in 1968.

Dr. Cole, "the winkles that you see on Mr. Fwost's bwow do not come from old age or wowwy, but the weight of the weath."

Sorry—one gets so caught up in quotation—many hands make light work. Before going any further, let me thank my sponsors for the wreath of today's occasion.

In my invitation to speak, something was made of this Class of 1980 being the first in Amherst history whose graduating women were completing the full four-year course. It left me wondering what could be said about the sexes, if only with regard to the poets, the men and women of this century, whose work means most to us. When we look at the men we notice a drift toward the more or less monumental. Sometimes a highly compressed monument, a sketch for a monument—I'm thinking of *The Waste Land* or *Notes Toward a Supreme Fiction*; sometimes, as with Pound or Lowell or Dr. Williams, a huge, unruly text that grapples ravenously with everything under the sun. Now these men began by writing small, controllable, we might say from our present vantage "unisex" poems. As time went on, though, through their ambitious reading, their thinking, their critical pronouncements, a kind of vacuum charged with expectation, if not with dread, took shape around them, asking to be filled with grander stuff. As when the bronze is poured in the lost-wax process of casting, what had been human and impressionable in them was becoming its own monument. I speak, alas, from experience, having felt a similar pressure at work in my own case, and seen also, though fighting it every step of the way, how little choice I had in the matter. And wistfully thought how while men have built monuments to themselves—as well as to women: look at the Taj Mahal—no woman has ever gone on record as wanting one. But that's too neat. Look at poor Anne Sexton who, submitting a poem to an editor, wrote: "I realize it's very long, but I believe it is major."

Another true story. In the early 1950s a Professor degli Alberti was conducting his last class of the year at a finishing school in Florence. He reminded his young ladies—as they were called in those days—that they'd learned a lot of history and seen a lot of art, churches, museums, and whatnot. Here now was their chance to clear up any remaining questions. Silence; all had been understood. No—a shy hand went up: "Professor, we've looked at these hundreds of statues and paintings of the Madonna and the Child, but the child in her lap always seems to be a little boy—

why's it never a little girl?" It would take only twenty years, until the publication of Mary Daly's *Beyond God the Father*, for that exact question to
turn from an ignorant into a profound one.

I've been too regularly bullied by women to believe in a male Mafia. Yet
when I come across language I dislike, it'll usually be a man's. We hear the
man in *manifesto*. We see, as I've said elsewhere, in such common expres-
sions as "to erect a theory" or "a seminal idea," the worst kind of Don Juan-
ism. Men write more universally than women, perhaps; but they also—at
least up until these years of the raised consciousness—take the cake for
ponderousness and complacency.

One exception would be Mr. Frost. He dealt with monumentality now
by smiling (or wincing) at how his mind worked, now by taking directly
into public life those attitudes he knew better than to inflict upon his
poems. Thus the friendships with presidents, the grand illusion that he
and Khrushchev face to face could settle the differences between their two
nations.

Then there's Elizabeth Bishop. There was, rather—she died last October: the last and, I think, finest of a generation that included John Berryman, Robert Lowell, Randall Jarrell, and Theodore Roethke. Lowell
called her one of the four best women poets ever—a wreath that can hardly
have pleased Miss Bishop, who kept her work from appearing in the many
recent "women's anthologies." Better, from her point of view, to be one of
the forty, one of the forty-thousand best *poets*, and have done with it. If I
raise the issue at all, it's to dissociate her from these shopworn polarities.

"I don't much care for grand, all-out efforts," she wrote to Anne Steven-
son. "This is snobbery, but . . . in fact I think snobbery governs a good
deal of my taste. I've been very lucky in having had some witty friends—
and I mean real wit, quickness, wild fancies, remarks that make one cry
with laughing. . . ." And from another letter to the same person: "I think
we are still barbarians, barbarians who commit a hundred indecencies and
cruelties every day of our lives, as just possibly future ages may be able to
see. But I think we should be gay in spite of it, sometimes even giddy—to
make life endurable and to keep ourselves 'new, tender, quick.' "

Not a manifesto—yet what honesty, what simple nerve it takes to put
such thoughts into words.

The threat of human indecency and cruelty can be felt always between
her lines. Her most popular (though surely not her best) poem is a first-
person account of catching "an enormous fish." As it hangs by the boat,

half in water, Bishop examines it, imagines it so closely—the skin like peeling wallpaper, and underneath, "the coarse white flesh packed in like feathers"—that the written conclusion could not be otherwise:

> I stared and stared
> and victory filled up
> the little rented boat,
> from the pool of bilge
> where oil had spread a rainbow
> around the rusted engine
> to the bailer rusted orange,
> the sun-cracked thwarts,
> the oarlocks on their strings,
> the gunnels—until everything
> was rainbow, rainbow, rainbow!
> And I let the fish go.

"Rainbow, rainbow, rainbow! / And I let the fish go." Two free associations here. The first: a friend of Elizabeth's gave the book in which this poem appeared to her husband, himself something of a fisherman. He singled out "The Fish" for special praise, saying "I wish I knew as much about it as she does." Four years later this man published a novella, a fishing story some of us will remember as ending quite differently from the poem. He called it *The Old Man and the Sea*. Now what are the facts behind such fictions? It would surprise nobody to learn that, in his long career as a sportsman, Ernest Hemingway let go far more fish than Elizabeth Bishop ever hooked. Besides, *her* fish wasn't let go at all, not in real life; she told in an interview about bringing it proudly back to the dock—intact. But both she and Hemingway, whatever their private strengths or weaknesses, were concerned in their work with attitudes, "emblems of conduct"—or shall we say, some form of moral headgear—for the reader who wanders out unprotected into the elements. Thus, both fish are invested with grandeur and wisdom, and the respective fishermen behave nobly, even reverently, according to their lights. That remark about her poem, Elizabeth told the interviewer, "meant more to me than any praise in the quarterlies. I knew that underneath Mr. H. and I were really a lot alike."

Rainbow, rainbow, rainbow . . .

My second association is a memory. After a solid week of rain in Brazil, ten years ago, out came the sun and Elizabeth proposed we visit a pretty town nearby. Presently a taxi was jouncing through sparkling red-and-green country, downhill, uphill, then all at once *under* a rainbow—like a halo on the hill's brow, almost touchable. She said some words in Portuguese; the driver began to shake with laughter. "In the north of Brazil," Elizabeth explained, "they have this superstition—if you pass underneath a rainbow you change sex."

And this memory in turn brings to mind one of her early, never-collected poems—written perhaps in the very hour when the young lady in Florence was asking her haunting question. Let me read it to you now.

EXCHANGING HATS

Unfunny uncles who insist
in trying on a lady's hat,
—oh, even if the joke falls flat,
we share your slight transvestite twist

in spite of our embarrassment.
Costume and custom are complex.
The headgear of the other sex
inspires us to experiment.

Anandrous aunts, who, at the beach

"Anandrous"—in Greek "without a man"—doubles as a botanical term meaning "having no stamen."

Anandrous aunts, who, at the beach
with paper plates upon your laps,
keep putting on the yachtsmen's caps
with exhibitionistic screech,

the visors hanging o'er the ear
so that the golden anchors drag,
—the tides of fashion never lag.
Such caps may not be worn next year.

Or you who don the paper plate
itself, and put some grapes upon it,
or sport the Indian's feather bonnet,
—perversities may aggravate

the natural madness of the hatter.
And if the opera hats collapse
and crowns grow draughty, then, perhaps,
he thinks what might a miter matter?

Here now come the poem's last two stanzas, where what's happening almost gets upstaged by the verbal bravura. A single past tense in their opening line; the unexpected adjective *avernal*—and it dawns on us that a certain uncle and aunt are no longer among the living, are rather shades in a classic underworld. The meter too has changed, iambic to trochaic. Most telling of all, each figure now wears forever the hat appropriate to his or her gender, a lone identifying attribute, limiting and melancholy, like the headstone on a grave.

> Unfunny uncle, you who wore a
> hat too big, or one too many,
> tell us, can't you, are there any
> stars inside your black fedora?
>
> Aunt exemplary and slim,
> with avernal eyes, we wonder
> what slow changes they see under
> their vast, shady, turned-down brim.

Before leaving that graveyard, here is its poet dressed for an occasion we shall all, by tomorrow, have participated in. "I bought a simple B.A. gown at the Coop yesterday," she wrote when she had to read the Phi Beta Kappa poem at Harvard in 1972. "It is so cheap and flimsy—it looks exactly like a child's witch costume for Halloween. But when I received my one honorary degree my hat was too big and the gown reached to the floor and covered my hands. Another recipient, an actress, had had the forethought to get a really mini-gown, above the knees, and she got the biggest hand and the rest of us felt jealous—so I thought I'd take one that more or less fits this time." Afterwards she described the tassel on her hat swinging back and forth across her line of vision "just like a windshield wiper."

So there we are, back at what goes onto and into the head, plus a characteristically functional image, the windshield wiper—merely a tassel perhaps, if not the whole academic experience: that series of rapid, brief, ongoing clarifications which allow us to face, through glass no doubt, but on our worst days, the inrush of emotion and event. It's an image we might want to recall tomorrow—the rest of us mostly bareheaded, in our natural (or unredeemed) state—when the Class of 1980's young men and women go forth under their identical mortarboards. These of course will be too square, too colorless, too obviously exchangeable. But one has to start somewhere.

Foreword to
Le Sorelle Brontë

This remarkable work, a libretto set to popular tunes of variable vintage and familiarity, will be known to few readers. Although over ten years old, it has never been performed for more than a handful of its Alexandria-born poet's friends. As editor I venture to hope that its beauties will attract a larger public.

It is designed for that small red theatre in the soul where alone the games of childhood are still applauded. The obsessive role of music in these games is well known. It gave them form, permanence, and power. Whoever first set the sentence beginning "Passengers will please refrain. . . ." to Dvorák's "Humoreske" made one of those tiny, vital discoveries for which thousands have been grateful ever since. Once made, such a discovery cannot be ignored. The music imperiously calls up the words, and vice versa.

Bernard de Zogheb has given us what may be the first extended works in this genre. A real difference lies between the conventional "ballad opera" and *Le Sorelle Brontë*. Here there is no dialogue; nothing is left to chance. Neither is there a musical accompaniment; the melodies begin and end in the reader's ear or the performer's voice. Experiments with a piano have convinced me of the wisdom behind such austerity.

Dramatically, these are works of high quality. On every page something is made clear about the tenacious inanity of human emotion. As we had gathered from Verdi, it can be set to any tune. We laugh and weep along

An edition of *Le Sorelle Brontë*, one of the home entertainments concocted by Bernard de Zogheb to amuse his friends, was published in New York by Tibor de Nagy Editions in 1963. When the puppet theater, The Little Players, wanted to produce *Vaccanze a Parigi* and *Phaedra*, two of de Zogheb's plays, as "operas," it was found that musical accompaniment suited them perfectly; and when they were performed, a variant of Merrill's essay served as a program note.

with M. de Zogheb's characters; they work like puppets upon us, being at once so much smaller and so much larger than ourselves. Actions are simplified and debased, as befits a "popular" retelling of famous lives. The idiom—no less popular, no less debased—in which they are composed is therefore of the essence. One would not want a syllable changed; I have altered only a few ambiguous spellings.

Le Sorelle Brontë, the earliest of these libretti, is in many respects the most genial. *Byrone* may be more massive, more epic; *Vaccanze a Parigi*, more consciously sparkling. But it is to *Le Sorelle* that one has turned time and again. The reader will search in vain for the gloomy, introspective Brontës of his literature class. In their place, three wild extroverts ride the familiar Mediterranean pendulum between the most lavish endearments and the coarsest recriminations. They are concerned with money, food, sex, and renown. It is what one had always suspected of great writers, and it is but a single strand in the web of truths that M. de Zogheb has woven.

Concerning the language:

From 1880 until just recently, nearly every house in Alexandria had an Italian servant—a Triestine maid, a Genoese chauffeur. It seems to have been the smart thing to do. Dutifully the native servants added the new tongue to their attainments. Count A——'s Osman, impressive in silk robes and white handlebars, spoke it excellently well, if with a Sudanese accent, while his master fancifully continued to address him as an imbecile or a foreign child: "Osman, caro, mi prendere bagno. Tu aprire la kanafia ['tap' in Arabic] adesso? Merci, caro." Thus, the idiom of *Le Sorelle Brontë*—so richly macaronic, so poorly construed and spelled—represents both the bad Italian cultivated by the upper class and a kind of lingua franca used by their domestics.

Overpliant as mistletoe, it is upheld by the stout tree of song. Like the feeble remora glued to the shark's back, it pilots those powerfully shaped, dull-witted tunes—those scavengers of music—toward our hearts' inmost haven, which they had never before attained.

Sometimes the words must shift for themselves. One can go weeks at a stretch without meeting anybody who knows "La Fille du Bédouin." Copyright laws, moreover, would discourage an index of tunes in the present volume. But even where the melody is unknown, the song's title may provide a suggestive rubric. "Civilization" marks the excited decision to visit Brussels; another decision, Anna's to enter a convent, is more cynically labeled "Fools Rush In." Wherever possible, of course, the reader is urged to fit the tune to the text. It will take patience and imagination. The first lines of the libretto, for instance, falling into the following pattern

are easily scanned. The third and fourth lines, rhythmically no different, oblige us to wrench the accents:

> Non ha lácciató nella casa
> Némenó le venti pará.

(What is *venti pará*? the Italian student will ask. It is in fact an old Turkish coin. Lacking such information, the Italian student could do worse than to think first of the French—in this case, *paravents*—so that later he will be able to fathom Carlotta's *falsa cuccia* and Dickens' *libro di chevetto*.) Displacement of accent occurs relentlessly throughout the opera. Let us remember Stravinsky's setting of English and neither scorn nor wince at M. de Zogheb's methods.

Foreword to
Nineteen Poems

Robert Morse was born on Christmas Day 1907 in Toledo, Ohio, and grew up in Evanston, Illinois. His maternal grandfather, a Swede, manufactured player pianos. His daughter married one of the craftsmen; they were divorced while Robert was still a child. As a boy he played the piano accompaniment to silent films in the local theatre. Going on to Princeton, he received an award for painting, and upon graduation was enabled by a grant to study for two years in Paris. Through his roommate there, he made friends with the son of Senator Joseph Cotton, whose daughter Isabel he was to marry some ten years later. They lived in Manhattan, in Bedford Hills, in Stonington, Connecticut; they traveled to Mexico, to Europe, to Bangkok, to Jamaica. Their son Daniel was born in 1942. Robert died in the summer of his seventieth year.

His accomplishments were just that, in the faintly amateur, nineteenth-century sense of the word. He used them, that is, for his own and his friends' pleasure. At the piano he played Mendelssohn, Bach, Schumann; Mozart (whom he regarded as the Second Coming); four-hand arrangements of the Haydn and Beethoven symphonies, the "Dolly" Suite, and "Pulcinella." His touch was modest and clean, his technique (as he liked to put it) "almost perfect." In painting he was a gifted, attentive portraitist. During World War II he visited hospitals, sketching the wounded. There were some who broke months of withdrawal, began to smile and speak again, under his mild, intent scrutiny.

Over the years Robert tried a number of literary forms. He collaborated

Robert Morse was for many years Merrill's talented neighbor in Stonington, and one of the dedicatees of *Water Street*. He appears as Andrew in Merrill's ballad "The Summer People" (included in *The Fire Screen*), and is himself an important character in *The Changing Light at Sandover*. After Morse's death, Merrill had a small edition of his poems printed for his friends and family, and included this memoir.

on a play or two, published some rather creepy short stories. An essay on Dickens appeared in *Partisan Review*. Throughout, he continued to write poetry. *The Two Persephones* was published (Creative Age Press, 1942) through the good offices of Eileen Garrett, the famous witch. These two pieces—the title poem and "Ariadne, a Poem for Ranting," each some hundred pages long—represent the fullest flowering of Robert's early style.

He knew, of course, that he was living in an age of artistic breakthroughs almost automatic in their regularity, of technology at the expense of technique, and "open-ended" content at the expense of closure; knew it, and went on, a touch perversely, as if the rules had never been changed.

It is upon that special bloom of accomplishment in Robert's early poems—their importance to Our Time is another question—that I should like to linger. Here originality is made to feel at home by little more than a modest turn of mind or phrase. The borrowings are—how to say it?—neighborly: a goblin nutmeg from Miss Rossetti, a bunch of lovage from old Landor up the road. (To watch Robert in the kitchen was itself an education.) The basic elements of verse are a second nature to him. He can put them to use in the same way that Queen Victoria along with thousands of her contemporaries, through having learned young how to wash-in that familiar blue or sepia distance, or scribble the spring foliage of an oak, could produce in one sitting a watercolor landscape both competent and evocative. There exist some translations into English of Cavafy by the poet's brother, not himself a literary man—and indeed the effect is a bit diluted; yet his fluent handling of the meters and rhyme schemes surpass that of any later versions known to me. These were things people once had at their fingertips. "Why do you keep doing it, if it's so much trouble?" one of Robert's sitters asked the artist muttering to himself over the difficulties of getting something on his canvas right—for to be sure none of this was as easy as it looked. Back came the answer in a flash: "Because I *can*."

A received style discourages quotation. The elegant plotting of "Ariadne," its interwoven voices, its action visible through the brilliant limpidity of the verse, can best be savored in depth. The tone ranges from Oenone's earthy aside during a speech by Pasiphaë:

> We hacked her bridegroom into steaks and chops
> many a year gone by, if but she knew.

to the Minotaur's touching soliloquy in the maze he has trustingly watched grow up around him:

My thigh grew thick and taut beneath its casing,
the varied hide like rough and patchy moonlight,
the black and white discordant pattern, printed
without, and yet more deeply stained within,
so that a slice or section of my soul
would still have shown the same two-coloured conflict . . .
Be animal! my mother's blood cries out,
my father's sperm replies, Assault the angels!
Between these double stones I grind the children,
and for this cause my only wish is death.

to the high concluding speech of a Bacchus straight out of Giovanni
Bellini:

Whichever goat-foot fingers best the flute,
let him stand forth. Whoever plucks the harp
with most melodious pain, maenad or centaur,
tune his unsullied string. For now to music
she who has slept shall wake, and wake to love,
and love shall crown her with a wreath of stars.

She who has slept shall wake. . . . Some interpreters of the Ariadne legend have it that, far from being saved by Bacchus in person, the poor griefstricken princess simply took to drink. *She who has wept shall slake . . .?*
Either way, the unruffled syntax and firm monosyllables ring true. Are we
on the verge of a discovery?

Having worked so long at these received patterns, fulfilling them line by
line and stitch by stitch, what on earth remained to do with the finished
needlepoint: stuff it with kapok? leave it to the children? Robert's inspiration was to reverse it, exposing then and there that hilarious and disquieting tangle, the underside of idiom. A certain consonant-transposing
slip of the tongue, named for its mortified old victim, produced the spoonerism. The slip lends itself irresistibly to our Anglo-Saxon—as it does not,
say, to French—yet decades went by before anyone thought to try it out as
a rhetorical figure. It may well be that Robert was the first. In any case
"Winter Eve" impressed Auden enough for him to include it in *A Certain
World*.

Although Robert chiefly relied upon the plain, garden-variety spoonerism (take a shower/shake a tower), his gaudy triple hybrids should as well
be admired (gay football fans/fey fatball goons) along with the occasional
freak (Super Bowl, superb owl) all but lost in the surrounding abundance,
and due less to phonemic cross-pollination than to a single sideways-flit-

ting Cabbage-White space. The fair blossom of a phrase and its dry or-
ganic fertilizer (my river's all light/my liver's all right) at every turning "exchange vitalities," as Hugh Kenner said of certain effects in Pound. What,
in a word, *isn't* going on in these late poems? With "Fugue," the last and
most complex of the four, came a diffident explication:

> I wonder what you will make of this . . . I have no opinion, but then
> I don't even know my Muse's first name.
>   The three voices seem to be:
> 1) A dark swamp with water birds, surrounding
> 2) an elevated church-crowned town by the sea, at dawn.
> 3) Burghers and beggars at Carnival time.
>   The skybirds are a kind of coda—the promise of Easter—all de-
> duced from the bird-steeple-rising-sun. It really *is* quite like a fugue
> in structure, which may be no excuse?

He also appended a "key," which reads in part:

> Marsh hen! unlighted still in the gloaming fen,
> lift your heads and eye the towers loosed from night.
> Ruff, ree, and sora! hark to the bells,
> the old clangor of baying bronze. Rails!
> hear out the tolls of shattered bells,
> crack-sided gongs, heart-riven gongs.
> Grey goose! from the half-light
> gander the halls of state, the floating gables.
> All Innocence, in fen-bound home (yes, bobolinks
> too) wonder at the rich-draped sables
> on regal backs, on loving minx and silky punks.

Notice that this version is hardly less bizarre than the original.

When the time came to look again at Robert's "straight" poems (with an
eye to making the present modest selection), at least one reader was so on
his toes that every phrase could be felt as positively trembling with its imminent subversion. In his own odd way Robert had made his lines command the textual scrutiny we reserve for the masters.

IV.

STORIES

Rose

After his second glass of wine he sat at the piano and became an insect. The children applauded his transformation—he had arrived for dinner looking much like any other young man. But as the visitor sat talking with their parents, they perceived suddenly that he had begun to resemble nothing as much as a rabbit, a brown rabbit with erratic eyes and an improbable nose. Robbie saw it first and whispered it to Rose who, because she was an albino and therefore something of a rabbit herself, a white rabbit with crimson eyes, refused to look in his direction until they entered the dining room where she was told to sit opposite him.

By this time, however, no longer a rabbit, he was alternately a frog, a groundhog, a bird, a goldfish. The children watched each evolution with delight, trying, as the meal progressed, to catch him in the act of change, at the moment when the bland greed of the groundhog should become the bland preciosity of the bird, or when, turning from his salad to his sliced oranges, the goldfish eyes were lidded and the whole face grew round and composed and unobtrusive like a fruit. And after dinner he took his wine-glass to the piano and became an insect. The music, too, was insect-music, as though the very notes on the page were eggs to be hatched. The light was faint, because of Rose's weak eyes, but the children could see him smiling and his eyes, which were now enormous, darted against them decorously, as moths beat on a windowpane.

It was their bedtime. "Good night," said Rose to the visitor. "Good night, Rhoda," he replied, resting his hands for a moment on the keys. He doesn't even know my name, thought Rose, all the way up the stairs. But as she stood at her bedroom window, waiting to see him leave, it occurred to her that, by his calling her Rhoda, he had in some way endowed her with a new identity, just as he had changed from one creature to another

Written in 1946. Published in the October 1949 issue of *Glass Hill*, a fugitive mimeographed literary magazine published in Buffalo. This issue also had contributions from Richard Wilbur, John Frederick Nims, Paul Fussell, Byron Vazakas, and James Schevill.

throughout the evening. She was pleased, and braided her white hair until she heard the door shut below, and saw him, faintly luminous, received into the night air. It was the last she ever saw of him or, if she did see him again, she never recognized him.

The next morning Rhoda woke early. When she finished breakfast she told her mother she was going to play at a friend's house; then, wearing her dark glasses to protect her eyes, she ran into the street and began walking toward the center of town. Through the deep green of her glasses Rhoda could guess the extreme brilliance of the day, and she found herself tempted to snatch brief glimpses of the dazzling street out of the sides of her glasses, with her bare eyes. It was cruelly bright; a white wall was brighter than she had ever seen the sun; the sun, flashing on a window-pane, cut into her eye as if it had been a blob of jelly. The sidewalk was strewn with bits of mica; she walked on knives. Her eyes watered from this first blink and she shut them in terror, yet at the same time laughing at the shy ghost of Rose, who had never risked such an injury: shy Rose, laughing, deceitful, wicked Rhoda. Passing a fountain, she looked over the rim of her glasses at the sun striking the jet of water; it was less painful than the time before. When she reached the center of town, she paused before a mirror in a shop window. Carefully she removed her glasses, stared for a moment at her red eyes, her white hair and lashes, her almost translucent skin, then turned deliberately and gazed for five seconds directly into the sun.

She remembered screaming from the pain, which somehow did not reach her until she had covered her eyes with her arm. She was sitting on a bench in a dark hallway, and the first thought that came to her was that she was no longer herself. A man stood beside her, his hand on her forehead. "What's the matter? Are you all right?" he asked softly. "I looked into the sun with my eyes," she whispered. "She's an albino, poor dear," said another voice, a woman's. "Light affects them dreadfully." "Tell me your name," said the soft voice.

She turned her face in the direction of the voice, her arm still across her eyes. "Rosalind," she said.

"Your last name?"

She paused. The question was repeated. "Rabbit," she said very quietly. There was a long silence full, no doubt, of expressive glances. Then someone lifted her arm from her eyes.

"Open your eyes," said the man with the soft voice. "Can you see my hand?" He stroked the air in front of her face; she could see his hand. "Yes," she replied.

"She'll be all right," the man said. He smiled at her—she could see him smile—and told her to stay there for a little while, and that if she wanted he would take her home. "No thank you," said Rosalind. "I'll be all right." They left her alone on the bench in the dark hallway.

In a few minutes she put on her glasses and returned to the street. She bought a bunch of violets at the corner. Rhoda had hated flowers. On all sides, Rosalind saw the streets, the fountain, caught up in a killing light. Surely somewhere a darkness was implied.

The museum was cool and dim. She stopped before each painting and entered it, sat under the trees by the river, fingered the tablecloth sprawling with apples, combed the hair of the naked lady in front of the mirror. In one picture a child lay asleep in the desert; above her an angel flew, holding close to the child's ear a large silvery snail, the graceful animal protruding from its shell like a talisman in some private ritual. The angel had eyes like last night's visitor as he played the piano, and her love for him grew very deep in the minutes that she looked at the painting. She became the child asleep.

A hand touched her shoulder. Turning, she faced a woman in green who gazed at her a long time before speaking.

"Are you prepared for death?" the woman chanted. Rosalind lowered her eyes. "Can you look into your heart and say: I am prepared for death? You are a child and a freak, and therefore the choicest of Christ's innocents, but even a child, even a freak, must be prepared for death which comes to all creatures." The woman moved away, smiling. Rosalind walked out into the sunlight, her violets gripped so tightly in her hand that her palm grew moist and stained by the green leaves. Her eyes still ached a little, as from an excess of sun.

Walking home, she repeated to herself the names she had assumed during the day: Rose, Rhoda, Rosalind. They were all wrong, now that she thought about them, just as it had been wrong to think of the magical visitor as any one of his multiple disguises. He had not been a rabbit, a goldfish, an insect, but something common to them all. And then she said aloud, "Death. Death."

When she reached her house she went swiftly upstairs to her room, and with her fingertip, in the dust upon the windowsill, she wrote her new name.

Driver

A single lesson converted me. I heard the call and would obey it happily ever after. This was in the summer of 1919. My father, back from France, gave me thirty minutes of instruction, after which I was on my own, learning by experience over a network of frail dirt roads flung outward from our village into the surrounding farms. I should be able to describe those roads, those farms. People we knew lived on them. Without question I must have stopped to talk, enjoy a piece of cake or, the following year, a cigarette, to stroke the long face of a stalled animal before, my own face brightening, I leapt back into the sputtering Ford. But I have no such memories. That summer of being fifteen, conjured up today, might have passed exclusively within the moving car. My teeth would clack together over ruts. Off to my right a discoloration of the windshield made for the constant rising of a greenish cloud. I inhaled a warm drug compounded of fuel and field. My feet, bare or sneakered, burned, grew brown, grew calloused. One day at summer's end I noticed in the rearview mirror a tiny claw of white wrinkles at the corner of each eye.

In those days to my embarrassment, as later to my pride, I was not mechanically minded. Other boys my age preferred the languorous exploration of parts to the act itself. I took as much interest in what lay beneath the hood as I did in visualizing my entrails; that is to say, none.

Quite simply, I adored to drive. Enlarged to the dimensions of my vehicle, I took on its blazing eyes, its metallic grimace, its beastlike crouch. Or am I ahead of myself? Were not, at first, humbler qualities instilled by those early models? They rattled but stood upright in sober garb. Fallible, they departed like Pilgrims out of faith, theirs and mine. But now I suspect I am *behind* myself: I have no real memory of that Eden of the Model T, in which the car was yet one more patient beast for man to name and rule. Temptations of Power, Speed, and Style were already whistling loud in

Published in *Partisan Review*, vol. 29, no. 4 (Fall 1962).

my young ears. A windshield clearing, I gazed through the forehead of my genie. Other drivers, rare enough still, I hailed silently as having drunk from the same fountain. At night each learned how to lower his gaze, conscious of what blinding foresights were to be read in the oncoming other's. A needle registered the intensity of the whole experience. When I saw my first wreck, complete with police and bodies under sheets, I found in my heart a comprehension, an acceptance of death that has never—or only lately—deserted me.

My parents were amused, if alarmed. "We gave you the wrong name, boy," my father would laugh (I am called Walker after *his* father), but he soon learned to make notes of mileage and to deduct the fuel I was using from my allowance. "Walker, if you're going driving at this hour of the night," my mother would begin. "Your mother's right," my father would add as I rose yawning from the dark oval table where we ate, brushing to the floor, like any destiny they might have arranged for me, a constellation of crumbs. For by then I had ceased to take seriously, or indeed to recall, anything that occurred while I was off the road. The abrupt standstill left me groggy and slow on my feet, as in dreams or on the ocean floor. My parents gesticulated, their lips moved. I cannot explain their helplessness. I was a boy, perhaps in my first year of college: I did not even—but yes! By that time I did have a car of my own.

Once more I have paused to see if I can remember how it came about; I cannot. I can shut my eyes and imagine odd jobs, see my hand, wrist bare and brown beneath a rolled-up cuff, pressing a plunger marked VANILLA— a shiny brownish stream braids downward into the glass; or holding a brush and rhythmically, as if to obliterate any detail that might distinguish such a moment from a million others like it, covering a clapboard wall with ivory paint. I can invent, if not truly recall, the death of a grandparent, a legacy in which I must have shared to the extent of a yellow diamond or dented gold watch immediately pawned. Anyhow, I drove to college in my first car, old-fashioned but sufficient, and finished my education with honors, having been promised a new car if I did.

What is strange is that my teachers complimented me upon my excellent mind. If only I could think of a single occasion on which I used it!

Towards the end of the summer following my graduation the question of what I was to do with my life must at last have arisen with some intensity. Evenings come back, of straight roads traveled in fury, the dog on the seat next to me listening while I rehearsed manifestoes aloud. "No," I told him. "You may be my father but I refuse to work in the business you have built up. I want to travel, get to know my country. Besides, I scorn both your methods and your product. What are these prosperous times for, if not to. . . ." It may be that I ended by delivering this speech to the right audience. More likely it sank without a ripple into those trustful brown eyes fixed upon me through the warm and whizzing night.

I became, in short—but it does not matter what I became. If I am to set down the truth about my life it will not be found in dates and labels but in this brief memoir of my supreme pastime and of those who now and then shared it with me.

My first passenger was the dog I have mentioned. He was brown, short-haired, virtually nameless—we called him Pal. He and I had loved each other for many years. By the time he began to drive with me, habit and trust had taken the place of passionate contact, kisses, exclamations. Neither now had any particular need of attention. Pal's head would be thrust, tongue flapping gladly, into a torrent of sunlit odors. If I reached to stroke him absently he would look round, not displeased but puzzled, then turn with one token thump of his tail back to the window. When I talked, he would, as I have said, listen, especially at night. His face, no longer transfigured by adoration, had grown serious, almost ascetic. I felt he wanted me now merely to illustrate certain still baffling but minor aspects of human behavior, against the day when his own turn came.

A truck hit him, one morning early, in front of our house. The cook kept marveling over how the driver, "crying like a baby," had carried him right into the kitchen. I found him there on newspapers when I came down for breakfast.

I am glad to say that in all my years of driving I have never been responsible for the death of an animal. Nothing pains me more than those little corpses that accumulate on our highways. The first one appears just after sunrise—a rabbit, or cat, glittering with fresh dark blood—but as the day wears on they become uncountable and unrecognizable, a string of faded compresses dried out by fevers they had merely intensified. All night they are mourned by shining green or amber eyes. And by dawn they have become part of the road itself.

Not long after the death of Pal I left home.

I still preferred to drive by myself. At college, the car had made me popular. Every weekend filled it with classmates, girls, banners, flasks. I drank from the flasks, I waved the banners, I kissed the girls. And yet it was all beside the point. Their emphasis was forever upon *destinations*—the conventional site of waterfall and moon and mandolin; or else of the shabby "club" where liquor could be bought and consumed, where one danced to a phonograph in the red dark. Hours would pass this way, pleasurably no doubt. But I think there were few in which I did not once ask myself: How long will it last? When can we go back to the car?

This is something that happened not long after I left home:
  One lovely autumn day I found myself on a road that dipped and rose through golden shrubbery and tall, whitened trunks, when out of nowhere, on a steep curve, two figures appeared. They were all but under my wheels before I could stop: an old country couple patiently signaling for a ride. I let them in the back door. They were brown and wrinkled, dressed in patched blacks and raveling grays. The woman wore knitted stockings. In both hands she held a coffee can planted with herbs. As we drove I would catch sight of her in the mirror, watching them, lips moving, giving them courage. The old man carried on his lap a basket of apples, pocked, misshapen ones that nevertheless had been beautifully polished. Perhaps he had not been in a car before; he kept looking about and moistening his lips. I asked how far they were going. When neither answered I asked again, this time turning to look square in their faces. They looked back. The old man rested his fingertip against the window-glass, appreciatively. I understood his pleasure and was pleased myself to have brought it about. We drove in silence for a number of miles.
  Then the old man began to utter noises of unrest. Seeing no house or road, I drove on. His dismay increased. "Master," said the woman eventually; and when I had stopped the car, "there was a road," she said, and waited. I realized that they had wanted to get out, and, rather than cause them an extra inconvenience, I backed some hundred yards to where, indeed, a narrow dirt road forked off.
  I followed it without hesitation. An emerald green ribbon grew between its ruts. Overhead, branches met. I felt a foolish smile cross my face. The road itself soon petered out. We came to a halt in the middle of a cluttered barnyard. Dogs, pigs, doves, and a few small, soiled children moved in and out of larger, motionless shapes, a rusty tractor, a cow. One lone peacock trailed his feathers in the hard dirt. To greet us, four young people rounded different far corners and stared taciturn and crimson-eared at the car. Were

they all descended from my old couple? I could imagine that, instead of expelling anyone from the garden, God and the angels had found it hand-somer to pack up and go themselves, for all that could be done without *their* guidance and example.

My passengers had alighted and were making signs of hospitality. Too young to be gracious, I could only blush and stammer a protest. The po-etry of the invitation depended upon its refusal. Each of us, in fact, must have felt as much. In a single gentle movement the old woman set down her herbs, took an apple from her husband's basket, and handed it to me. As I circled the yard they stood waving. A dove fluttered out of my path.

I got back to my original road. The sun, pale and lowering, was waiting for me beyond the first crest. The apple tasted bitter, hard; it could not have been an eating apple. I tossed it away with a shudder. Night fell before I came to a town.

From now on I would offer rides to people. Absently at first, discouraging talk, moved chiefly by the missionary's fervor to acquaint others with Rev-elation. I drove well—too well, perhaps. As I rounded curves with a grace-ful one-handed gesture, certain passengers would look admiringly at me instead of at the road. I was young, husky, I had a pleasant face; people told me their stories. Having little to say myself, I became, depending on the occasion, grandson, son, big brother, kid brother, and would do my best not to destroy the illusion while striving to deflect attention back to the main points, those Olympian secrets of Fuel and of the Wheel. Until one day, inevitably, I added to these a role that by its nature and at my age was less easily given up than the rest: the role of lover.

She sat beside me at a counter one early evening, blonde, full-blown, and looking heartbroken. She had to go to another town, not far, but had missed the last bus and was I headed that way? Well, she paid for my coffee and I drove her off. Soon she was chatting and patting her hair. "I thought you'd be gone when I came back with my grip. Sure are a nice boy to do this. Shouldn't call you a boy, though. Bet you know more than I do!"

I can smile now at my innocence. She guided me past her town, past the next. Night was falling, I wanted to stop. Even when I understood and drove without protest, indeed with my heart thumping, down the dark dirt road, her hand reaching across me to turn off the lights—even then I had a surprise in store for me. Opening my door, I started out. "Where you off to?" said my friend coyly. I stood frozen with stupefaction. It was going to happen in the *car!* I forced a casual reply and turned from her to the underbrush, lifting my face to the stars, letting her imagine what she liked, while I tried to make sense of my feelings.

I knew that love was made in cars. Mine, though, *my* car—could I put it to these uses? And were the uses high or low? As for love, I can use the word today, but a molten gulf separated its earlier meanings (a girl to be kissed between drinks, an imitative couple in the backseat) from *this* experience, wringing and intense, that within an hour had left the dry track of a tear on either cheek as I drove deeper and deeper into some dark Western state. The woman nodded at my side. I did not know whether I had degraded or fantastically enlarged the road ahead.

That first love rose and set, establishing a pattern others were to follow. First came days, or weeks, during which the fact that we desired, but did not know, one another, kept us both good-humored. Then, gradually, at the woman's insistence, our passion overflowed into rooming houses and hotels, although with luck I was still able to confine it to the car, reserving our shared bed for sleep. Mornings, we drove on; the woman would not mind, not at first, waiting in the car while I transacted my business. Thinking it over, I shall not emphasize my profession by concealing it. I was a salesman, of countless different things, encyclopedias, garden supplies, trusses, religious texts, all or none of these. I would reach into the backseat for my case. The car door shutting behind me threw a switch. Two minutes or two hours later I would be back, whatever had passed between me and "the lady of the house" forgotten now unless translated into clues: money in my wallet, a thumbnail blackened by a slammed door, more than once liquor on my breath and lipstick on my ear. The patience of the woman in the car came to be tried. We would drive on doggedly, a capsule of discord, she questioning, pleading; myself silent, not guilty, amazed by the recurrence, from one to the next, of the same demands, the same voice first injured then sarcastic before its final sickening fall into a nastiness without nuance or remedy.

I would want only to be rid of her.

I soon learned to avoid these climaxes. At the first sign of strain—when the woman, say, was no longer content to do her nails in the car, but sat making lists of food to buy or friends to surprise with postcards—I would persuade her that I meant to stop several days in a certain town. On being shown to our hotel room, I would make impetuous love to her before going down to "see about the car" (in which I would happen to have left my things) and driving off into the night alone. Those were hours of resolution, of pride in my lonely calling. The renounced woman roared in the motor and wailed in the fleeing dark.

Somewhere I have read that driving is a substitute for sexual intercourse. I am as good an authority as the next man on both subjects, and can affirm without hesitation that for thrills, entertainment, and hygiene the woman is no match for the automobile. There is furthermore the efficient, even temper of the latter, and the fact that you may obtain a younger and more beautiful one as often as you like.

There were bad moments, though. I had no ties. My parents were dead. I was thirty-five years old, one moving body inside another. What does anyone do in my position? I got married.

Muriel.

This poor, foolish, virgin librarian had staked her job, her room, perhaps her entire future, on a summer's trip West. Up to then she had spent her best moments scanning the heavens above Iowa, filling her little heart with the play of clouds and tints, and her little head with the certainty that if once those skies were seen reflected in some vast expanse of water—the Pacific Ocean for instance—all would be changed, life would no longer pass her by, she herself would turn lovable overnight.

Again, that curious faith in destinations.

She never saw the Pacific, she may or may not have become lovable, but life definitely did not pass her by—*I* stopped for her. She had been resting on her suitcase at a crossroads; a placard round her neck read *California or Bust*. She saw the car stop, saw that it was powerful enough to take her where she wanted to go. She was too tired, hungry, and sunburned to wonder about its driver. That came later, offshoot of the basic physical infatuation with the machine.

We *headed* West—my intentions were honorable. We might have gone all the way but for that billboard somewhere in Nebraska advertising a "Motorists' Chapel. Worship in Your Car." My weakness for novel experience within the traditional framework, or chassis, together with Muriel's empty, peeling face, caused me to stop, propose to her, and, once accepted, make inquiries that led to the first marriage ceremony ever performed in an automobile. A national magazine paid all expenses. For weeks people recognized us wherever we went. Many wished they had thought of doing the same thing.

My marriage was not unhappy, it was unreal. Legally each other's dearest belonging, we spent, as I might have foreseen, more and more time in rooms, eating places, shops, or under trees with sandwiches and books of verse. "And if thy mistress," read Muriel aloud, "some rich anger shows,

> Emprison her soft hand and let her rave,
> And feed deep, deep upon her peerless eyes."

Parked up a hill, the car shimmered in waves of heat, gazed wrathfully, peerlessly out over our heads.

Muriel's underclothes hung drying on a cord rigged across the backseat. She wanted to settle down. I tried to dissuade her from this step, the one of all that would lose me to her. Had she forgotten California? Ah, she didn't *need* California now! The denouement can be imagined. One cool blue morning that fall, or the next, I left our secluded cottage—a last rose blooming by the gate, a letter of farewell written and ready to mail when I stopped, if I ever stopped. I got into the car for the first time in three days. A miniature Muriel waved from the house into my rearview mirror, then staggered abruptly and lurched with a whine out of sight. I was off, life lay ahead once more! In the nearest town faces stopped me. It was the morning after Pearl Harbor.

A voice on the radio was already predicting the rationing of fuel.

I quickly appraised the situation. Six months too old for the draft, I could settle down where I was, with Muriel, in the middle of our continent. This life at best would permit me the daily drive of a few miles to and from some nearby parachute or food-packaging plant. I decided on the spot to enlist in the Ambulance Corps. Weeping over the telephone, Muriel promised to wait. Laughing, I promised to send money. A year later I was driving in North Africa.

I think of landscapes, of roads erased by sand forever rippling under washes of light. A grove of palms, women in veils, the tank burning on the horizon. Above all, a vastness in which hovered black birds of indeterminate size. Whatever the scale, it was not human. This comforted us; we permitted ourselves colorful, passionate acts, at once proving and outweighing our tiny statures.

Made up of volunteers, our company had an odd, aristocratic flavor. Books were passed around—Tolstoi, *Les Liaisons dangereuses*, collections of fairy tales. These showed me how far I had gone along certain roads never noticed while concentrating upon their macadam counterparts. I found in myself traces of the sage, the pervert, and the child.

Nothing bored me, nothing frightened me. Up from a half-hour's sleep in the shade of a wall, I would face into a warm wind blowing at the exact speed of my life. The laugh and the wound, the word of the wise man and the bullet's sunburst through glass, converged and drove me onward, light as a feather. It became all but superfluous to take the wheel again in search of casualties.

I see now that I did not belong. My heroics were prompted by exuberance, not humanity. My passengers suffered and prayed and died like the natives of a country I was content merely to visit. I had myself photographed smiling in front of grand Roman arches preserved for centuries in that climate. And then I went home. Sand covered them quickly. The war was won and lost, both.

Ours was now the oldest in a cluster of similar bungalows, each occupied by an older couple or single woman waiting, like Muriel, for her hero to return. This colony, having taken my wife to its heart—"you clever, darling child," I heard her addressed with my own ears—welcomed me avidly. Neighbors came to the door bearing covered dishes. Muriel kissed them, led them to where I squirmed. Poor, popular, outgoing Muriel. I was outgoing, too, in a sense. "Sorry," I would say, leaping up. "You caught me on my way to work."

My restlessness neither fazed nor puzzled them. It did me. Often I turned back after an hour on the road. People were buying anything, I could have sold rocks. And yet—

One day I drove home to witness the following scene. A car had stopped, motor running. My wife stood leaning across the gate, talking to the driver. A bleak wind lifted her hair and skirt, she was having to raise her voice. I heard nothing. As her eyes darted my way the car moved on. Its driver had got lost, Muriel said; she had given him directions. I shrugged. We did live off the main road.

Two nights later I heard the truth. We were returning from a drive-in movie. We had sat, not touching, in the car and watched a couple of starlets barely out of grammar school learn "the hard way" (burned biscuits, Madame de Merteuil for a neighbor, a miscarriage leading to a reconciliation under moonlit palms) that it took two to make a marriage. A mile from home Muriel spoke. "Walker, let's stop here." She had to touch my arm. "Can't we stop."

"If that's how you feel."

"I mean the *car*."

"Of course you do." I pulled uneasily to the side of the road.

"Now let's get out."

"What's got into you? We could be home now."

"Just for five minutes. I want to talk to you."

"All right, talk to me."

"Not in the car. *Please*. I can't think in the car."

"You said you wanted to talk. Make up your mind."

Muriel started to weep.

With my feet on earth, my head emptied automatically. The night stung and shone. Something of that cold clarity may have prompted her words; of those distances, too, without a sense of which the starry sky would be just another town on a hillside, soon to be entered and left behind. I tried to take her hand. These were things she did not need to tell me. At one point a silence fell, long enough for a small oblivious animal to amble past us on the icy road. I looked wistfully after it.

At last we were heading home. "You can keep the house," I said.

"You haven't understood, Walker," said Muriel in a higher, sadder voice than usual. "I don't want you to go. I don't love him—yet. But you're driving me to it."

"Driving you?" I stepped on the accelerator, wanting to turn it into a joke. "You mean like this?"

The car jolted forward.

"Yes!" Muriel screamed. "Exactly like this!"

Then, in our lights, two amber-green eyes were glowing. I pulled out of the creature's way. We turned over.

Muriel was not killed—I have never killed a living thing. But there was no further question of staying together. And early the following summer she and her new husband were drowned in a storm on Lake Tahoe.

Towards my next car, as towards the next and the next and the next, I felt a kind of disabused tolerance. Each could have been my heavy, middle-aged person—not yet a source of suffering, no longer a source of delight.

In fact I have nothing more to relate except the incident which decided me, some weeks ago, to write these pages. Today I wonder if what I have set down leads anywhere, let alone to that warm, bright morning.

I had bought a convertible—not that it promised to change anything— and had thrown back the top before setting out. It was late June in the South. My road led without warning to a group of old-fashioned buildings, shaggy with ivy and vacant behind pale buff window shades. A black and gold sign in their midst read STATE TEACHERS' COLLEGE. I had slowed down for no reason—the place was clearly deserted—when a young man stepped from under a lintel that bore in large block-lettered relief the word POULTRY. He raised a careless hand, as if saying, "There you are!" to a friend.

Although I take no riders nowadays I stopped for him. He was dressed with an undergraduate's nattiness: white shoes and seersucker. In my day he would have carried a mandolin. After we began to move he named a town some fifty miles distant—some fifty miles out of my way, too, if a "way" was what I had—then closed his blue eyes, enjoying the ride, I supposed.

He opened them soon enough and, turning to me, made, in the pleasantest of voices, a series of wholly uncalled-for remarks. Cars had grown (he began) too ugly for words. So pompous, so unwieldy. He only rode in them when absolutely essential. The seats were no longer covered in cloth or leather, but some hideous synthetic material. The dashboards were cushioned. As for the color schemes—well, why not put a bedroom on wheels and get it over with? I decided he was a fairy. I suppose *you* fly, I nearly said.

As if he had read my mind he burst into laughter. His name was Sandy, he continued. He had known I was coming. Hadn't *I* felt, too, that something unusual lay ahead that morning? "Look," I said firmly, but he went right on. I could expect something far more unusual than him. A woman, a Princess, was waiting for him—for us. Already I was part of their mission, his and hers. I felt him watching me closely. The Princess was a medium. I knew what that meant? Good. They had been for many months in communion with a guide—did I understand?—a guide who at last had judged them ready to receive and carry out a set of elaborate instructions. They were to fly that very afternoon to the West Coast, thence to an island in the South Pacific. They had been given quite a timetable of duties, contacts with strangers minutely described by this guide as to both appearance and spiritual pedigree—one of the most useful was to be a thirteen-year-old fisherboy who in a previous life had been Sandy's grandfather. Just what they hoped to accomplish he was forbidden to say. But the general aim, I might as well know, was to save mankind from annihilation.

I shot him a startled look; he was smiling. Beneath his tanned cheeks the young color danced.

"You've seen the newspapers," said Sandy. "The end gets nearer and nearer. Nobody else is really trying to stop it."

Casting about for a badly needed plausible touch at this point, it occurs to me to mention his "hypnotic voice." It was nothing of the sort, rather a boyish, matter-of-fact voice, yet I hesitate to put forth any *serious* explanation for what was happening. My early impression of him had vanished. In a strange apprehensive sleepiness I found myself hanging upon his words. I thought of the "missions" of my own youth, the awakenings I dreamed of bringing to my fellow man. Rooted behind my steering wheel of white, sun-warmed plastic, I had a glimmering of how those others would have reacted, as I did now, half with the drowsy numbness of Muriel's favorite poet, half with a heart shocked by its sudden pounding.

He talked the entire hour. Of that crazy quilt only scraps come back today. Good and Evil existed, pitted against one another. He, Sandy, had seen an angel routed by Lucifer in the New York Subway. The beautiful white yarn of vapor trails was being used to entangle us all by statesmen, adult impersonators, lurching from one trouble-spot to the next. Their explosions in the press and on TV caused a kind of horrible psychic fallout in people's living rooms. Forces in the next world were fighting to reach us with messages rarely heard, almost never heeded. The resurrection of the body was at hand; we were no longer to be slaves of—personality? nationality? His exact word escapes me; no matter. We had reached the town. The Princess might or might not see fit to tell me more. Sandy had already implied—with a touch of condescension which, in my increasingly pliable state, turned my very bones to wax—that I had been chosen from among thousands to help them through this stage of their mission.

"A lot depends on what she thinks of you," he said earnestly.

We parked in front of a willow-shaded Tourist Home. From the car I watched Sandy leap up the steps to the porch and into the house without knocking. A fly lit on my face. I could not have driven away.

He held open the screen door for a girl in a black, armless dress. She was using a cane and watching her feet, in sandals, descend the porch steps. At the car door she hesitated, then turned upon me the face of a middle-aged woman, sick-eyed and freckled, but not by this year's sun. I got out to help her. She motioned Sandy into the rear seat and settled herself awkwardly up front.

I looked back at the house.

"No baggages," said the Princess. "This." She patted a bulging leather purse. It sprang open. She took out a scarf of milky chiffon to keep her hair in place. "Everything gets done for us, so we travel light. You are very kind," she added in the same breath, ridding herself as neatly of the obligation as of the unwanted suitcases. "We—I can say?—*anticipate* kindness."

"I think she means," Sandy began.

"He know what I mean," said the Princess grandly. "He understand my English." She gave a formal signal to depart.

Idiotically, I relished my place in their little aristocracy. It was all so effortless! Poor clods (I thought) who had still to rely on telephones and timetables. I drove with my whole heart, bent on getting my passengers to their destination.

The airport was thirty miles farther on. Noon had struck; the plane would leave at half past one. Leaning forward to make himself heard, Sandy pointed out turns. Once on the straight road he announced as if casually, "This isn't a scheduled flight. A DC-4 picks us up at this field and takes us to New Orleans where a connecting jet to San Diego will be waiting."

I nodded too quickly. We were driving through broad fields.

"Oh, not waiting for *us*. We mean nothing to them. Any delay will be dismissed in the usual way—a motor check, a confused weather report. Don't you know what goes *on* at airports? Let me tell you, it's a scandal. They're debasing something pure and rare. I have to say this in spite of times like now, when their obtuseness works to our advantage."

Here Sandy digressed at length on the subject of flying. I was too much a part of the adventure, by now, to feel the annoyance his earlier speech about automobiles had provoked. Instead, I listened humbly, as ready as not to accept the judgment implicit in his words. I shall not try to reproduce them. The impression he gave was of intense, disquieting enthusiasm for aircraft, for certain models over others, for the view one came, as a pilot, to take of things. In the Islands, he remarked, they would be flying their own plane.

My self-respect spoke up: "But you don't even drive a car!"

I never felt it took great perception to tell the drivers from the rest. All the same, Sandy shouted with delight. "You knew that! What a beginning! Did you hear him, Anya? He's one of us!"

At my side the Princess started—had she been asleep?—and spoke in a new gruff voice whose accents were not hers. "The road first traveled is the longest road," said this voice.

Sandy touched my shoulder. "It's Uncle Sam."

"Who?"

"Our guide. We call him that. She's in a trance."

I looked at her in alarm. Beyond the whipping scarf her jaw hung open.

"Don't worry," said Sandy.

"It is a long and painful road," intoned the Princess. "It will seem shorter and easier a second time."

"Is this message for us, Uncle Sam?" Sandy inquired.

"For your friend. Wait."

"He's such a darling," said Sandy. "He followed the Princess to America last year and *loves* it. He wants to be the fifty-first state."

Suddenly from the Princess came a high, plaintive, uncertain voice: "Walker, have you learned to walk yet?"

I gripped the wheel for dear life.

"I couldn't teach you. Learn to walk, Walker. Learn."

"All right," I said stupidly. "Where are you, Muriel?"

"Here beside you. There's someone else."

"That's the Princess, Muriel."

"Not *her*," the voice giggled. "Someone *here*. Someone who loves you."

I could barely whisper, "Who?"

The Princess whimpered excitedly through her nose.

"It's Pal," said Muriel's voice. "Your little dog."

My throat filled with tears. My hands fell from the wheel. Sandy must have kept us from driving off the road.

We sat there. The Princess was inspecting me with vague, puffy eyes. She gave me a Kleenex from her purse, and shifted her attention to her own appearance where deeper ravages had been sustained. Into a large oval mirror she peered, touching a fingertip to her various features, testing their firmness. Soon she was intently painting her mouth.

Without a word I pressed the starter. They were watching, waiting to bind me closer and closer to them, but I kept gazing straight ahead, mile after mile. I had borne all I could. I already believed.

I believed, too, at the deserted rural airport where I deposited my passengers and waited with them. I believed well after they had exchanged that single faintest of frowns with which one tries to shake a stopped watch into running. When I left at their insistence—as if my presence had thrown the wrench into the works!—I drove away still believing.

The road climbed. At one turning I was able to look back and distinguish, in a dream's deepening light, the two figures motionless outside the locked hangar.

Something glittered on the front seat; the Princess had left her mirror. I peered at myself in it—I am nearly sixty—and threw it down. Phony, hysterical pair! There was no more to be learned from them than from those fat "psychical" studies of the last century, with titles like "Footsteps behind the Veil of Life" and "The Nine Stages: Dante's Vision Corroborated." Though I had never opened one, I have only to think of their Victorian embonpoint, their black or purple bombazines, to invest that whole day with the worst kind of dowdy ineffectuality. Uncle Sam indeed! Would the American Way of Life save mankind from annihilation? Was *that* the level of arcane innuendo from beyond the grave? One thing I knew, though no prophet: their plane would be a long while coming. They might have gone further by horse and buggy.

If I am angry now it is because I still believe, but not in them.

Driving, I kept glancing skyward, prepared, in spite of everything, for the glint of wings. Cross with myself, miles from my road, how gladly I would have hailed an order of machine superior to mine. To this day I cannot see a plane without stopping to wonder, to reenter those last lonely hours in the car—the mirror, face up beside me, shooting provocative flashes into the bare heavens.

Peru:
The Landscape Game

Our cub plane growls and quivers for the pounce. K has fallen asleep, out of simple nervous tension. It is still dark. Lima twinkles under its habitual dense ceiling.

The luggage label of the Hotel Périchole is a much reduced page from the Offenbach score.

There. We're off.

Last night after dinner a white-haired lady from Zurich had us play that psychological game in which each person describes a house he then leaves in order to take an imaginary walk. One by one he discovers a key, a bowl, a body of water, a wild creature, and finally a wall. Free association is invited at any stage, and nothing explained until the last player has spoken.

The house is your own life, your notion of it. Trees roundabout stand for Other People.

The key is Religion. The bowl, Art. The water, Sex.

The wild thing is Yourself—the unconscious.

The wall is Death.

Our companion, K decided, was really Jung's widow. She noted our replies on a paper napkin:

> K—apartment whose vine-covered terrace overlooks a piazza with fountains;
> small gold key, to a lost diary?
> goblet of iridescent glass, quite undamaged, which he kneels to fill at
> a clear deep river;

Published in *Prose*, no. 2 (Spring 1971).

a polar bear—K runs away;
high brick wall complete with electrified alarm system, enclosing
the estate of an industrial magnate.
J—Victorian house, many rooms, gingerbread, topiary garden;
key to grandfather clock;
mixing bowl, cracked—fearing botulism, I kick it out of my path;
a pond stagnant in appearance but full of activity: lily pads, tad-
poles, buzzing dragonflies;
a raccoon, masked, washing its little black hands on the far side—
it runs away;
stone wall exactly my height, over which appear eaves and chim-
neys of a house much like the one I started out from.

"Are you sure you haven't played this game before?" asked the Frau
Doktor, not unreasonably. Yet she interpreted our answers at length, scanning our faces for the intelligence we were too far gone to muster.

"What was it your bowl meant?" K yawned, up in the room.

"I'm a good mixer. But liable to go to pieces."

Sunrise. The foothills of the Andes—crumpled brown paper everywhere
mended with lighter or darker oblongs of the same, and riddled by a can-
yon's bookworm course.

At once and stupidly, we succumb to the altitude. K's nose is bleeding, I
cannot breathe. Small unreal men emerge from the hotel. Are they por-
ters, these meerschaum apparitions in espadrilles and ponchos striped
pink and rust, who lift our bags onto their heads and trot off in what can't
be the right direction? Two others in black alpaca cutaways advance like
penguins—¿permiso?—and taking our elbows guide us, with frequent
pauses, up a flight of steps. It must be early still. Tiny gold crumbs adorn
my Samaritan's white piqué waistcoat. The steps, of stone like our legs,
are seven in number and sparkle with frost.

Opening the register at random I see a familiar name: Mary Klohr, August 1938. A window behind the desk frames scenery for which words will
be found another time. Our room is ready. K is handed a profusely tasseled
iron KEY.

We give onto a courtyard. Ice films the dung-spattered water-trough.
Next to an "unhinged but brilliant" green door hangs an armadillo—quite

incurable, K suspects as he unpacks vial after vial of pills. His nose bleeds on. The maid, impervious to our pantomime, leaves a star drowned in the thick glass decanter on the chest of drawers. She has no "soul" in *our* sense, of individual resonance to this or that. But she knows how to live 12,000 feet above the sea. We shoo her away and lie down, overcome.

The Cuzco market is a grass-and-cobble arena outspread among baroque, whitewashed ramparts. Smelling of the tinsmith, the tanner. From under their awnings Indian women whistle and coo to attract us. No young one without a baby. Wherever you look blouses have been unfastened to expose a single breast, full, soft, and of the pearliest gray.

This booth sells only skeins of string dyed burnt orange. Instead of letters the Incas used knotted cords. The "yarn" as history. No older woman without a bobbin in her hands.

Poverty, death—the great shears everywhere poised and parted.

Mirrors. Papayas. Ponchos. Nescafé.

Woven stuffs by the bolt. The Incas lived in communes. Ornament was forbidden in their houses, mothers were forbidden to dandle their own children. Lives crisscrossed, warp and woof, with *relevance*—coarse dense fabric of the state.

A witchcraft booth. Herbs. Candy hearts. A bin of dried-up doll dinosaurs. The llama fetus has powerful juju.

On back streets you will see unlit, dirt-paved shops which contain a single sewing machine, nothing else. Or a tall glass cupboard piled full of unleavened loaves. Silence. Or the click of billiards behind closed doors.

A booth where newts and lizards of all sizes hang in festoons, their baby limbs twitching. An Indian delicacy? Necklaces for the ogress?

Shiny purple-black beans in piles. Piles of white maize. Great petrified tubers splattered with grayish mould.

I walk and walk, buying none of it. Entirely cut off, entirely at one.

Mangled portions of meat. Skins stiff with blood.

Saddlebags. Ponchos. Oranges.

The silver ornaments smell of cardamon. K buys a bracelet for L. Farther on, I pick out a shallow unglazed BOWL for DMc. It has one vaguely genital lip, for pouring, and a stern, long-suffering face worked into the opposite rim. The handles are two arms akimbo.

RECITATIVE

Four exquisite young llamas eye the crowd as in a ballroom. Four Natashas.

A sentence from Prescott:

> The animals were no less above their comprehension; and when the cock crew, the simple people clapped their hands and inquired what he was saying.

The train, after doggedly trailing for hours the rapids of the Urubamba, gives up with a sigh. We get out.

(Far, far north, this capricious water, swollen beyond recognition, scummed with topaz and hostess to ten million razor mouths, becomes unalterable law. The river steamer blisters and moans. The banks suck their gums endlessly as it shudders upstream.)

"Good day," says a small man in whose amber features we discern the fossil slave. "I am your guide, Porfirio."

The site of Machu Picchu would make a blind man's heart pound.

You must imagine an unscalably huge system of interlocking pyramids and cones, clawed, raddled, packed in dry ice all smoking and swirling in the high damp green. Where you stand their upper twentieth has been battered almost level to form this rock garden of touching gravity.

Bamboo. Thatch. Cloud. A primitive Japan. Le Douanier Sesshu.

Monoliths made to fit like a puzzle. The Katsura palace built by trolls.*

Innumerable terraces rake Huayna Picchu's vertical jungle like any temple garden. This paradox of steaming nature at the most rarefied level is something we have all had to contend with in our day. As in the person of an epileptic monk serene amid utter instability—for earthquakes take lives by the thousand in these young, visionary mountains—danger and prayer assume a single face.

Which comes and goes in mist—a floating world. Suddenly you are left alone with the Inca-Kola bottle cap underfoot.

Then, the great eye focusing as through a burning glass, you plunge on, goaded.

K says, "I don't see any of that. Why complicate things? This place is simply heaven. I mean, you go up through clouds to get there, and what do you find but all these good old friends—begonias, hydrangeas, gladiolas,

*By hobbits, say the Swedes we meet in La Paz. Each to his own, says K.

Spanish moss. I'm serious. That's a red gladiola right over there. It's our own fault if we thought they were tacky in the world below."

Meanwhile Porfirio keeps emphasizing History—heads on pikes, imperial flatulence, drinking parties, disease—until what's to choose between past and present. We know these stories, we would hardly be here if we didn't. To make him stop, we inquire about his own life, and he obliges with a smiling tale of hardship, obedience, decency, such as one tells to any stranger *just in case*. Only now do we notice how far off the path he has led us. He gestures for us to wait outside a tin-roofed shack. "Here," says K, "is where Porfirio kills yet two more Yanquis." But from the stifling dark interior the little man emerges with a BABY in his arms—"mi niña." She is complete with eyelashes and earrings. Her complexion is some magic chocolate made out of pink rose petals.

While lunching on seven kinds of tuber and a sweet bean tart, K and I play the landscape game with the genius loci:

His house is Sagittarius. "Mutable, fiery, and masculine," according to K's horoscope paperback. "Travel, self-projection to new horizons," are indicated.

His key. Here we disagree. I want C-sharp minor (the three Urubamba-maidens lamenting the theft of their gold by international museum directors), but K would settle for a key to the puzzle of the stones.

His bowl: golden.

His body of water: a drop of eau de cologne; he bathes in it.

His wild creature: the condor (K); Porfirio's baby (J).

His wall: cloud masonry he ascends and paces, gleaming fitfully down upon all our houses.

Indeed, Huayna Picchu is now altogether lost behind a WALL of mist. K slings his binoculars and strides off in its direction.

J: You're not thinking of climbing it! Whatever for?

K (already indistinct): Because it isn't there . . .

Midafternoon. I found in a pocket certain leaves Porfirio had given me when I asked what he was chewing. Leaves the shape and green of bay, only more pliable; bitter to the taste. From a westerly terrace this steep trail led downward, dizzily, never looking back. Steps cut into rock, matchstick railings, slick ledges curling like smoke above the chasm. I chewed my leaves, assurance flowed through me, and I sent grateful thoughts back to Porfirio as down and down I zigzagged, all but dancing.

I see now that this place is a vast theatre turned inside out, its lichened granite and green plush parterres, balconies and smoking rooms thrown open to the elements. Not far from a chandelier forever dimming and brightening I am seated among ferns in an acoustically perfect loge. A gala by Berlioz is under way. Having whipped the pit to a shimmering spate, he now introduces daring new effects (tropical birds, chug of that toy loco-motive) among the strings and reeds, the gongs and cymbals—

And something nearer? The pounding in my ears is after all / Not so much terror as a WATERFALL / Shaking and shimmering till the blond / Air has been atomized to diamond—

An icy mountain stream. Voice of mercury. Elvire Cascadin singing the "Nuits d'Été"—

> Tu me pris encore emperlée
> Des pleurs d'argent de l'arrosoir,
> Et parmi la fête étoilée
> Tu me promenas tout le soir

                                        —and I think of you whom I am too old to love, yet love so intensely. No. From *within* inten-sity: a dry place, a niche behind the waterfall, yes.

Stream forever at the end of its rope. Frayed. Unafraid. The nudged pebble touching earth once or twice only in the course of its long, slow-spinning—

Ah!

Broken out through spray, this fantastic thing, green fire in a soap bub-ble, wings slowly beating, in spirals up up up—

Utters in Quechua a single cry:

I am the QUETZAL. I will never die.

In this virgin hemisphere the bath drains counterclockwise and a man fac-ing the pole will see daybreak on his left hand. Does the fingerprint's whorl flow backwards, too? Does the very hair grow otherwise on the scalp? Those new stars rising in their new way all night long—can't you feel an illusion risen with them, my dear one, of fatal processes reversed?

Of springs great and small being unwound? Slowly but surely. Until the anaconda and the music box lie down together.

K joins me at this point, his binocular case full of wild strawberries.

How to find the right words for a new world?

One way would be to begin, before ever leaving home, with some antic-ipatory jottings such as these. Then, even if the quetzal turns out to be ex-tinct, if surefooted grandmothers from Tulsa overrun the ruins, and Por-firio's baby has a harelip and there are cucarachas in the Hotel Périchole, the visitor may rest easy. Nothing can dim his first, radiant impressions.

Back in New York, K and L will have finished dinner. They hold hands, they giggle. Perhaps they have been playing the landscape game.

My jet veers sickeningly into the "habitual dense ceiling" above Lima. So far, so good. Now the capital's slums, squares, and fountains twinkle beneath me. This is Peru—a déjà vu to be revised henceforth like galleys from the printer, in solitary pleasure and exasperation.

A Note
about the Author

James Merrill was born in New York City on March 3, 1926, the son of financier Charles E. Merrill and his second wife, Hellen Ingram. He was raised in New York and Southampton, and attended St. Bernard's. His parents were divorced in 1939, an event with reverberations throughout his poetry. After Lawrenceville, Merrill enrolled at Amherst College, his father's alma mater; he took a year off to serve in the Army, and graduated with the class of 1947. He taught at Bard College in 1948, and at various later times has taught briefly at Amherst, the University of Wisconsin, and Yale. In 1954, he moved with his companion David Jackson to Stonington, Connecticut, and for two decades starting in 1964 spent a part of each year in Greece. Since 1979 he has wintered in Key West. His different homes, and the displacements and discoveries of his travels, are the subject of many poems. Merrill was elected to the American Institute of Arts and Letters in 1971, has been awarded honorary degrees from Amherst and Yale, and in 1986 was named Poet Laureate of Connecticut.

Merrill's earliest writings—contributions to the *Lawrenceville Literary Magazine*—were collected and privately printed by his father in 1942 as *Jim's Book*. And in March 1946, a group of his poems first appeared in *Poetry*. *First Poems* appeared in 1951. He turned next, though, to playwriting. His one-act play *The Bait* was produced at The Comedy Club in New York in 1953, and *The Immortal Husband* at the Theater de Lys in 1955. His first novel, *The Seraglio*, appeared in 1957. These experiments with voice and narrative were also reflected in a chapbook of poems called *Short Stories* (1955), most of which were included in his next collection *The Country of a Thousand Years of Peace* (1959; a revised edition was issued in 1970). *Water Street* appeared in 1962.

If *Water Street*—its title is Merrill's Stonington address—had a domestic focus and marks the culmination of his early work, his next several books reflect a more exotic, and a more ambitious, side of his work. His novel *The (Diblos) Notebook* was published in 1965, and a collection of poems, *Nights and Days*, in 1966—a volume that was given the National Book Award, whose judges cited Merrill's "scrupulous and uncompromising cultivation of the poetic art, evidenced by his refusal to settle for an easy and profitable stance." *The Fire Screen* appeared in 1969, and *Braving the Elements* (1972) was awarded the Bollingen Prize for Poetry. *Divine Comedies* (1976) won the Pulitzer Prize.

The long narrative poem "The Book of Ephraim" included in *Divine Comedies* turned out to be the first installment of an epic on occult themes whose other two parts are *Mirabell: Books of Number* (1978), which won for the poet his second National Book Award, and *Scripts for the Pageant* (1980). In 1982, these three long poems were brought together, and a coda called "The Higher Keys" added, in a comprehensive edition of the poem, now entitled *The Changing Light at Sandover*, which won the National Book Critics Circle Prize. That same year, a selection from his earlier books, *From the First Nine: Poems 1946–1976*, was issued. His most recent collection, *Late Settings*, appeared in 1985.